ENGLISH AN

ENGLISH AND HISTORY

CAIT WOODS

YOUCAXTON PUBLICATIONS

OXFORD & SHREWSBURY

ISBN 978-1-912419-45-6
Printed and bound in Great Britain.
Published by YouCaxton Publications 2018
YCBN:01

YouCaxton Publications
enquiries@youcaxton.co.uk

THIS BOOK IS DEDICATED TO

GEORGINA PENNEY, WHO KICKED MY IMPOSTER
COMPLEX SQUARELY INTO TOUCH.

ACKNOWLEDGEMENTS

GEORGİE, FOR HOURS OF EDUCATİON AND
ENCOURAGEMENT AND EXCELLENCE.

MY PARENTS, FOR ENDLESS LOVE AND SUPPORT.

MY BEAUTİFUL, BRİLLİANT CHİLDREN.

STEVE, WHO TURNED THE LİGHTS BACK ON.

CHAPTER ONE

'Morning, Mr. Elliot. How are you today?'

Elaine's voice startles me, and I spin round, knocking my phone off my desk.

'Sorry I gave you a fright,' Elaine says, perching on a nearby table. She's our depute head, small, angular and Glaswegian. She releases commands like volleys of bullets and the pupils are terrified of her.

'Morning.'

'What's wrong, Chris?' She's also brutally perceptive.

'Nothing. Just tired. What happened last night, then?'

'Mr. Kamisky's English is a bit broken. He thought you were Katia's form teacher, because she talks about you a lot. Maybe a wee schoolgirl crush or something? He wanted to see you because he's worried she isn't doing too well in school. I said you'd call him about her progress in English. I hadn't had any concerns flagged up until now.'

'No, she's fine.'

She clears her throat as she notes that I'm fidgeting, pushing highlighters into neat lines on the desk.

'There was one other thing. We're getting a student teacher. I just heard from the uni yesterday afternoon. A mature student, about your age, I think. His profile looks decent. Can you make up a timetable for him? You know: the usual spread of classes? There's some stuff from the university that I'll pass on to you.'

'Sure, yeah, no problem.'

'He starts next week. I'll forward you the email from his tutor. Hope we get a decent student this time.' Elaine smooths the fabric of her dress over her knees.

'Does Dr. Laurenson know I forgot about Parent's Evening?'

'We discussed it, Chris, briefly. I didn't lie for you. There are also a couple of things that are late from your department.' She speaks gently but directly. 'The tracking analysis still isn't in, and none of your reports were proofread. You need to tell me if we can do more to support you as the acting principal teacher; that's what we're here for.'

'Yeah, yeah... I know. I just need to get a bit more organised. Sometimes I get behind with emails. I've not been... I've not been sleeping very well, and I think it's that. I... just need to get it together a bit.'

'It's very stressful, I know. We've all been there. You just need to ask for help. There's no need to sweat it out alone—senior management is meant to support you. And if you're having trouble sleeping, you should see your GP. You look pretty washed out. I hope you're looking after yourself?'

There just never seems to be time for that. I forget to eat; shopping and cooking are impossible. I survive on wine and crisps and takeaway. Most mornings I wake up with a hangover, and there never seems to be time to shave or iron my shirt before work.

'How's Eilidh doing?' Elaine asks.

'Eilidh's fine. I might go out and visit her in the holidays.' I start clicking on emails, hoping she'll leave. She talks for another five minutes until her mobile phone rings and she leaves the room with a hurried goodbye.

My overwrought brain is repeating my omissions and shortcomings. I scribble a to-do list and begin unpacking the essays from my marking bag ready for period one. An email from Elaine lands in my inbox with the subject 'Trainee Teacher: English.'

Dear Mr. Elliot,

PGDE Student Placement: Aberlayne Academy, Department of English

Forenames: Alasdair Stewart

Surname: McClay

I read the name repeatedly, holding my breath. Can there be another Alasdair Stewart McClay, about the same age as me, in the northeast of Scotland? No.

I'm fucking losing the plot. I can't work with Ally McClay.

I'm split open. Panic is clamping onto my throat. This email means that he will walk into this school in a week's time. I can't even think about this right now. I hold myself around the waist, folding forwards and brushing the to-do list and highlighters onto the floor. The only sound I can hear is my own laboured breathing.

'Mr. Elliot?'

I see her come in, but I can't speak. 'Mr. Elliot, sir? Will I get another teacher?'

'No!' I pull my glasses off and wipe the stinging sweat from my eyes with my shirtsleeve.

Katia scrambles in her rucksack and presses a tissue into my hand.

'Thank you, Katia.' I clamp it in my palm, willing her to leave.

'Sir? What can I do?'

I try to tell her to come back later, but no words pass my dry tongue.

She crouches down next to my desk. 'I am going to get Mrs. Curran. You wait here.'

'No!' I shake my head, wave her away.

She stands up, swaying awkwardly. 'I just came to speak to you, but I can come back.'

'It's fine, honestly. I just need a minute...'

Katia reaches into her rucksack and this time produces a bottle of water, which she presses into my hands. 'I came to see you, sir, because of my dad,' she says. 'He thinks I'm not having enough homework, and he really wants me to do good in English. I'm coming to ask you to please tell him I am working very hard in class.'

'You do work hard.' I'm still breathless, and scarlet with shame.

'He don't believe me. Maybe you can give me more work for doing at home? He says I not working hard enough to get best grades.'

My breath escapes. 'Let me think, Katia. I'll try... em, do you read? I mean, do you like reading?'

'Yes, sir,' she says.

'What do you read?'

She looks unsure as to whether I'm trying to catch her out. 'I read for school. I read sometimes in Russian, some books in Russian. I read Scottish newspapers with my dad to know about things in the world...'

'Books help you know things about the world, too. Why don't I lend you something to read? Can you leave it with me?'

'Of course, I come back tomorrow. It's good, I can tell my dad you give me extra work to do.' She looks relieved, smiles shyly and closes the door behind her.

The email is still there. His name is still there. Ally McClay. I take a long, cold drink of water and shiver.

CHAPTER TWO

Not even the school bell shuts Dr. Laurenson up. The meeting in the airless boardroom has dragged on all through last period, and I'm clueless as to why we needed to be here in the first place. I've so much to do that I'll be up until the early hours again, yet we have to sit through another fucking meeting. The other principal teachers of Aberlayne Academy look as bored as me, but, unlike me, they are managing to stay awake.

It's a struggle to keep my eyes from shutting, my head from tipping forward. Elaine is sitting next to me. We've been having a conversation via notes scribbled on our refill pads, about something far more pressing than the school mission statement, which is what our head teacher is droning on about.

It's so warm, and I'm crushed with the weight of my exhaustion. I have a problem with sleep. I wish I could replicate this desperation to let my eyes close when it really matters. Elaine nudges me, and it jolts me awake.

'Chris!' she whispers. 'Wake up!'

I sit up with a start and knock over my coffee. It puddles murkily around Dr. Laurenson's laptop, staining the draft of his improvement plan and dripping onto the carpet tiles. The head teacher pushes his chair back to avoid staining the cuffs of his shirt.

'Shit! I'm sorry.' There's nothing in here I can use to mop it up. I look like a total dick. 'I'll go and get some paper towels. I'll be right back.'

Pushing the chair backwards, I stumble over Elaine's handbag and only just avoid headbutting the wall. Sweat slicks the small of my back—I'm mortified. I forget to breathe as I scramble for the door. The staffroom will be quiet. I need somewhere to compose myself, some icy water from the cooler to wake myself up. Surely the meeting can't go on much longer?

Outside the wind is whipping rain off the narrow, single-glazed windows high up the brick walls of the hallway. The school day ends as the darkness falls on a dreary November afternoon. The corridors are still clearing after the final bell, and I dodge between knots of pupils who are talking shrilly as they layer hoodies and coats over their navy blazers. They are all checking their smartphones, tech-starved after one fifty-minute lesson.

Two skinny First Year girls with matching braces on their teeth smile at me as they pass. 'Hi, Mr. Elliot!' they say in unison, giggling and whispering to each other.

'Hi, Chloe. Hi, Danielle.'

I hear the click of high heels behind me.

'Mr. Elliot, have you got a moment?'

Louise is the probationer teacher from my department, and she's clutching a pupil's phone and a red behaviour-referral slip. She's pink and out of breath. I wait for her beside the staffroom door.

'You know they gave me your class last period while you were in that meeting? I had a bit of an incident. I've kept a couple of kids back, and I think it would be better if you talked to them.'

My heart sinks. That Period Six class has always been an incendiary nightmare. Louise is not experienced enough to cope with them alone. I've been teaching for years and I can barely keep them in their seats. I check my watch, then look back down the corridor to the boardroom.

'Yeah, sure. What happened?' I ask her, reminding myself to give her my full attention when my brain is in a tug of war with itself.

'I'm so sorry, Chris. I know you're meant to be in a meeting.' Louise shifts from one foot to the other. I can see they've damaged her.

'It's okay. Who was it that kicked off this time? Was it Jordan again?'

'No, I put him through to Callum's class after about ten minutes. It was Ryan. He pushed Craig off his chair, and Craig says that his iPhone got smashed, but Ryan says it was smashed before. Then Craig started crying, so I put him in the base to calm down. Callum's with him now.'

'Oh, for fuck's sake.' I'm dizzy with exhaustion. This is going to take hours to follow up. 'It's not your fault. They shouldn't have given you that class again. They're completely mental. I'll speak to them both, and I'll phone their parents. Could you do me a favour and just look up the phone numbers while I'm talking to the boys?'

I'm hurrying back towards the English corridor, when I realise that Louise's eyes are filled with tears that she's biting hard on her bottom lip to keep in check.

'Lou, come in here a minute.' I steer her into the first door on the right.

The English department's bookstore is just a glorified cupboard, but the soothing smell of old books makes it an ideal sanctuary.

'Are you alright?' I ask her.

Louise starts to cry. Her lips tremble, this morning's coral lipstick now just a faded smudge.

'You're not, are you? I'm so sorry you were landed with them again.'

She dabs at her heavily made-up skin with the sleeve of her black suit jacket. 'They made me feel like I can't teach to save my life. They know I'm just a probationer and they think I'm fair game.'

'Yeah, but they make me feel like that too. They make everyone feel like that. It's not you, Louise. You're a great teacher—look how well you're doing with your own classes. And 'Please Takes' are a nightmare, even for experienced teachers, because the kids aren't used to you and you don't know them. I'll speak to Management about how many cover lessons they're giving you. I know there are a lot of people off sick, but they shouldn't be using you like a supply teacher.'

'It doesn't normally get to me so badly. I'm just... shattered. I took home all the prelims to mark last night and didn't get much sleep.'

'I know the feeling,' I sigh. 'I'll go and deal with these wee shites, and then I'll come and see you. But try not to stress about it. You did what you could. They're a fucking nightmare.'

She dabs under her eyes and checks her fingers for smears of makeup.

'Is my... can you tell I've been crying?' she asks. She smooths back the fringe of her pixie cut. I feel the heat creeping up the back of my neck as I look her straight in the face, check her big, dark eyes. There's only a slight shadowy smudge of mascara under her lower lashes.

'No.' I look away before she catches me blushing.

Two hours later, I've reprimanded two sulking fourteen-year-olds, pacified their irate parents, and filled out the raft of paperwork that accompanies every behaviour incident when you're head of a department. I've so much still to do, but the janitor is waiting to lock up, and my mind is adrenalin-drunk, flitting ineffectually between tasks. I sign out and let myself into the staff car park. The walk home can be soothing after a day like today, but tonight it's bleak and freezing cold. I hunch against the slicing November sleet.

It's a twenty-minute walk. My hands are raw and marbled as I fumble with the key. Inside I peel off my dripping wet jacket and drop it over the back of the folding chair. The flat is catastrophically messy. I stumble over a solitary trainer by the sofa and kick it under the table. The place stinks of the bin bags I meant to carry downstairs before work. Last night's takeaway is congealing on the coffee table, keeping company with an empty wine bottle.

I drop my bag of marking and collapse onto the sofa, crushed by the weight of my weariness. I'm exhausted, but I mustn't stop. My stomach is proving a doughy lump of dread, and my chest is tight. I'm bone-tired from the effort of pretending that I am alright.

The marking I've brought home will occupy my mind and keep it from the darkest places it's so often compelled to go these days. I wonder if Eilidh will call tonight. If she does it will be after nine p.m., and even if I sink a bottle of wine by then, I'll struggle to say anything interesting.

I imagine it's loneliness. I miss Eilidh, especially in the evenings. It feels like such a long slog through the night. Eilidh thinks I am stressed, that teaching is stressful enough without managing a department with the minimum of experience. Days pass by in a relentless blur of classes, meetings and behavioural crises, and so the marking and prep spills into evenings and weekends. My sense of inadequacy at work spills into the nights, when I barely sleep.

Eilidh has gone to teach in an international school in Madrid, because Eilidh felt she was wasted in the Languages department at Aberlayne Academy. She's seven years younger than me, and she's just finished her probation year. I miss the sex and the talking. Eilidh talks a lot; she's well-read and well-travelled, much cooler than I am. The unwelcome thoughts in my head have free rein when I'm sitting here alone.

I sit on the window ledge to heel off my soggy shoes. The cold glass presses my hips as I lean over. I have a stabbing pain behind one eye, accompanied by the grinding of an escalating tension headache. I slide to the floor, cover my face with my hands. My thoughts are looming, but I cringe away from them. With my head between my knees, I focus on the sound of my heart. It's lurching in my chest. *You're so fucking useless. You idiot.*

Half a bottle of wine submerges the worst of my restless self-loathing, enough to anchor me to the sofa with a pile of marking. Katia's essay is the first one I pick from the sprawling pile of A4 jotters. She writes in pink pen, which aggravates my headache. Tragically, there's nothing special about her essay despite the obvious care she's taken with it. She has summarised the plot of the Harper Lee set text and described the characters, but there's scant analysis; the essay question is avoided, unanswered. She makes excusable spelling mistakes because English is her second language. Her title is diligently double-underlined with a ruler—'*To Kill a Mockingbird*: Katia Kamisky, 4C, Mr. Elliot'—and she marks the dot on each 'i' with a star.

What is particularly significant about Katia? She has wavy brown hair, NHS glasses and is usually nursing a cold sore. She works devastatingly hard, is polite and eager to please.

At eight thirty I check my phone. There are texts from Callum and Louise. I open my laptop again and am relieved to see a short email from Eilidh.

Sorry, I can't call you tonight, as I'm out for dinner after work and a concert later. How did Parent's Evening go—bet you're shattered? You sounded a bit strange last night. Did you finish that James Robertson book yet? What did you think? E xx

It must be loneliness, because the first thing I feel is her physical lack. I want her here, and I want to touch her. If I touched someone, I'd know I wasn't a ghost. We seemed to have the sex thing sorted, and that's a big deal for me. She left the odd bottle in my shower, and an extra toothbrush appeared, but Eilidh left separately for work whenever she slept over. She lived with flatmates who I never met. Outside my flat, she never held my hand. Kids and colleagues whispered about us, but we didn't spend time together at work. I kick myself for never asking her the right questions. I really like her.

Getting maudlin and mildly aroused is not getting any of my marking done. I drink more red wine, eat some crisps because there's nothing else in the flat, and watch the news instead. I get no further than flicking through Katia's jotter again.

Poor Katia, desperate to please.

'I think that Boo Radley is a frighten man that have some reason not to come out of house. I think he want friend but has much fear.'

CHAPTER THREE

MONDAY

On the first day of Ally McClay's placement, I wake up—or rather give up trying to sleep—at four a.m. I half fill my water bottle with vodka and top it up with orange juice. I'm disgusted with myself, but today, nothing is taking the edge off, nothing is working.

I drink half the bottle as I wait for the morning briefing meeting to finish. I came in late to avoid him for as long as possible. I'm staring at the floor and fidgeting as Dr. Laurenson stutters through the school bulletin.

'This week we welcome PGDE student Alasdair McClay as a trainee teacher. He'll be based in the English department for the next eight weeks. I'm sure Chris and his team will look after him well. He may be observing classes or in attendance at meetings to learn more about the school. Can you make yourself known, please, Alasdair?'

In the far corner of the staffroom, he stands up.

'Hi, it's Ally', he says, and coughs apologetically.

Rachel and Claire from Geography whisper to each other and smile. He's still instantly likeable, smiling and self-effacing. He looks good, hence the whispers and giggles. His suit is expensive.

I wait nauseously for the ripple of pleasantries to die down. The bell rings, and the crowd in the staffroom begins to disperse. Dr. Laurenson steers Ally in my direction. I stay seated, tucking my shaking hands between my knees. If the reunion is causing him any anxiety, it's not showing.

'So, you haven't travelled too far, then?' Laurenson asks him routinely, his eye already wandering to the staffroom door.

'No, I'm local. I went to school with Chris.' He's insistent with his smile and his eye contract. I swallow and look at the floor because I just can't bear it.

'Oh, so you already know each other? Well, you'll be aware that Chris is acting as principal teacher while Lorraine is on maternity leave. I believe Chris has made up a timetable for you, and I'll catch up with you later. All the best.'

Dr. Laurenson nods, glancing from me to Ally and back again before slapping Ally's back and bumbling off.

If I take off my glasses and rub at the lenses, I won't have to make eye contact. Ally smells of cigarettes muted by aftershave and mint.

'Didn't you recognise me?' Ally asks.

'Yeah. I did. I knew it was you. What are you doing coming into teaching? Are you nuts?' I force a laugh.

'I heard the holidays were good,' Ally says, deadpan. 'How long have you been here?'

'Six years. You'd better come and meet everyone. It's this way.'

My frosty discomfort registers with Ally. He bites his lip and swallows, follows me in silence.

The rest of the morning drains my scant reserves, and I achieve next to nothing. At lunchtime, I neck some painkillers along with the alcoholic orange juice left in my water bottle before loosening my tie and heading for the English base. I left Ally with Callum and his First-Year class at eight forty-five a.m. I can hear the good-natured chat and hearty laughs coming through the wall. He even brought fucking *biscuits* with him. Louise is laughing, open-mouthed, at something Ally is saying as I walk in.

'How's it going?' I ask him.

'Really good, thanks. Everyone's made me welcome. The kids seem nice here,' Ally says.

Yeah, wait till you meet my Third Years, they'll fucking eat you alive.

'Yeah, mostly. Where was your last placement then?' I ask him, shifting a delivery box off my chair.

'Cairnhill Academy. Even that didn't put him off,' Callum says, shovelling the contents of a Pot Noodle into his face. 'Tell him what the wee guy called you in your Crit lesson, Ally?'

Ally blushes behind the apple he's eating, studying the threadbare carpet between his expensive-looking shoes.

I grudgingly change the subject for him. 'So, what do you make of the fine specimen of pedagogical perfection that is Callum Urquhart, Ally? Inspiring, eh?'

'Cunt,' says Callum, mouth full of noodles.

'Don't call your line manager a cunt,' I reply with mock severity.

Louise tuts, and sips at her Diet Coke, scrolling through her iPhone. The stuffing is leaking out of the English base's ancient chairs, and I notice that some of the yellow spongey pieces have adhered to her opaque black tights.

'Line manager, my arse. Have you seen Louise teach yet? Now she is shit hot. You should watch her—she'll still be doing all that crap you have to do in college.'

16

Callum's right. Louise is twenty-two, efficient, innovative. The pupils love her; the girls want to be her, and the boys fancy her.

'What did you do before, Ally?' Louise asks him.

'I work for a local company doing sales and marketing, a bit of PR. Hoping to get out, though. I've been with the same company for years. Too long.'

'What kind of company is it?'

'Binnie Homes. The building firm. Family run; like the mafia.'

So, he's still in the job that paid him through his English degree. Binnie Homes employ a lot of people locally. The Binnie family are notoriously hard-nosed. They keep new-build housing estates mushrooming around all the old county towns in the area. Still, I'd thought Ally would have achieved something more. He's one of the brightest people I've ever known.

I finish the spiked drink in my water bottle. I can't bring myself to unwrap my lunch, so I pull a Kit Kat from the packet Ally brought. I hold it until it melts, drawing my thumbnail up and down the silver paper.

'It'll be pretty exhausting trying to hold down a job and get through your placements, I imagine,' Louise continues, looking up from her phone again. 'I had to give up my shifts at my dad's restaurant last year.'

Ally shifts in his seat, looking for the bin. He aims and neatly drops his apple core into it. 'Yeah, it's pretty tiring, but I've got a mortgage to pay.'

The mention of a mortgage makes me glance at Ally's left hand. He's not wearing a ring. He hasn't really changed, just looks more polished. His fair hair is neat, trendy, his clothes are immaculate and he's wearing a Rolex Oyster that must have cost more than a new car. He has the same clear, pale skin, and he still bites his nails. From where I'm sitting I can see the red, ragged cuticles and swollen nail beds.

Louise and Callum ask him lots of polite but interested questions: Why is he re-training? Why teaching? What does he think of Aberlayne? His answers are careful and guarded. Periodically, he tries to make eye contact with me. I grit my teeth and look out the window at the rain.

I'm sweating from the stress of making small talk with him. I make an excuse and leave them to chat. I shut my classroom door and take out my phone to text Eilidh. I need a distraction. She's left me a voicemail message, and a gnawing anxiety pushes me to call her straight back. She rarely calls me during the day.

'Eilidh?'

'Did you get my message?'

'No, I haven't listened to it yet. What's wrong?'

'Nothing. Why would anything be wrong? Can I stay at yours this weekend? I'm coming home for a few days.'

She waits for me to react favourably.

'Oh God. Yeah, yeah, sure. Is everything... I mean, why are you coming back?'

A few seconds of silence indicate I haven't responded as she'd hoped.

'It's half-term here. I managed to get flights with birthday money my dad sent me. I thought it'd be a nice surprise.'

You fucking idiot. Now you've upset her. 'Yeah, of course it is. I can come and get you from the airport after work, and we'll go out for something to eat. When do you get in?'

Her fingers are tapping a keyboard as she speaks. 'Er... I think three-ish, but I'll get a taxi. Did you have other plans, Chris?'

'No, of course not. I mean, yeah, work's busy and stuff, but I... no, no other plans. It'll be great to see you.'

A few moments of dead air.

'You've been really funny lately, Chris. You've not been replying to my messages, and then you hardly say anything when I call you. Elaine messaged me on Facebook the other day. She was asking me if you were alright, and I didn't know what to say to her.'

'I'm fine. Honestly, I'm just... well, I can't sleep just now; it's screwing with my head a bit. I'm sorry I've been shit. I can't wait to see you.'

'Chris, I keep telling you: you need to go the doctor!'

'Yeah, I know. I will... I've really missed you.'

She laughs a little awkwardly. Everything will be alright. I will see her this weekend.

CHAPTER FOUR

THURSDAY

'Ally, where the fuck are you?' Scott Binnie sounded deeply unimpressed that Ally's phone, which he paid for, was going to voicemail every time he called. 'Phone me back. I'm not fucking sitting here all night waiting for you.'

Ally groaned—the tepid shower hadn't done much to revive him. Scott's message gave him a nervous jolt, and he fired off a placatory text as he dressed, then broke the speed limit on the drive out to the Binnies'. As he barrelled down the dark, deserted roads, he smoked out the window and forced down sickly synthetic mouthfuls of energy drink.

The Binnies lived just outside Bridge of Layne in a huge, sprawling seven-bedroom house with ostentatious railings, gates and colour-by-numbers landscaping. Their prestige cars with personal plates were conspicuous to all who passed on the B road out of town.

Ally reached into the glove box of the A3 for the control to the automated gates, flicking his cigarette butt out the window as he waited for them to open. His fingers trembled with apprehension and too much caffeine. He'd been wired all day, fuelled by the effort to impress at Aberlayne, and that deeper hope, too. Now, drained and on edge, he parked beside Scott's Range Rover and, quickly checking his hair in the rear-view mirror, dried his slippery palms on his trousers.

Campbell Binnie's parking space was empty. Mrs. Binnie was on a shopping trip to Dubai with Scott's sister, Serena. As he got out of the car, Ally could faintly hear the bass of the expensive sound system in the kitchen. The frost had bloomed already, and Ally started to wheeze as the cold gripped his smoker's lungs. He fumbled and dropped the keys as he hurried towards the front door. Light spilled onto the driveway as the door opened, and Scott stood silent and shirtless, waiting.

Ally stepped past him, over the threshold. As the door shut behind him, he started to heel off his trainers to avoid muddying the cream carpet. Scott backed him roughly against the wall and pinned him by his arms. His head met the exposed stone with a crack.

'It's half nine, Ally. Where have you been?'

Scott was lost to twin addictions, cocaine and working out; his cultivated muscles were hard and unyielding. Ally could barely breathe.

'You can't just fuck me around now. I don't pay for that phone so you can ignore me all the time.'

'Jesus, calm down, I can't—'

'You can't what? Can't get your arse round here when you say you will?'

'Let me go, you daft cunt! I told you I'd be late. Jesus, what's wrong with you?'

Scott shifted forward. He cupped Ally's face in his hands and traced his jaw line with his thumb before leaning in to kiss him, sliding his hands from their pinning grip on his biceps to a possessive tug on his hips. Ally let his tongue meet Scott's, running hands through his thick dark hair before reaching down for the buttons of his jeans. As his hot palm enclosed Scott's straining cock, Scott's hand pressed too hard against his collarbone, pushing him back.

'Jesus, you make me so angry sometimes. Please don't fuck with me like that. I need you.'

'I know,' Ally whispered.

'Why are you being such a dick to me just now, eh?'

The hand on his collarbone circled his throat. 'It wasn't like this before. It's like you think you're something special now, and you can do what the fuck you like.' Scott snatched Ally's fingers from his pants where they were desperately working to distract him.

With his head forced up by the pressure on his throat, Ally could see the white dust clinging to the tiny hairs inside Scott's nostrils. 'You're off your fucking tits. Let me go!' Unease, quickly becoming fear, pushed his voice up a tone.

'You make me wait all fucking day to see you? You know you're going to get fucked right into next week. Stay still, you wee slut...'

Keeping one hand at Ally's throat, Scott used the other to undo Ally's jeans and free the pressure on his hardening cock, rubbing at it as he kissed up the side of Ally's neck and nipped his ear. Ally unbuttoned his shirt and was rewarded with a sharp rake of blunt nails on the softest skin of his sides and hips. Scott marked his neck with his teeth before dropping to his knees. The moist heat of Scott's mouth turned his spine to syrup where he slumped against the wall. Letting his head tip back, Ally closed his eyes and gave in to the sex. It was the only thing that still made sense.

Scott dozed beside Ally in the king-sized bed, pinning him uncomfortably under his weights-sculpted arm. Scott's dark hair fell across his forehead, the flush of sex still staining his prominent cheekbones and lightly stubbled face. Scott liked taking chances like this, being together at Kirkton, where his parents lived, but there was no excitement in it for Ally. There was nothing really.

His feelings for Scott had been strangled by Scott's addictions and insecurities. Scott had become pathologically possessive and controlling, and, as time passed, even more fiercely closeted. Fear and sex kept Ally from breaking away. Apart from Scott's volatility, there were the photographs and videos taken when he'd been so loved-up and sex-drunk that he'd never imagined Scott would keep them as collateral.

For Scott, being found out meant the loss of everything. His ultraconservative family accepting it seemed unlikely. The Binnies were high- profile in the local media. Mr. and Mrs. Binnie had found God in recent years, and He had pushed them even further right of centre than ever before. They had fingers in numerous local pies—the town council, the football team, the police force—as well as shares in various businesses and nefarious connections. Ally had started working at Binnie Homes as an office junior during his university vacations, then had been offered a permanent marketing position post-graduation that was meant to tide him over until he could go back to university and do his teacher training.

That was almost eight years ago. Scott had helped him with promotions several times over; now Ally had a good salary, a smart company car, and a house in Bridgend, a commuter village between Bridge of Layne and Aberlayne. Money was never a problem, and it was hard to pull away from that. Campbell Binnie was a devious bigot, but Scott always had Ally's back, and Campbell seemed to accept his son's judgement and leave Ally to do his job.

Scott bought Ally the Audi for his birthday, the Rolex on a business trip to London. He paid for designer clothes, gym memberships, weekends in expensive hotels. He took Ally, who had never been abroad, to Marbella and filled him full of gin and Valium to get him on the plane.

It was heady and exciting until it became stifling. Then Ally found out that Scott was taking girls home for sex.

'I'm not gay, Ally. What did you expect?'

He tried to accept that there was nothing he could do. The balance of power between them had always been skewed. He'd shown his hand, and now Scott knew Ally was too scared of losing him to throw his weight around anymore than necessary.

Ally inched across the bed and reached for his phone. The slight movement was enough to make Scott's fingers close on his arm.

'Where are you going?' he asked.

Ally propped himself up on the pillows to check the time on the screen. It was after midnight already. He needed to get home, and somehow get enough rest for the next day of placement.

Having spent a few days observing Chris and Louise and Callum, tomorrow they would let him work with a selected few classes in preparation for the dreaded Crit visit from his university lecturer. He was in awe of how Chris, especially, could hold his student's attention, minding the minutiae of their learning while also dealing firmly and calmly with the difficult characters. Callum got by on his charisma and wisecracks, had a great rapport with the less academic kids and pulled together a lesson ten minutes before the class arrived. Louise poured her heart and soul—as well as most of her waking hours—into making exemplary lessons, but how could she sustain that? He ran through the timetable for tomorrow, his plans for each class, and the few last-minute things he needed to print off and copy.

'I need to go home. Got to get some sleep.'

Scott's fingers tightened and this time his eyes opened. He seemed fully aware that Ally's mind had drifted elsewhere. 'I'm not finished with you, you know.' Scott started to kiss him, hovering over him and stroking his face.

'I've got to be up early. I need to go home.'

'We've got the house to ourselves. Stay.' Scott raked his nails down the inside of Ally's thigh, pulling him closer. His breath was sweet and medicinal.

'I can't. I'm on placement now. I really need to get home.'

Scott tugged softly at Ally's bottom lip with his teeth and then met his tongue, flicking it with his own and running it over the gap between Ally's front teeth.

'I don't know why you won't get your teeth fixed,' he said. 'I told you I'd pay for it. I know you're scared of the dentist, but they'd knock you out. You'd be even prettier with nice teeth, babe.'

'I like my teeth, thanks.' Ally began to sweat at the thought of the process behind Scott's perfect white veneers. 'I really need to go. I've got stuff to do for tomorrow.'

Scott pushed Ally down onto the pillows and let his full weight pin him as they kissed. 'This is bullshit, Ally, this teaching thing. The kids are wee bastards and you get paid fuck all.' He nuzzled under his chin, nipped his ear. 'It's bullshit. You know it is. The old man says he'll make you a director eventually; they're on seventy grand, basic. You think you're not happy now, but wait till you're stressed out your brain, marking and making up lessons every night for absolute peanuts. There's no car, no bonuses, no perks. You think you're doing some greater good, on some fucking amazing ego trip changing the world, but you'll just turn into a sadistic, burnt-out old dick like those teachers we had back in the day.' His fingers pressed hard on Ally's lips, so he couldn't reply. 'You need to get real, pal. You're not cut out for it. You'll get crucified because of what you are. How many gay teachers do you know? Once the kids at school find out you're gay, then you're toast. It'll be around the place like wildfire. It'll be all over Facebook. The parents will think you're a pervert going to fiddle with their wee boys. You said it yourself: those lads at Cairnhill read you like a book. You didn't like it much, being called a faggot to your face, did you? It's bullshit. I'm telling you. You should listen to me; I know what you're like.'

Scott pressed a kiss under Ally's ear and grazed his teeth down his neck. Ally shrank from him, his skin crawling with ire, but his guileless cock responded, poking into Scott's hard, muscled stomach. Scott raked his fingernails through Ally's fair hair, making him shudder with visceral pleasure.

'You think you want this, but it's bullshit. I know you too well. You'll not stick at it. I know all the stuff no one else knows about you. By the way, your dad's not doing so well right now. I had to speak to him today, had to give him his First Verbal. Didn't he tell you about it? Fuck me, he's got some lip on him, eh? Like father like son, I suppose. And he's half-cut at work most days, so he can't help the backchat.'

'What? No, he's not. I'll talk to him tomorrow, I thought—'

'He's definitely off the wagon, Ally. I'm surprised you've not noticed, but you've been so up your own arse with your teaching course lately. He's not turned up for work a few times, and he's late as a standard. Tell him he'd better watch himself. Most firms would have given him his cards by now. I just keep putting in a good word for him because of you, even though I know full well he's a useless, alky bastard.'

'Scott, leave it!'

He pulled away from Scott's grip, savagely digging his fingernails into the palms of his hands to stop himself responding. The only quarter left to him was denying Scott the satisfaction of reading his humiliation and his fear. There had to be something that was still his to control, even if it was just his own reactions.

Scott rolled sulkily across the bed, and the silence in the dark bedroom lasted for a full ten minutes.

'Christ, Ally, can't even get a decent fight out of you these days.' Scott got up and opened a window. He reached into his jeans for cigarettes and a lighter, tossing one across to Ally, who caught it neatly between his thumb and forefinger.

'You're pissed off about me going to uni, and I can't change how you feel. I don't know what you want me to say.'

Scott lit his cigarette and sat down, naked and cross-legged, hugging a pillow to his stomach with one hand as he flicked ash into an empty tumbler by the bed. 'I know what I want you to say.'

Ally groaned with frustration. 'I'm not going to quit what I've always wanted to do because it freaks you out.'

'I didn't mean that.'

'What then?'

He hadn't even lit up yet, too exhausted to remember what it was he was craving. Scott took the cigarette from his hovering fingers, lit it on his own and passed it back. 'You used to say that you loved me all the time.'

Ally concentrated hard on producing the most strategic response. 'Yeah, I did.'

'Why don't you say it anymore, then?'

'I just... it's... that's not really what we're about these days,' he said.

'What d'you mean, not what we're about?' Scott reached across and tipped Ally's chin up with his fingers, tense lines forming around Scott's almond-shaped eyes.

'What about Leisha?' Ally asked.

'What about her?'

'You must be in love with her or you wouldn't have asked her to marry you.'

'That's completely different.'

'No, it's not. Once you're married to her—'

'I can hardly fucking marry *you*, can I?'

'I didn't say that! You don't seriously think you're going to get married to Leisha and we're just going to carry on as normal?'

'We have to,' Scott said. 'I need you, and you're not just going to leave me now. Fuck's sake, Ally! Don't threaten me! Don't try giving me fucking ultimatums now, because you know why it has to be this way!'

'I'm not threatening you. You asked why I don't say that I love you anymore. I've pretended to be something I'm not for you, to protect you. I'm thirty now, there are other things I want, and I'm fed up of sneaking about. There's nothing in it for me anymore.'

'Nothing in it for you? You ungrateful wee shit! You're fucking spoiled rotten! You pay for nothing, and I give you

28

everything you want, even now that you're walking away from the business. I employ your useless dad when no one else would, and I don't know how many times I've given you money to bail your mum out when he drinks all her benefits.'

'You're off your face again. You're not listening, Scott.'

Scott elbowed the pillow and dragged irritably on his cigarette. 'Go on then, why don't you say it anymore?'

'How can you expect me to? When it's totally one-sided and you fuck other people whenever you want. Then you meet a girl and ask her to marry you? Jesus, I must have been in love with you, or else I'd have run a mile a long time ago. I can only keep it up so long. I don't get why you expect me to go along with all this.'

'Don't be so fucking dense, Ally. I love you. Of course I fucking love you!'

There was the declaration Ally had once longed for, now hollow with violence and desperation.

Ally shivered and pulled the duvet up. Dragging for comfort on his cigarette started a fit of coughing.

'It's just the way it has to be, and you know that. It doesn't mean I don't... I mean, I'm not into saying it all the time, but I thought you knew. Leisha is... something else entirely. You know what my folks are like. It's just how they are. They think it's unnatural, what we do. They'd go apeshit if they knew about us. I really thought I'd grow out of this, out of wanting to be with you, but haven't. I do want to be with you. It's shit we can't be open about it, but that's just how it is.'

Scott stubbed out his cigarette, got up and pulled on his boxer shorts. He paced to the other side of the bed to kneel and cup Ally's face in his hands. 'Do you still love me, then?'

Ally filled his lungs deeply with smoke and slowly exhaled over Scott's shoulder. 'Like I said, I haven't thought about it for a while.'

Scott dropped his hands. 'Always got to be a smart-arse, don't you?' He reached out and tousled Ally's hair, letting his fingers come to rest in the nape of his neck.

'Not that smart, obviously.' Ally yawned expansively.

'I can't believe you don't love me. You're still hot for me, you dirty wee slut. You've got a hard-on right now.'

The ultimate humiliation was that Ally's lethal combination of low self-esteem and sky-high libido kept him unhealthily addicted and coming back for more. His need was on a par with Scott's cocaine habit, the draw of a mind-blowing fuck with someone superior and unattainable.

'Just go home, Ally,' Scott said. 'You look knackered. I'm not a total cunt, you know.'

'Yeah, that's debatable.' Ally yawned again and pulled Scott to him in a fragile truce, feeling Scott's heart thump, drug-revved, through his chest.

Scott tried to kiss him again, grabbing Ally's jaw in his fingers. 'You'd be lost without me, you know.'

'I need to sleep. I'm so tired,' Ally whispered, pulling away. "God, I didn't think I'd be so tired.' He stubbed out his own cigarette, leaning across Scott to reach the ashtray and turn out the light. Scott caught him up in his arms.

'I do love you, Ally. I really do. You know that. You always knew that.' He talked so fast it sounded like another language.

Within a few minutes, and despite Scott's hopeful fondling, he couldn't keep his eyes open any longer.

CHAPTER FIVE

FRIDAY

In a way, it's worse when I do manage to sleep a bit. The alarm wakes me, and I'm sick with disappointment, convinced that I've just closed my eyes.

Every morning it's harder to get out of bed. There's a heavy weight on my chest as I reach for my glasses, and the cold floor under my bare feet makes me recoil. After the Parent's Evening fiasco, I can't stay off work. Everything is piling up, and everything that was already hard anyway is now fucking impossible because of Ally. He seems to have backed off a bit, stopped any personal chat and avoiding any reminiscing, thank fuck. I can't be unprofessional, but I don't have to be friendly.

I've been avoiding him, spending my lunchtimes and breaks in my classroom trying to catch up on prep and paperwork. Today he'll take on a couple of my classes as part of his placement, so I have that to deal with. To be fair, in the classroom, he doesn't bother me quite as much. He seems to genuinely like the pupils, and he obviously wants to teach. Yesterday, my senior girls asked me who the 'hot new teacher' was in English. *Fuck's sake*, I thought. *Must be nice to turn heads.*

I shower and dress and force myself to eat toast and drink some black coffee. It's early and pitch-dark, but before the kids arrive is the only time I get peace and quiet. Outside, the grass is heavily frosted, so I take the car. My car has seen much better days. It's a ten-year-old Golf with a bumper held on with black tape. It always takes a few minutes to start on cold mornings. The radio comes on, and I remember that Eilidh is coming tonight. My flat looks like a bomb hit it and I've no food in the fridge. I haven't changed the bed since... well, that doesn't bear thinking about. *Fuck it, I just need to get into work. It'll be okay. It must be okay.*

En route to school, the car reminds me noisily that it needs a new exhaust. I don't know when I'll find the time to get that done. Usually at seven a.m., it's just the janitor's car in the car park, but today there's a conspicuously new and expensive-looking car by the side door. It's a red S-line Audi A3 with nice alloys, a high-spec trim and a personal registration: S4 ASM. I shake my head.

Just when I start to think he might not be a complete tosser.

Ally gets out of it holding a thermal coffee mug, bumping the door shut with his hip because he has a lit cigarette in the other hand. Fuck, I'll have to talk to him. It would be too obvious to pretend I haven't seen him. There's no one else around.

Ally waits for me to cross the car park, huddled over his cigarette.

'Nice car,' I mutter, stepping back a little from the haze of clinging smoke.

'Thanks. It's a company car. You're in early,' Ally says.

'Yeah, loads to do. You're keen.'

'I woke early... Well, I didn't sleep much.'

He flicks the fag ash into the gutter as we walk.

'Me neither.' The mention of sleep generates a yawn.

'I was thinking about your Third Years,' Ally says. 'Can I show you my lesson plan again? I don't know if it's a good idea doing group work to start or not. What about Josh? If he's autistic, then maybe it's not great for him?'

'Josh likes to work on his own, but he will work with Kieran if he has to. I'll have a look. Just make sure you've got extension work planned today because Simona, you know, the quiet girl who sits at the back with Kelly? She's always finished fast. If you put her in a group, she just does all the work for the rest of them.'

'Will you stay with me?' Ally asks.

I'm holding the door for him, already thinking ahead to something else I need to do. 'Sorry?'

'You'll stay in the room while I take your class? That's how it works here, eh? They tended to just leave me to it at Cairnhill.' Ally flicks his cigarette end into the bin at the front door.

'Yeah, if you like. I'll take notes.'

'Oh, that'd be really good. I'm bricking it, to be honest.'

'I won't let them totally destroy you.' I allow myself a wee, grim smile. 'Not on your first day, anyway.'

In fact, Ally's lesson plan is impressive, although when you have twenty fourteen-year-olds in front of you, no amount of planning makes a lesson watertight. I grudgingly reassure him and send him off to do his photocopying. He's got Callum's biddable First Year class to start, and then he's team-teaching Louise's Highers before lunch. Settling at my desk, I neck my coffee and check my emails before the first class of the day line up at my door. The sky is starting to lighten, and the corridor is still silent.

At lunchtime, I'm buoyed by the thought of seeing Eilidh in four or five hours, and I brave the English base to make more coffee. Louise and Callum are talking about

Ally as I walk in. Louise is perched on the edge of the desk, and Callum is eating his sandwich with his phone in one hand.

'Give him a chance, Lou. Not everyone's as perfect as you, eh?'

'I don't mean it in a bad way, Callum. It was a good lesson, and the kids really like him. He's such a nice guy. '

'Yeah, I can tell you like him too. You'd tap that, missy.'

'Shut up, you absolute cretin!' Louise flips her middle finger at Callum, who just laughs.

'So, what's the verdict on Mr. McClay then?' I ask. 'Where is he, anyway?'

'Gone out for a fag.' Callum is waiting for the kettle to boil. 'It'd be like snogging an ashtray, Louise. I wouldn't go there if I were you.'

I laugh at him despite myself. Louise gives Callum a withering look.

'I'd say he's, well... overly self-critical. He ripped his own lesson to bits before the kids were five minutes out the door. I couldn't persuade him to take anything positive away from it.'

'Oh well, HMIE loves the reflective practitioner. He'll be fine.' I shrug, turning away to scoop instant coffee into my mug. I've forgotten lunch again, but I'm not hungry.

'Are we going to the pub after work?' Callum asks.

'I am,' says Louise. 'I'm not staying late though. Driving home to Edinburgh tomorrow.'

'Eilidh's coming home this weekend,' I say.

'Oh, aye,' Callum sniggers. 'Mr. Elliot's getting laid tonight then. Will she let you come to the pub?'

'I might see if she wants to come too.'

'Will she be okay with that?' Louise asks. 'She might just want to... you know—'

'Fuck his brains out?' Callum laughs. 'Nice one, Lou.'

'Jesus, Callum, shut up! I meant she might want to just go out for a meal alone with Chris or something.'

The thought of going out in company is reassuring. I don't know why I feel nervous about seeing her. I sink into the most comfortable chair in the base and tuck my knees up, nursing a hot coffee.

'You not eating again, Chris?' Louise asks.

'I had a something earlier,' I lie.

'Are we asking Mr. McClay to the pub?' Callum asks. 'You know, so that Lou can get him drunk and have her wicked way with him.'

I roll my eyes. I can see Louise squirming.

'Callum. Seriously, mate, give it a rest, you're embarrassing her. He'll probably need a drink or three after taking my Third Years next period.'

Ally's lesson with my Third Years goes tolerably, but right at the end, Jordan Franks asks to go to the toilet, loudly, as Ally is talking them through their homework.

'Sorry, Jordan, but you can't go right now.'

Aggrieved, Jordan swivels around in his chair and appeals to me. I'm marking jotters at a spare desk at the back of the room.

'Mr. Elliot?'

'Turn around, Jordan, you're interrupting,' I tell him.

Jordan turns around and tries Ally again.

'Please, sir, or whatever your name is again, I really need to go.'

'I said no, Jordan.' Ally doesn't sound convincing enough, and Jordan latches on to it. Soon, Ally's lost his place, looking flustered and shuffling his notes. It gives the pupils a chance to begin muttering.

'This is bollocks,' Jordan shouts. 'You're not our teacher, Mr. Elliot's our teacher. You're not even a proper teacher. You can't tell me what to do!'

He pushes his chair back and flounces out, slamming the classroom door. I get up to follow him, but Ally's not sure how to react or how to get the rest of the class refocussed.

'Listen.' I raise my voice just loud enough, not a shout, no loss of control. 'You need to be quiet and note your homework in your planners for Mr. McClay. Right now, okay?'

They're not completely settled or silent for the last few minutes, but I don't have to intervene again.

Once the class has noisily pushed their way out the door, leaving seats turned over and books untidily scattered across the front desks, Ally leans against the whiteboard, scuffing the chewing gum-studded carpet with his foot.

'Oh my God, that was a disaster,' he says, grey and deflated.

'No, it wasn't. Get it in perspective; one wee guy kicked off because you said no to him. He's so dyslexic he can't copy from the board and he was acting up so he didn't have to. You can't make it personal.'

'Yeah, but I should have remembered that he was dyslexic. I've read their profiles. I should have remembered to print his homework out for him.'

'It's only your second placement. All that stuff comes later, once you have your own classes and work with them all the time. That class isn't easy. You did fine.'

'You think so?' Ally doesn't look convinced, and I'm not surprised. I'm too prickly around him to sound reassuring.

'They're not an easy crowd. I've got a meeting now, but I'll speak to you about it later.' I turn my back on him, gathering papers from beside the computer. I hear the tremor in his weary exhalation and relent a little. 'Are you coming to the pub tonight?' I ask him.

Ally looks down at the floor, his adrenalin visibly draining. 'Yeah, I might, just for a bit. I have to work this weekend.'

'You mean at Binnie?'

Ally looks distant, as if he hasn't heard me, so I leave it. 'Are you going straight from work?' he asks me.

'To the pub? No, I need to go home first to pick up my... I need to go home first, but I should be there by five.'

CHAPTER SIX

Ally tidied Chris's classroom after he left, picking up dropped pencils and scraps of paper, pushing chairs in under desks and stacking abandoned books and jotters. It helped his mind settle. He now had a better idea of how he could tighten his lesson up for next week

At Binnie Homes, he worked mostly from his desk, and he had, with supreme naivety, assumed the shorter days in school might be less taxing. He hadn't reckoned for the adrenalin spikes throughout the day, or for the hours of extra work before and after every lesson. That said, 'Mr. McClay' was becoming a kind of alter ego, one that gave him a bit more authority and a bit more hope.

Despite the exhaustion, he was quietly excited at the prospect of going out for a drink after work. He didn't have a social life because he kept evenings and weekends clear in case Scott called; they could only meet when Scott could get away without being missed.

Scott regarded both male and female friends as a threat, so Ally didn't see any. He couldn't even remember the last time he'd sat in a bar with friends. Having anyone to confide in was a distant memory. Chris was closed off from him; he knew he was being tolerated on sufferance. The way things were left years ago, it wasn't unexpected.

Closing Chris's classroom door, he wandered along to the base to begin gathering his things. Louise was there, typing and frowning at the screen. She looked up as he came in. 'I think your phone's been ringing,' she said, nodding toward his bag hanging by the door.

'Oh God, sorry, I meant to put it on silent.' He fished it out to find three missed calls from Scott and a succession of texts. Slipping the phone into his back pocket, he took himself back to Chris's classroom and read them, pacing the carpet tiles.

11.01: Woke up with a hard on for you, baby. When you coming back?

12.44: Phone me at work. I need to see you tonight. Thinking about your pretty mouth on my cock.

2.17: Why aren't you picking up your phone?

2.58: Why the fuck are you ignoring me?

Glancing at the door, he wrote a reply knowing it wouldn't be enough.

Been so busy, not ignoring you. What time tonight?

Ninety seconds later his display lit up with 'Scott: Office,' and he was compelled to answer it. 'Hey, are you okay?'

'No, Ally, I am really not fucking *okay*,' Scott said. 'I'm not okay with your bullshit right now. I know what you're trying to do. Why did you sneak off this morning without saying goodbye?'

'I had to get ready for work.'

'Bullshit. It's not work. You don't get paid for it. We never get to spend a whole night together, and you didn't have to leave so early. Now you're ignoring me all day because you're suddenly so fucking important. You'll have had time to drink coffee and smoke fags, so you don't tell me you were too busy to text me. It's like you just don't give a fuck about me anymore.' It sounded like his voice was cracking, but it could have been the signal.

'I do, it's just... come to mine later. We can talk then. You can stay over tonight, eh?'

'You know what? Fuck you, Ally. I'm sick of you doing this to me. I don't need you that much. Seriously, just go fuck yourself.' Scott hung up.

Ally sat down at Chris's desk, another adrenalin rush to his sleep-deprived brain making him weak and light-headed.

'Shit.' He let his palms cover his sore eyes. The last bell of the day sounded, and then the thunderous noise of eight hundred teenagers vacating the building. What was it out there that had them shrieking and shouldering one another off the walls? They left layers of teenage scent behind them, musty and chemical- cloaked.

He looked around Chris's classroom at the piles of books, the dog-eared posters and the untidy desk with its mess of paper, jotters, loose pens, and an aged mug of cold coffee. A very tatty paperback had fallen on the floor, under the swivel chair. Ally picked up *The Pearl* by John Steinbeck. It was deeply familiar. Inside the front cover, there was a yellowed sticker.

Christopher James Elliot, For Excellence in English, Duthie High School, 1998

Chris and Ally had shared a double desk in Mrs. Stewart's English classroom, a Portakabin with a view across the dual carriageway to where they were building the new houses on the moor. Mrs. Stewart read aloud to them from *Sunset Song* by Lewis Grassic Gibbon in her authentic Doric dialect. Ally had a vivid memory of looking sideways and watching Chris be enthralled as she described Ewan's ghost ascending the brae for an otherworldly reunion with Chris Guthrie at the Standing Stones. *'Oh lassie, I've come home.'* He caught

Ally looking and blushed. Chris was shy and studious while Ally was often bored at school, fidgeting a lot and getting them bawled at for whispering or writing notes.

Mrs. Stewart's bark was much worse than her bite. It must have been her who put Chris forward for the English prize. Sometimes he wrote even when he didn't have to, and, like Ally, he read voraciously. He played the guitar very well, which stopped him from being bullied and made him tolerably popular with the girls. The last, heady summer before university, he confided in Ally that he'd lost his virginity, finally, to Carolynn Flett, and it had been a total disaster.

'You coming, then?' Louise appeared at the door with her coat and scarf on. 'Chris is meeting us there. He's got to meet his girlfriend first.'

CHAPTER SEVEN

Eilidh's text to say her flight has been delayed wins me a bare half hour to buy some wine and crisps at the corner shop and deal with the squalor of the flat. I change the bed and throw all the dirty clothes into the bottom of the wardrobe. Mouldy mugs and discarded tissues have colonised the floor beside the bed, and I scoop up as many as I can and take them to the kitchen. The kitchen situation is hopeless. There's no time to start on the pile of dishes or the sticky floor, but I bundle up the fetid, overflowing bin bag and take it downstairs to the wheelie bin by the front door.

As I'm ditching it, a taxi pulls up and nerves rake my spine. I'm still in my work clothes, sweaty and dishevelled, and now my hands are stinking of rubbish. Eilidh gets out of the cab with a small wheeled case. Her hair has grown and lightened in the sun. She looks slimmer, and when she turns to look up to my flat window, her face is tanned and freckled.

I wipe my hands on my trousers and give my glasses a quick rub, wishing I'd remembered to put my contacts in before she arrived.

She waves, crossing the car park to meet me.

'Hey. You look great.' I go to hug her, feeling awkward.

She steps back and studies me, her eyes narrow. 'Are you okay, Chris?' she asks.

'What?'

'You look so... different. Have you been ill?'

God, I look like shit. I knew I looked like shit.

'No. Em, it's just I... well, it's been a bit of a rush and I've come straight from work. I meant to go shopping, but I couldn't get away from school. So I thought we could just go out to eat? If that's okay?'

Eilidh tilts her head, assessing me. 'Yeah, whatever, I don't mind. Is that nice Chinese place still open? We can walk there, eh?'

I nod, scrabbling for a way to avoid taking her inside the flat right away. 'I'll take your case upstairs and grab my coat, and then we can head there. You could just wait here; I'll only be a second.'

'Yeah, that's fine. Are you sure everything's okay?'

'Mm-hmm, yeah. I'll be quick.'

I sprint upstairs, heart racing, and drop Eilidh's case in the bedroom. In the bathroom, I splash my face and wash my hands before rummaging for some aftershave and a comb. Worriedly checking my breath, I do a patch job with my finger and some toothpaste. After grabbing my coat and wallet, I arrive breathless in the lobby where Eilidh is waiting, scrolling through her phone.

'What have you got on your face?' She dabs at my cheek with a finger. 'Toothpaste?'

We drink a lot of wine with dinner, and I start to find it easier. Eilidh talks about her new job, her new friends, her apartment in Madrid and the nightlife there. She seems happy to keep talking. I listen self-consciously, reaching across the paper tablecloth to play with her fingers. She's wearing a silver and aquamarine ring on her right hand, and her nails are painted a glossy red. I get so restless with need that I can barely concentrate on what she's saying.

She's wearing a wrap dress with opaque tights and knee-high boots. I undress her repeatedly as she tells me another anecdote I know I should laugh at. The exposed skin of her neck and chest is a biscuit colour, licked with Spanish sun. I've been obsessing about her breasts all day, and they look lush as she leans forwards to tell me another anecdote.

I can't stop myself from interrupting her. 'You look so pretty, Eilidh. I've really missed you.'

Eilidh laughs and looks away. 'Thank you.'

'Things are pretty full on at work, I feel like I haven't talked to anyone properly in ages.'

'It's not the same talking on the phone,' she says.

'No, it's not... I'm not very good at thinking what to say on the phone.'

As if to prove my point, a silence grows and looms between us.

'What's new at Aberlayne then?' she asks.

'Not much.' I shrug.

'Elaine says you have a student teacher in the department. What's he like?'

'Ally?' I shift in my seat and top up her wine glass. 'He's alright. The kids like him. Louise likes him—'

'She would,' Eilidh says pointedly. She's not keen on Louise for some reason. 'Sounds like there's a 'but' coming?'

'No, not really. Just that I... I know him from before. We went to school together, but we lost touch ages ago. He's... yeah, he's alright. Will we get another bottle?'

The more she drinks, the more she talks and laughs, and the less I need to contribute. She's so beautiful when she laughs. I stroke her forearm and the back of her hand, squeeze her knee under the table and brush her hair out of her face with my fingers so that I can see her dark eyes more clearly.

'You're so quiet,' she says, pausing between stories. 'You look exhausted.'

'I'm just tired.'

'Still not sleeping?'

'Not much.'

'Have you seen anyone about it?'

I shake my head and close my fingers around her wrist. 'Let's get the bill. I've got more wine at home.'

'God, more wine? I'm pissed already. I drink beer all the time now. I kind of forgot what wine does to me.'

'I like what wine does to you.' I squeeze her fingers and lean across to kiss her. Her lips are so soft.

She smiles. 'Hmm. I take it I'm not crashing on the sofa then?'

I am utterly horrified by this idea. 'Why would you be sleeping—'

'I didn't want to assume anything. It's been five months.'

'Eilidh...' A lurch of dismay unsteadies me.

'Come on then,' she says briskly. 'Let's go back to yours.'

Outside the restaurant, I kiss her insistently, until the strangeness of it diminishes. My hands travel over her until she smooths them back against my sides.

'I'm freezing, Chris. Let's go back to yours.'

Despite the alcohol and horniness, I can't settle. Her comment needles me as we walk home. I stop her for kisses that should reassure me. She kisses me back, giggly and business-like.

Inside the flat, I shepherd her to the bedroom, not giving her time to see the mess elsewhere. She takes off her boots and sits on the bed, appearing to sniff the stale air. I kneel in front of her and push the dress down off her shoulders, so I can scoop her heavy breasts out of the satiny push-up bra. I thumb over the dark nipples.

'Oh my God, Eilidh, I love your tits.'

She sighs as I fondle and kiss them before moving to nuzzle her neck and kiss her mouth. She helps me get her dress off and strips to her knickers. My tie is already lost, but as she unbuttons my shirt, I remember that I haven't showered, and she'll encounter the layers of dried nervous sweat on my skin.

'Jesus, you've lost so much weight!' She palms over my shoulders and torso, prodding my bones, tugging at my waistband where it gaps and sags.

I'm thrown, but distract myself again with her breasts, sucking on each nipple and fumbling in her knickers.

'Have you got condoms?' she asks, undoing my belt and zip.

My heart sinks. 'I don't know—there might still be some in here.'

Eilidh rummages in the drawer of the bedside cabinet and finds a couple of dog-eared foil packets.

'Bloody hell, Chris, these are out of date! I didn't even know that condoms could go out of date.'

'Well, now you do.'

I have never been an unqualified success with women.

She tears the corner of a packet with her teeth, one arm around my neck. 'It's okay, I'm on the pill now anyway, so if it disintegrates with age we'll be okay.'

Eilidh's confidence puts me on edge sometimes, so I concentrate on the immediacy of her naked skin to stop my mind racing off in the wrong direction. She kneels on the floor to pull my pants off and put the condom on, sexy concentration on her face.

'You're so pretty.' I help her to her feet and cup her face in my hands to kiss her. 'I've missed you so much.'

'Yeah, so it seems.' She arranges herself under the quilt, wriggling out of her knickers.

Sex with Eilidh was all I could think about. Now that she's underneath me, I'm worrying that I'll come too quickly, and it produces the opposite effect. After Eilidh's distinctive arch and squeal finally satisfies me that there's been something in it for her, at least, I turn away and quickly bundle the condom under the bed out of sight. It doesn't matter—there's all weekend for shagging. She's here in my bed, and I want to talk, to hold on to her. I'm alive because I'm touching her again.

Eilidh arranges herself in my arms and smooths my hair with her fingers, studying me with languid eyes. 'So, you don't shave for work these days?' She thumbs my face with its four days' worth of stubble. 'I'm not sure about this new look, to be honest.'

'I just... I've been a bit stressed out lately. Work is mental. I'm so tired the whole time; I need to get some sleeping tablets or something.'

'Is it just work, then?'

'Kind of...' I kiss her again, sliding my fingers through the silky lengths of her hair. 'I didn't realise how much I'd miss you.'

'That's sweet, but it's not why you're like this.'

'It doesn't help that you're so far away.' I feel her stiffen a little, her eyes becoming distant.

'The thing is, Chris, you're talking as if we're... I mean, we get on well, but we never talked long-term or anything.'

Cold sweat trickles between my shoulder blades. 'Have you met someone else? Is that... is that why you're on the pill?'

She's nibbling her bottom lip. 'No, it's not that. I'm just concerned that you're thinking this is something different to what I think it is. It's not that I haven't missed your company, but I haven't been locked away pining for you, and if I had met someone else, I wasn't planning on feeling bad about it. I assumed we were just casual, because of me moving away.'

'Okay,' I swallow back my hurt. 'That's my fault, I never asked you about that.'

Casual is what things are to begin with, I console myself. This is my chance to put things straight. 'Maybe you're right. I should have told you how I felt before you left.'

'That wouldn't have helped, Chris,' she says. 'I was going anyway.'

'I've money saved to come across and visit, and we've been doing okay with the phone and emails.'

Eilidh frowns, tucking her hair behind one ear. 'I don't know—you never seem to have much to say to me on the phone. You just pretend like everything is okay when I call. Elaine told me you didn't turn up for Parent's Evening, but you never mentioned it. You need to find someone you can talk to.'

'Honestly, Eilidh, I really look forward to talking to you. If I don't have much to say it's because nothing much is happening here.' My voice is struggling past the sadness crushing my throat.

'If you're having a hard time, why are you pretending everything is okay?'

'I just want to spend the weekend with you and not think about work. We can't leave it another five months. I've got enough money to come and visit you, and it's not even that far, really. There's no reason we can't see each other more often, even if it's just for the weekend. It was just bad timing, me getting the PT job just before you left. I let work take over. Before you leave, we'll book flights for me to come across next month, for the Christmas holidays. I've never been to Madrid.'

She sits up in my bed, smoothing creases out of the duvet cover. The ends of her thick dark hair brush the fullest part of her breast as she bends over. I breathe her synthetic cinnamon biscuit scent and stroke the buttery flesh of her upper arm as I wait for her to agree.

'Well... maybe. We'll see. I haven't really decided what I'm doing for Christmas yet.'

A prickling sensation crawls over my back and neck. The sour taste in my mouth might be rejection. 'We'll work something out.' I kiss her shoulder, my conviction and my grip wavering as the alcohol and sex begin to leave my system.

CHAPTER EIGHT

'Looks like Chris isn't coming,' Louise said as she came back from the bar with their third round of drinks. She tossed a couple of bags of crisps onto the table.

Callum immediately fell upon them, tearing open the packages. 'Naw, he'll be balls deep in his wee French teacher.'

After a couple shots of Jack Daniel's, Louise allowed herself to laugh. Ally picked the ice out of his gin and reached for a handful of crisps before Callum devoured them all.

'Poor Chris, it's a shame. He must miss her. It's funny, everyone knows they're going out, but he never speaks about it at work, and neither did she.'

'Did you work with her?' Ally asked. 'What's she like?'

'Not bad. Bit of meat on her bones, nice tits,' Callum summed up.

Louise rolled her eyes and flicked a crisp across the table at Callum's face. 'Yeah, she's nice enough. I don't know her that well. She went to work in Spain.'

'What about you, young man?' Callum pushed the remaining crisps across the table to Ally. 'Are you spoken for? Louise is asking.'

He blushed. 'No.'

Callum revelled in causing embarrassment. 'There you go, Lou, he's single!'

'Yeah, well, kind of.' This had become the conversation Ally tried hardest to avoid.

'Well, he's kind of single. That'll do you, eh?'

50

'Just ignore him, Ally. He's being a dick,' Louise said into her drink.

He quickly checked his phone—no messages yet. Maybe Scott would stay in a sulk long enough to let him relax and have a few drinks. But then again, Scott was horribly unpredictable these days.

'Has anyone texted Chris?' Louise asked. 'Should I text him? Maybe they're just running late. I'm starving. If they're not coming, we could just order some food.'

Ally's stomach growled in agreement; hunger was really making the drinks go to his head. 'Is it okay if we just order anyway?' he asked. 'I think I'm going to pass out if I don't eat something soon.'

'Yeah, good idea, pal. What d'you want, Lou? Ally and I can go up and order.'

She was already scrolling through her phone to find Chris's number.

'Scampi and chips and another JD and coke, please.'

Ally offered to pay, and Callum was happy to accept. They chatted perfunctorily about cars, mainly Callum making admiring noises about Ally's. Louise was on the phone when they got back to the table, so Callum finished off describing his own modified hatchback as Ally feigned interest.

'They're not coming,' Louise said as she hung up. 'I spoke to Eilidh.'

'Is everything okay?' Ally asked.

'I don't think so. Eilidh sounded a bit tetchy.'

Callum shrugged. 'Lovers tiff.'

'No. She thinks something's wrong with him? Was he okay at work today? I didn't really notice; I was so busy.'

'He was quiet,' Ally said. *He's always quiet around me.*

'Yeah, and he didn't eat anything at lunchtime, did he?' Louise said.

Callum looked at his phone, half listening.

'I hope he's okay. He has been a bit strange recently, and he's starting to look pretty run-down,' Louise pushed her third drink into the middle with the other empties.

'Never realised what he was taking on doing Lorraine's PT job, eh?' Callum said.

'He's stressed out. It's a good thing Eilidh's back this weekend. He never seems to do much but work,' said Louise

Ally had no insight to Chris's life over the last eight years. He had expected more for Chris than what they were describing, and it made him sad.

'No one else smokes?' he asked, getting up and shrugging on his coat.

Outside, alone in the dark car park, he lit up and leaned against the wall. It was a starry night with lashes of icy wind. He'd missed his nightly phone call to Jamie, his younger brother, and, feeling guilty, screwed his eyes shut tight. He'd kept a lid on what Scott had said, but it wouldn't go away. If Scott wanted to hurt him, then he just might by exploiting his dad's historically fragile sobriety.

The fourth gin and tonic had gone to his head, and he hoped to find the food had arrived when he went back in, just to soak it up a bit. He wondered how things might be if he could pass this year and find a permanent job. He could even move away and... well, no, he couldn't move away, not the way Jamie was now. Maybe Scott would get the message without losing the plot, he thought as a sharp gust of wind brought a few snowflakes with it, causing him to hurriedly finish his cigarette and go back inside.

Gone half eleven, Ally waited outside the pub for a taxi home with Louise. Callum had already left on foot. The world was turning, and Ally was blissfully relaxed. He wrapped an arm around Louise's shoulders and gave her his hat to keep her warm. She leant against him in the cold wind, and he helped her into the taxi when it arrived. She was unsteady on her feet. In the back of the taxi she rested her head on his shoulder and reached for his hand. Hers was tiny and marble-cold.

'So much for you going home early then.' Ally said.

Louise was looking out the window pasted with snowflakes.

'You okay?'

He rubbed her cold fingers to generate some warmth.

'Can I come home with you?' she asked.

He took a moment to register what she meant. 'Louise, I...' she pulled her hand away, mortified, and he tried again. 'You're beautiful. I can't believe you don't have a boyfriend.'

It wasn't helping. She was shrinking away, her hands clawing around her middle.

'I'm gay, Louise. It's just... I don't want anyone at school to know.' He snatched her hand back, needing reassurance as much as she did.

For a second, she studied him. 'You're gay? Really?' She hiccupped and laughed at herself. 'Good-looking, well turned-out; I should have guessed.'

Thanks to the alcohol they both found this disproportionately hilarious.

'Oh my God, who do you fancy at work then? Have you *seen* the Art probationer? No, really, you have to; he is so fit it's ridiculous.' Louise shrieked with laughter. The mute cab driver glanced over his shoulder.

As they pulled into Ally's street, Louise wrapped her arms around his neck. He chastely kissed her goodnight as the cab door opened, winking at her and squeezing her hand.

'Goodnight, Miss Macari.'

'Goodnight, Mr. McClay.'

Unsteadily, he crossed the road and rummaged for his house keys. The street was silent; most of the neighbours' lights were out. He pictured himself in bed with a mug of tea to warm him before he'd sleep through to the next morning.

The figure on his doorstep stood up, dropping a glowing cigarette end on the path. Without saying a word, he unlocked the front door. Scott followed him inside.

'Who was she?' he asked as soon as the door closed behind them.

'I work with her.'

'Yeah, apparently you do more than work with her.' Scott's face was white and pinched in the harsh light. 'Caught you bonny there.'

'You know I don't fancy girls, Scott. She's my friend.'

'You've been drinking. Look at you. You're half-cut.' Scott backed him into the living room, gripping him hard by the shoulder.

'Yeah, I am. I am half-cut. Louise is a lovely girl, and I had a really good night.'

Sullenly, he wrenched himself from Scott's grip and turned his back to walk away. Scott shoved him so hard that he lost his balance. When he fell, his head met the sharp edge of the glass coffee table with a substantial force. He blacked out on the hardwood floor.

When he opened his eyes, he was naked in his own bed, and he urgently needed to throw up. Lurching to the bathroom, he hugged the toilet seat until he couldn't be sick anymore. His head was agony, but there was a different pain, radiating and red-hot. He pulled himself up to his feet and looked in the mirror. A two-inch gash on his hairline was covered with dried and clotting blood, and he'd bitten his lip until it was bleeding stickily, too. His mouth tasted vile.

'Can't hold your drink,' Scott said, perched on the side of the bath. 'I suppose I'd better take you to A & E to get that stitched. What a fucking state you get yourself in, Ally.'

Ally held on to the sink; he could barely see straight, let alone move to get dressed. His throat was raw, and his jaw ached. He sank back down on the cold bathroom floor.

'Ally, come on.' Scott dragged him to his feet again. The whites of his eyes were bloodshot, the black of his pupils obliterating the flinty hazel colour. He was dressed but dishevelled, with blood smeared down his pale shirt. He dabbed ineffectually at Ally's face with the corner of a towel. As he helped Ally gingerly pull a T-shirt over his head, Scott tutted. Ally winced, turning to hide the tears gathering above his bloody cheek.

Ally started to shiver, and felt sleepy again, so he let his weight rest against Scott's shoulder for a moment. From the waist down, he was sore and slimy. He sat on the edge of the bed and tried to remember. Agitated, Scott threw him the rest of his clothes.

'Can you get me some water?' He pressed tentative fingers to his burning throat.

'There's a bottle in my car. Hurry up.'

After a tense and silent drive across town, Scott dropped him at the A & E entrance and drove away. Once Ally had haltingly given his details to the receptionist, he was seen almost immediately by the triage nurse. The other occupants of the waiting room glanced warily at him as he hugged his sides in agony. He was battered by nausea and struggled to stand unaided when his name was called. In a small room with a sliding door, a middle-aged nurse cleaned and stitched the cut on his head, stopping twice to let him throw up in a cardboard container.

'What happened to you, then?' she asked, handing him some paper towels to mop his face.

'I fell,' he whispered hoarsely. 'I'd had a drink.'

'How did you get here? I hope you didn't drive yourself?'

'My friend drove me. He couldn't wait around.'

'Your friend?' Her eyes raked him up and down. 'You've had a head trauma. Your friend shouldn't have left you alone.'

Ally swallowed and winced, his throat raw from throwing up. 'He had to go.'

'But he was there when you fell?' she asked, palpating the angry red marks around his throat.

'Um... yeah.'

'These look like finger marks on your neck here, and up there on your arms. You're burned too—looks like from cigarettes. Doesn't it hurt?'

Ally glanced down at his bare arms. He didn't remember getting undressed, but he wasn't wearing the clothes he'd come home in. She was right, there were marks colouring up around his wrists and biceps.

'Can I have some water?'

The nurse filled a white plastic cup. After she passed it to him, she rested a hand on his shoulder, speaking softly. 'Alasdair, you know, we're not here to judge anyone. You can tell me what's happened to you. I notice there's some blood on your jeans, and it's not from the cut on your head.' She moved her hand to gently touch his forearm. 'I think you need to tell me a bit more about what's been going on tonight, and then maybe we should have a look?'

His stomach contracted violently when the doctor who came to examine him paged for someone else to come as well. She was a counsellor of some kind, but Ally covered his face and hugged his knees when she tried to talk to him. The doctor diagnosed shock and concussion from the head wound. The stitches were tight and painful, a keener tugging among the overwhelming soreness. The nurse brought him more water and strong painkillers. The wanted him to stay overnight, they wanted him to talk, but he was crushed with the shame of it. He walked away as they protested, sodden with nervous sweat, feeling as if everyone he passed recognised what he had allowed to happen to him.

He called Scott, leaning unsteadily on the wall of the foyer. 'Can you come and get me? I didn't bring any money for a taxi.'

The Range Rover appeared twenty minutes later.

'You shouldn't drink,' Scott said as Ally arranged himself in the passenger seat. 'Look at the state of you. I'm going to take you back to Kirkton.'

'I want to go home,' Ally said.

'You don't know what you want, so try doing what you're told for once, you muppet.'

'Take me home.'

'You're concussed; you can't stay on your own.'

'I don't want to be with you,' he said. 'I don't want to be with you anymore.' He wasn't convinced that he was saying the words out loud.

'What?' Scott took his hands off the wheel, the keys still in his lap. 'What did you say?'

Ally took a deep breath. 'I don't want to be with you anymore.'

'Don't be so fucking stupid. You don't know what you're saying. What did they give you in there? I'm taking you back to our place and you can stay the weekend until my folks get back.'

'What did you do to me when I was out cold?'

Scott looked at him, his eyes widening. 'Ally, you were drunk and horny.' His voice wavered. 'You just don't remember.'

'The nurse saw I was bleeding. I was sitting in my own blood, Scott! Look at my arms and my neck. She wanted me to give a statement. What the fuck did you do to me? '

Scott froze in horror. 'You didn't, did you?' Please tell me you didn't say anything.'

'No, I didn't. Take me home, for fuck's sake.' He was crying now.

'You give out mixed messages, Ally. I picked you up to take you upstairs and I just wanted to get you into bed, see you were okay. You hit your head pretty hard when you fell. There was blood all over your work clothes, so, yeah, I undressed you and got into bed with you, because you were shaking so much. You just don't remember, but you wanted it. You just don't remember. I know what you're like, Ally—you don't want to admit that's how you like it. I just... I was so fucking angry with you. I love you, you know I love you.' Scott grabbed for Ally's hand.

'Don't fucking touch me! Take me home now, or I will go back in, and I will make a statement.' The tears were making the fresh stitches sting.

Scott drove through red lights, smoking, muttering under his breath. Just outside Ally's house he locked the Range Rover doors.

'Please let me come in with you. You shouldn't be on your own. I love you, baby, and if everyone and everything would just fuck off, we could be together all the time and it wouldn't be such a fucking mess. Please, Ally, just talk to me. I can't let you go like this. I know I lose my rag sometimes. Please let me come in with you, just to talk.'

He shivered. 'I don't want to talk. Let me out.'

'No! You can't just do this. You can't just do this.'

He refused to look at Scott, tugging at the door handle. 'Let me out.'

As soon as Scott's thumb flicked the central locking, Ally stumbled out onto the kerb in the brooding winter dawn. He locked his front door behind him, pushed a heavy chair up against it, pulled the curtains and switched off all the lights. The bed was stained with blood and sex and smelled of Scott, so he pulled all the blankets from the spare room downstairs and passed out under them on the sofa.

CHAPTER NINE

SATURDAY

I wake bathed in Eilidh's warmth and the coconut smell of her hair. She's propped up on pillows, scrolling through her Facebook newsfeed on her phone.

'You slept a bit. Feel any better?' she asks.

'So much better.' I play with her hair, suddenly and desperately horny. She puts her phone down and shuffles back under the duvet beside me. I'm almost tearful with gratitude as she takes my cock in her mouth. I come within minutes, and it knocks my words away. I wallow in the treacly post-coital ooze of wellbeing while it lasts.

'That felt so good.' I pull her tighter against me, kissing her hair.

'Hmm.' She wriggles a little. 'My turn?'

I don't need a second invitation. I love that Eilidh knows what she wants.

'Do you want some coffee?' she asks me afterwards.

'There's no milk.'

'There is, I went to Tesco while you were sleeping. Do you want a bacon roll too?'

'That would be amazing, but you don't have to, sweetheart.'

This is what's wrong with me. I miss her, I'm lonely, that's all. If she were here all the time, things would be so much better. She makes to get out of bed, but I catch her fingers and pull her back for another kiss. Her bemused expression nags at me like a toothache.

'The flat looks as though you'd been burgled. I tidied the kitchen a bit,' she says, smoothing her bed-ruffled hair with her fingers.

'You didn't need to do that.'

'I counted about twelve empty red wine bottles in the recycling, but you had absolutely no food in your fridge. No wonder you're wasting away.'

'I'll give you money for the shopping.'

'Don't be silly,' she says. 'What do you want to do today?'

I wrap my arms around her, so she can't leave. 'Hmm, probably make love to you about twenty times, if that's okay?'

'Yeah, that's not going to happen,' she says. 'We're out of prehistoric condoms.'

She comes back with two mugs of coffee and we watch an old Coen brothers film on my laptop. I can't stop touching her, smelling her hair and kissing her neck and shoulders as she reclines against my chest. We have sex in the shower and all my hormones scream that I love her, that I should have the guts to tell her.

Wrapped in towels, she brings me more coffee on the sofa, and this time, we talk a bit about the film. Eilidh opens a packet of chocolate brownies and I eat five, one after the other. 'You're amazing, thank you,' I tell her, cupping her face in my hands.

Eilidh stiffens and pulls away, flicking crumbs off the sofa cushions. 'Chris, I know you're going to be angry at me, but I've been speaking to Elaine. She's really worried about you. She said I should persuade you to take this week off school and get a GP appointment. I think she's right, you know. You don't seem very well. I was pretty shocked by the change in you.'

I shrug. 'Yeah... I need to sort out my sleeping. I've been shit at work because it's hard to function when you're so knackered. And I think... well, I've been thinking maybe I'm just lonely, you know. I feel great today, because you're here. I feel so much better.'

She's distractedly studying her fingernails.

'I just didn't realise it would be so hard not having you here all the time,' I tell her.

Eilidh coughs abruptly and extricates her fingers from mine. 'Chris, I never was here all the time. I only ever stayed over a couple of times a week. I won't always be here anyway; I'm going back on Monday, and you know, I—'

'Don't speak about it now. I don't want to think about it.' I kiss her mouth to stop her.

'So, what will happen then? Elaine thinks you're depressed. She says—'

'I'm not depressed, Eilidh. I can't sleep, I miss you and work is a bit stressful, that's all.'

'But you'll go to the doctor, at least about the sleeping?'

'I will. I'll make an appointment. Honestly, I feel so much better now you're here. Like I said, it was stupid to leave it so long without seeing each other.'

She nods, cautiously. 'Come on, let's get dressed and go out. I fancy a wander round the shops and you can buy me a Starbucks.'

I hate shopping and Saturday crowds give me the fear, but I agree. I want to make Eilidh happy.

I grip her hand as I carry and pay for her shopping (a dress, some makeup), but I'm relieved when she suggests stopping for coffee. The cafe is crowded with couples like us, some with children, carrier bags and pushchairs. I queue for our drinks, letting Eilidh settle at the table. When I return with two mugs, she's chatting to a young woman who's taken my seat at the small table.

'Chris, this is Megan, my friend from uni. Megan, this is Chris.' I wait for her to explain who I am. She doesn't.

'Hi,' Megan says. 'Sorry, have I got your seat?'

'It's okay—I need to go back and get the cakes. Do you want a coffee?' I ask.

'Oh, that would be brilliant. Can I have a skinny latte?'

She reaches for her handbag, but I tell her not to worry. She's Eilidh's friend.

When I return, they're deep in conversation. Feeling a bit left out, I drink my coffee and scroll through my phone. There's a voicemail from Elaine. Struggling to hear her message over the noise in the coffee shop, I excuse myself.

'Hi, Chris, Elaine here. Apologies for contacting you over the weekend. You'll know I've spoken to Eilidh. I just wanted to let you know we understand at this end that things aren't easy just now, and whatever you need to do, just do it. If you need a bit of time off, don't feel bad. At least your student seems pretty switched on, so hopefully no problems there. You know I'm just at the end of the phone if you need me. Look after yourself, and just let me know how you are if you get a chance.'

I'm distracted, watching a couple across the road as they look in the window of the jewellers. They have their arms around each other's waists, his hand in her back pocket, and her head on his shoulder. They're picking out a ring.

I'm compelled to watch as they squint in the window, pointing and crouching down to see one lower on the display. I can't see the girl's face, but she has lots of curly blond hair under a black cable-knit beanie. I can tell from the way those curls move that she's feeling joyful and animated, and that's mirrored on her boyfriend's face. A blast of icy November air scours the street, sending leaves and litter tumbling across the paths of Saturday shoppers. I shudder and go back inside the warm cafe. Eilidh doesn't look up.

CHAPTER TEN

SUNDAY

It was late on Sunday evening before Ally ventured any further from the sofa than the toilet or the kitchen. He'd slept and sweated through the last thirty-six hours, waking only to smoke and make the odd mug of tea to wash down more painkillers. Every sound outside made him jump, and he hadn't tried looking at himself in the mirror yet. The living room was heavy with stale smoke because he didn't dare open a window. His body was rank with dried blood and the mess Scott had left him in.

Overwhelmed with hopelessness, the smallest action seemed impossible. His phone had run out of battery, and he couldn't bear to think of switching it on. His laptop with all his lesson plans and placement work was in the boot of his car, still abandoned in the school car park since five p.m. on Friday evening. He couldn't show his face at the school tomorrow looking and feeling this awful. Really, there was no other option but Scott.

At about eleven p.m., he finally mustered the energy to start cleaning up the blood on the living room floor; it had dried dark and flaky. He noticed his stained blue shirt lying half under the coffee table, and he picked it up to find it was torn. Aggressive make-up sex after a fight, torn clothes, bruised skin, nothing unusual. He followed the erratic trail of blood splatters up the stairs.

The rest of his clothes had been gathered up and dropped at the end of the bed. His bed was revolting, sheets and quilt twisted and smeared with a horrifying palette of bodily fluids. He went to throw up once again, and the effort of the futile retching left him sore and spent.

He spent a sleepless night on the sofa with the TV on mute, playing over the options in his head, smoking and biting his nails. At four a.m., he allowed himself a quick twitch of the curtains to peer out to the street. In the darkness, he could see nothing but the neighbours' cars parked outside their silent houses and a cat padding across his front garden.

You need to get yourself together and to school. This is what you really want, and he wants you to fuck it up because he knows he's your only other choice.

After a final cigarette, he went upstairs and braved the bedroom again to find clean clothes for work. Almost all his wardrobe was designer stuff bought with Scott's money. In the shower, he had to kneel and hold the side of the bath as the hot water hit him. He watched the water disappearing down the plughole turn from dark pink to clear. In the mirror, he saw the bruising from the cut on his temple had spread to his cheekbone. His left eye was swollen shut and ringed with dark blue. The bruises on his neck were finger-shaped and too high to be hidden by his shirt collar.

He ordered a taxi for seven a.m. and waited, smoking and biting his nails.

After the initial hurdle of facing people and explaining his injury away, the school day went surprisingly well. By getting in so early, he managed to resurrect the lesson plans, neck lots of coffee and have a talk with Chris that, for the first time, wasn't terse and perfunctory. Of course, Chris wanted to know what had happened, asking about the stitches and how he was feeling now. He seemed warmer and less defensive.

'Anyway, how was your weekend? Had to be better than mine,' Ally asked.

Chris's smile was genuine. 'My girlfriend was home for the weekend. She's working out in Spain. It was really good to see her.'

'How long is she back for?'

'She left this morning. I dropped her at the airport before work.'

'Does she come home quite often?'

'No, this is the first time she's been back since August. She worked here before; she's a Languages teacher.'

Chris looked and sounded different when he was talking about her. Ally turned away, deflated, pretending to smooth the tatty edge of a poster on the door.

'We usually have a department meeting on Monday nights,' Chris said. 'You don't have to stay for it.'

'I'll stay, yeah. That'd be great.' There was nothing he wanted to do less than leave the school building and go home.

'I've got to run to the office, and then I'll grab a coffee and we'll get started in ten minutes?'

'Okay, I might just nip out for a fag then.'

It was getting dark already as he stepped out into the car park to light up. The breeze was bitter, so he turned to face the wall and huddled under the collar of his coat. His disposable lighter guttered three or four times, and his hands were clumsy with cold. He swore under his breath and tried again.

'Here,' said a voice behind him.

Ally spun around. The cigarette was removed from his fingers, lit with an expensive Zippo and handed back. He took a breathy drag on it and edged away from Scott.

'Why did you come here?' Ally wheezed.

'I have to talk to you, and when you weren't at home today, I knew that you'd be here.' Coked up, he talked faster than normal. 'I just need you to listen to me, Ally. I need you to know I'm serious about you. I know I've been a dick and I know you've had to put up with shit you should never have had to put up with. I'm going to make it right.'

Ally scuffed the tarmac with his feet. 'Scott, for fuck's sake, not here...'

'Please, just listen to me, because I did listen to what you said on Thursday night, and you're right. I know you're not happy. I'm going to make it right. I finished with Leisha today. She knows there's someone else, so she's pissed off, but I don't care. I'm going to tell my mum and dad tonight; I'm going to tell them I love you and we're going to move in together.'

Ally glanced around them. The dark car park was deserted.

'Oh God, your face is such a mess, Ally.' Scott reached out and touched his bruised cheekbone, his burning fingertips making Ally cringe and drop his cigarette. 'Your pretty wee face.' He cupped Ally's cheek in his hot palm. 'Shame it wasn't your teeth. You'd have had to go and get them fixed then.'

Ally recoiled, sidestepping out of his way. 'Leave me alone. You can't be turning up here.'

Scott grabbed his wrist. 'Ally, listen to me! You know I can make things shitty for you if you won't.' He took out his iPhone with his spare hand and scrolled through his videos. 'You look pretty in this one. You know, the boy who was your birthday treat, down in London? He liked you, didn't even take the extra cash usually required to stay the night. Think your headmaster would like to see it?'

'Let me go.' Ally wrenched against Scott's grip.

Scott jerked him in close and whispered in his ear. 'I'll come to yours later, and we can talk some more. I'll tell Mum and Dad tonight, then you can move in with me straight away. I've got it planned, baby, I've got it all planned.'

'Ally?' Chris called across the car park. 'Ally? You okay?'

Scott spun around, glaring at Chris. 'He's fine.'

'Are you... are you coming back then? We're waiting for you.'

'Yeah, I'm coming,' he whispered, appealing silently to Chris. Scott stood impassively between them.

Oblivious, Chris shouldered past Scott and looked Ally up and down. 'You look frozen. Seriously, you should stop smoking. Let's get back inside.'

Chris was in his shirtsleeves, and he wrapped his arms around himself for heat as Scott studied him, muttering and scuffing the ground with the toes of his boots.

'I'll see you later, eh?' Scott stroked his fingers down Ally's arm, turned and walked away into the darkness.

Ally was shivering as Chris led him back inside.

'That was Scott Binnie, eh? What's he doing here?'

'I... I handed in my notice this weekend.'

When the warm air of the school building hit his lungs, he started coughing, wincing as the stitches tugged through his skin. He sank down onto a low window ledge and covered his face with his hands. He fought not to let tears spill out from the pain and frustration.

'Hey.' Chris sat down next to him. 'Are you okay?'

Ally shook his head. 'I just need a minute.'

'Stay there. I'll get you some water.'

He listened to Chris's footsteps and the glugging noise of the water cooler from down the corridor. His hands were salt-wet now, but he rubbed his face dry as the footsteps returned. 'Thanks.' He took the plastic cup from Chris. 'It's a bit of a mess.' He tried to sound dismissive, but his voice was uneven.

'Yeah, it never was a good idea to fuck about with the Binnies, was it?'

Ally looked up at him, wide-eyed. 'You have no idea. Chris, you have absolutely no idea.'

'He can't just turn up here, though. It's a school, he shouldn't be hanging around. Why didn't he just call you?'

Ally shuddered and stared. 'There is no reason why you should do this for me, Chris, but I really need some help,' he said. 'I need to give the car back to him tonight, and I don't want to go alone. Plus, I don't know how I'd get back once I dropped it off. I'll leave it at their place, but it's out in the sticks. Could you follow me out there and drop me home?'

Chris shrugged. 'Yeah, I suppose so. I'd just be marking essays and watching crap on TV.'

'I'll give you petrol money.'

'Don't be daft.'

Chris's distant smile made Ally feel less hopeless.

CHAPTER ELEVEN

Following the tail lights of the red A3, I drive onto Ally's street, and park up while he goes inside. It's a smart little semi-detached on a quiet cul-de-sac. The harling and windows are new, and the front garden has been paved over so he can park his flashy car off the street. I think briefly of the squalid council house he grew up in. He was too ashamed to invite me home after school.

Eilidh hasn't texted, and I can't stop checking my phone, expecting to hear from her. Sleep evaded me as usual last night, so I left her breathing peacefully in my bed, and sat cross legged in the living room, drafting and re-drafting a love letter for her.

I don't want casual; I want you to be my girlfriend. I want you to come home to me and stay. I think I love you.

Then I spent the rest of the night watching her sleep, wondering at her warmth and softness, inhaling the fading scent of perfume on her neck. Maybe her flight has been delayed or maybe she's just tired from travelling and has forgotten to text when she landed.

Ally emerges from the front door of his house with a cardboard box, which he puts in the boot of the Audi. He glances behind himself, beyond the pool of light from the streetlamp. He's changed out of his work clothes into jeans, a dark coat and a woolly hat pulled down over his ears. He gets in his car and I follow him out onto the dual carriageway in the direction of Bridge of Layne, the town where we grew up. It's just after six and the traffic is heavy. I weave across lanes so as not to lose sight of Ally's car. I think I know where the Binnie's place is, I've driven past it often enough and it's so ostentatious you can't miss it.

Like everyone who grows up here, I was always aware of Binnie Homes and the Binnie family's status. Ally got a job with them after he graduated, which seemed to me like a complete waste of a First in English. Back then we were friends and I told him as much. Ally is ridiculously clever. He should be doing something other than selling overpriced kit houses. It seems like someone else's past, and I shut the gate to it.

There's still nothing from Eilidh.

Filtering off the dual carriageway, I cross the roundabout and follow the ring road which bisects the estate of executive four and five-bedroom Binnie homes where my mum and step-dad still live. Since the Seventies, Binnie Homes have dominated local development, and the town has exploded in size so that its traditional core, is now dwarfed by new estates and the developments radiate out into what was once farm and moorland.

Campbell Binnie made his first million by selling all his farmland for development, just after they found oil. Then the local area, with its small fishing villages huddled around rocky harbours, low hills where whins and gorse and silver birch grew, little farming towns and defiant standing stones, was eroded steadily by burgeoning Binnie housing estates.

Ally signals left at the road sign for Kirkton of Carlyne and takes the B road out of town which crosses the remaining narrow, undeveloped strip between the town and the North

Sea. It's a twisty, unforgiving section of road notorious for accidents and black ice in winter. I'm driving faster than usual, keeping up with the Audi, and I concentrate on negotiating every corner.

After a narrow bridge in a dip in the road, there's a long straight and about a third of the way down it, the brake lights ahead flash red in the darkness and I brake and pull in behind the red A3. There's a half-moon of tarmac in front of the wrought iron gates, where Ally stops and immediately turns off the headlights. He parks hard against an imposing granite block etched in black with the name 'Kirkton House'. I roll down my window.

"Aren't you going up to the house?' I call to him. He hushes me frantically. I watch him drop the keys and his Rolex onto the passenger seat of the A3, before shutting the door and jogging around to the passenger side of my car.

'Come on, let's get going.' He fastens his seatbelt and starts coughing, until his eyes water.

'You're really just dumping it there? With the keys in it?' I ask.

'Come on, let's split before they see the headlights.'

'I don't understand what's going on? Why are you just dumping your company car and phone at the end of their drive?' I start my aged car's noisy engine. 'What have you done?'

'Something wrong with your exhaust.' Ally winces. 'Hurry up, they can hear that in Dundee.'

'What are we hurrying away from? You'd better not have gotten me into any dodgy shit.'

'I will tell you everything, but please can you nip on? If he sees your car, then he'll... honestly, he's lost the plot, Chris.'

Ally studies the mirrors, nibbling at his scabby cuticles until we're back under the streetlights on the outskirts of town.

'I need petrol,' I admit after a few more miles.

'Fucking useless getaway driver you are.' Ally's shoulders sink a little and I note a hint of a smile.

While I fill up, Ally goes inside to buy cigarettes and chocolate. He pays for my petrol and dumps the sweets in the footwell when he gets back to the car.

'Can I smoke?' he asks as I pull out of the service station.

'Open the window then.' I checked my phone again while Ally was inside. Still nothing. He notices the glow of the screen radiating from inside the glove box.

'Did she get back okay?' Ally asks.

'What?'

'Your girlfriend, did she get back home?'

'Far as I know,' I say shortly. It's none of his fucking business. A backdraught of cigarette smoke catches in my throat. I make a face, and Ally apologises and leans further out the window.

'Can't believe you smoke. When did you start? You didn't smoke before.'

'Don't really remember... I suppose I must have started because Scott smokes. It's been about eight years,' he said.

I drop one hand from the steering wheel and wind down my window. *Because Scott smokes.* The penny drops. I feel sick and wish he wasn't in my car, sitting next to me.

'Eight years ago is when I last saw you,' I say, not bothering to hide my disgust. 'Scott Binnie is your boyfriend? Seriously? Since when?'

Ally finishes biting his thumbnail. 'Boyfriend' is probably

stretching the point a bit. Nobody knows about it. Pretty much since I graduated, since before I last saw you.'

Apology creeps into his voice as he waits for the reaction he deserves. I won't give him the satisfaction. I drive on silently.

The stretch of dual carriageway that links Bridge of Layne with Aberlayne and the smaller satellite town of Bridgend, where Ally lives, is quiet now. Ally smokes and stares out the window morosely. I try not to look at him, willing the drive to be over. As I merge off at the exit for Bridgend, I change down the gears for the thirty-miles-per-hour stretch leading through the industrial estate on the outskirts of the town.

On the sharp bend before the first roundabout, headlights appear close behind me, and then a red car shoots past me on the bend, engine shrilling as it overtakes us.

'What a dickhead.' I shake my head in disbelief. It's a red Audi A3.

'Oh fuck!' Ally sits up abruptly, flicking his cigarette out of the window and shutting it. 'That's my car. He must have been there and seen me drop it off. Oh my God, he was coked off his tits.' He looks at me in a blind panic. As if I could help him.

'So he's going to your house now? Why?' I ask.

'I don't want to think about that,' Ally indicates the wound on his head. 'He was waiting for me on Friday night, and...'

'Fuck's sake, Ally! He did that to you? What happened?'

'It doesn't matter what happened,' Ally snaps. 'There's nothing you can do about it.'

'He assaulted you. You have to do something about it!'

'Please don't lecture me right now. I don't know what to do. I can't even go home. It's a complete fucking mess, Chris.'

'You need to go to the police then. He can't just do this.'

'No. There's no point. Campbell Binnie golfs with the chief inspector. Plus, Scott has all this stuff he'd use to get back at me.'

'Stuff?' I can't believe what I'm hearing.

'Photos, videos.' Ally looks away, covering his mouth with his fingers.

'Jesus, how fucking stupid! I can't believe I used to be jealous of how intelligent you were. Why would you let anyone do that?' As a rule, I don't talk to people that way, but he fully deserves it. He clearly hasn't changed.

Ally goes to pop his seatbelt. 'You're right, and you don't owe me anything. Thanks for the lift. You can just drop me off anywhere round here'

I want to do that. I want him out of my car. I don't know why I agreed to help him tonight. I'm a mug. If he wants to fuck about with Scott Binnie, then what does he expect? I should just leave him here, let him sort his own mess.

'This is bullshit, Ally. I can't believe you've dragged me into this. It's kind of the last thing I need right now.'

'Well, just let me out then.' Ally's fingers are wrapped around the door handle. 'I didn't mean for this to happen, I just needed a lift. Let me out.'

I brake so hard that he likely regrets taking his seatbelt off; he only stops himself from crashing into the dashboard by throwing out his hands. He swears and shakes his head as I turn the car around.

'We're going back to my flat. You'll be out of his way there.' I crunch a gear change and lose my temper. I never shout but I can't help myself. 'You're a fucking idiot, Ally! You've just told me that Scott Binnie knocked you out at the weekend; he threatened you outside work and now he's stalking you, high on drugs. Do you really think I'm going to be okay with dropping you off and letting more crazy shit happen to you? You know, I wish I'd never had to see you again, but for whatever fucked up reason, here you are. I fucking knew you'd be bad news all over again.'

Ally turns away, rolls down the window again and lights another cigarette. His hands are shaking. He exhales out the window and his free arm is clamped protectively round his stomach. I know he's crying, and it incenses me. I hate that he cries so easily.

CHAPTER TWELVE

Ally left school with six Highers and the Dux medal, and I got five Highers and the English medal. We had both applied to study English at University, I got my place at Glasgow and Ally got his in Aberdeen.

It was the summer between the end of school and the first term of university, the last summer before we left to study in different cities. Most weekends that summer we got drunk with the other outgoing Sixth Years. We had crappy part-time jobs that we attended sporadically, and unreliable cars that we drove far too fast. We were both academic, loved reading, and had gravitated to each other because we could talk about books. Ally was shabby, mysterious, didn't talk about home. He never talked about girls but would listen patiently as I agonised over my fumbling shyness with them. At sixteen, I gratefully disposed of my virginity with Carolynn Flett. I liked her, but she wanted to keep her options open, so it came to nothing. Ally hadn't much to say about her, other than that he thought she was a bit shallow.

I only visited his home a handful of times. I understood that Ally was ashamed of the cramped, dirty council house. Ally's dad was an alcoholic who found it hard to stay in a job, and his mum was fragile and struggling. She had Ally at sixteen, and that summer she was expecting Jamie, his little brother. 'A happy mistake,' she said, but she didn't seem very happy. Ally's mum was elfin and unkempt; she

78

always seemed nervous and jittery, expecting the worst. I called her Mrs. McClay and she blushed and said I was so polite. 'I hope you are polite like that when you go round people's houses, Alasdair?' she'd chide.

Ally's room had black mould high up in the corner by the window, where he couldn't hide it with Manic Street Preachers posters. The stale, musty smell clung to him. He'd made himself bookshelves out of MDF and breeze blocks and tried to paint the peeling woodchip. When we went upstairs, Ally would always push open a window to let out the fug of smoke and unwashed clothes. We had to be quiet when his dad was sleeping off a hangover in the next bedroom.

My mum, on the other hand, has crippling OCD, and kept our house like a show home. The cream carpets and fresh flowers made Ally uneasy. In the pristine kitchen, he'd dab worriedly at the marble worktop with his cuff when his mug of tea splashed. 'Your house is amazing,' he said. 'It's like a hotel.' Then he admitted he'd never stayed in a hotel.

Increasingly, he spent time at my house after school finished, eating my mum's home cooking and listening to me practice my guitar after we finished our homework.

Sometimes, Ally turned up unexpectedly and just wanted to sit and read in the corner of my bedroom. He didn't talk but seemed apologetic for the space he occupied. If I asked him, he would explain what had happened at home, why he'd walked out, but I knew that, to Ally, this would seem like a betrayal of his parents. I stopped asking.

My stepdad worked offshore for a month at a time, which was a relief to both of us, as then we didn't have to pretend to be interested in watching or talking about football. 'He could be worse,' said Ally. 'He could be like my Dad.'

'What does your mum do when your dad gets really drunk?' I asked him one Friday evening, as we sat in my primly landscaped back garden.

'Shuts herself in the bathroom or comes in with me if it's through the night.'

'In with you? Like, in your bed?'

Ally nodded. 'Where else is she going to go? She's so pregnant now, I sleep on the floor, or on the sofa. Don't know what she'll do when the baby's born.'

'Is she scared of your dad?'

'She always says she isn't. He doesn't hit her, but you should hear the way he speaks to her. He's a total dick. I fucking hate him.' Ally pulled handfuls of grass and piled them between his crossed legs.

'Was he always like that?'

'No, he's got worse since she got pregnant. Mum's so fucking stupid having a baby with him.'

I hated to see Ally so morose, so I suggested picking up some friends and a carry-out and going down to the river to drink up the beautiful evening. There was a deep pool in the river where we could swim on hot days. It was a sheltered suntrap by a bridge, with beautiful old silver birch and rowan trees. Someone brought disposable barbecues, and there were tons of cheap lager and cider and alcopops cooling in the shallows.

Carolynn was there, and I made a good show of being nonchalant about it, making breezy comments and acting as if I had never cold-sweated with terror and felt her naked body completely rigid beneath me.

As she chatted to me about her exam results, I noticed Ally staring at the little fish thronging around the tins and bottles propped in the shallows. He never learned to swim, so he just sat there on the edge of the water watching us splash about in the river. The others were further down the bank still, waist-deep in the pool and messing about like kids. We'd been drinking for a couple of hours and Ally looked flushed. The sun had caught his temples, and the nape of his neck was pink. His feet and ankles trailed in the river, and he dangled a bottle of cheap cider in his fingers.

I can remember what he was wearing, I remember pushing my sunglasses up onto my head as I talked to Carolynn. I was still shirtless and barefoot from swimming in the river. I watched Ally skimming stones and had a sinking feeling that he was distancing himself from me, preparing to go our separate ways as we left for university. I depended on him—I didn't talk much to anyone else—and I was scared. I have never made friends easily.

Heather called to Carolynn from down the current that they were going up to the car to get changed. Carolynn gave me a brief, ambiguous hug and scrambled up the bank after the others.

'Hey.' I sat down on the sandy bank next to Ally and reached into the water for a beer. 'You're quiet tonight.'

'Hmm.' Ally drained his cider and turned the bottle upside down in the wet sand.

'What are you thinking about?'

Ally didn't look up; he was shifting pebbles along the riverbed with his toes. The air smelled of gorse flowers and barbecue. Exquisite colours of evening light played on the peaty surface of the water.

'What's going on with you and Carolynn then?' he asked me, studying the currents.

'Nothing.' I shuffled nearer to him, trying to catch his soft voice over the rushing of the river. 'I think she got off with Dan Fraser last weekend. He's coming down later after his shift.'

'Do you still like her?' Ally drew his wet feet out of the cold water and hugged his knees, curling his toes on the short, warm grass.

I shrugged and sipped my beer, which had gone flat. 'I kind of hoped she would go away,' I said.

'Me too,' Ally said, and his voice sounded strange. He turned and looked straight into my eyes, unblinking for a few long, tense minutes. It's mad, but I knew what would happen. I looked away, down at my lap, resisting. But he was like a magnet. When I looked up and met his eyes again, my lips moved but no sounds came out. As Ally tentatively moved closer, shivers swarmed between my shoulder blades. When his fingers alighted gently on mine, I flinched.

'Shit, sorry! I'm sorry,' he whispered, but I grabbed his hand, pulling him towards me. Fireworks went off at the base of my spine as I brushed my lips against his, nudging and grazing until I felt him respond. His mouth opened, and his head tilted to let me closer, the first taste of his hot tongue ebbing and flowing with the pressure of his own.

'This way,' Ally said. Lacing his fingers into my clammy hand, he pulled me to my feet and led me down the riverbank to where the tall, purple willow herb and silver birch branches shielded us from view. Fizzing with desire, we came to a stop under a gnarled rowan. Ally's fingers cupped the nape of my neck. I ran my fingers through his fair hair and felt the heat and sweat on his bare shoulders.

A soft moan came from my throat, gone tight with need. I shifted my weight so that I tilted Ally's head back until he deep sighed into my mouth. We kissed frantically, like we were running out of time. He gripped my fingers so tight they went numb. Then, gently laying his palms on my collarbone, he pushed me back so that he could reach for the zip of my cargo shorts. My breath caught in my throat, and I choked on my own fear. I grabbed his wrists to stop him. *Not this way,* I thought, *not like this.*

'Hey, slow down.' I tried to smile, but Ally's eyes brimmed with frustrated tears. 'They could come back anytime. You could stay over at mine tonight.' I kissed him again, trying to make sense of what was happening to me.

'It's fucking unbearable, Chris. You have no idea how much I want you.'

Ally's voice was husky with disappointment. I apologised, but I couldn't explain, not even as we lay under the rowan on a fragrant mat of crushed ferns, watching as the last of the summer twilight faded, entwining our fingers and kissing until our lips stung. The darkness closed around us, and the distant voices grew closer, echoing off the surface of the river. Downstream from where we lay together, someone had lit a fire.

That night, in my double bed, I let Ally kiss my neck and chest and stomach, and I ran my fingers all over his pale skin, my hands hot and shaking. When Ally's hand strayed to move beneath the fabric of my shorts, I flinched away again. I felt sick.

'What's wrong?' Ally asked with a tender smoothing gesture down my cheek.

'I don't know. I really want to.' I wasn't lying. I wanted him to touch me. I wanted us to get naked and try everything I was thinking about, but I was paralysed. 'I'm scared, I think. Have you done it before?'

'No... No, I haven't.'

His disappointment brimmed over this time, tears streaking his cheekbones so that he tasted salty when I kissed him. I tried to explain, but I didn't understand it myself. He lay in my arms and listened to me talk, comforting himself by playing with my hair.

'I do want you,' I told him. 'I'm scared. I don't know if I can do it yet, but it is what I want.'

'It's okay,' he said. 'All I think about is you, Chris. There's no hurry.'

'What will happen now?' I asked him.

Ally yawned expansively, his breath still thick and sweet with alcohol. 'I think we'll fall asleep like this, so I hope your mum doesn't come in to wake you up tomorrow.'

'No, I mean, when term starts. When I go to Glasgow.'

'Everything will be okay.'

Ally moulded himself against my naked back, nuzzled into the nape of my neck and fell asleep.

CHAPTER THIRTEEN

NOVEMBER 2010

It started to sleet as Chris reverse-parked outside his
flat, and the beam from the street light bisected the car
window, casting orange glow across his face. Ally glanced
sideways at him, so remote behind a shell of hostile anxiety.
His face was etched with tension, his hands clawed on the
steering wheel.

Ally silently followed him up the stairs and waited
while he unlocked the door and switched on the lights.
Standing awkwardly just inside, Ally looked around the
flat for somewhere to sit. It wasn't homely—in fact it gave
him the feeling that something had been removed abruptly
and not replaced. Basic furniture, bare white walls and no
photos, or anything else too personal. There were a couple
of pin-tacked posters and rickety, overloaded bookshelves,
which had spawned a few dusty favelas of stacked-up novels
on either side.

Chris came back from the kitchen with a plate of cheese
on toast and a bottle of red wine and two glasses. After
setting it down on the coffee table, he poured Ally a glass
and passed him a pack of painkillers.

'Is it cold in here?' Chris asked.

Ally shook his head. Shivering uncontrollably, he hugged
his sides for warmth.

Chris pulled a fleece throw off an ancient, threadbare
armchair and laid it over Ally's lap. 'Here.'

Ally pulled it around himself and sank the painkillers with most of the glass of wine. 'Thank you,' he said, and necked the rest of the glass.

Chris refilled his glass and grabbed a slice of toast, folding himself into the armchair. 'It's okay, shit happens. Especially to you, it seems.'

Ally fidgeted under the blanket. 'I really need to phone Jamie. I call him most nights, and he won't understand what's going on if I don't. I gave my phone back to Scott with the car. Could I use your landline?' he asked.

'Yeah, of course. It's in the bedroom.' Chris indicated the first door off the tiny hallway.

The room was small, with just enough room to walk around the three sides of the unmade double bed. Ally sat on the side nearest to the door, where the handset lay next to a discarded baby wipe covered in black and tan makeup stains and the corner of a condom packet.

Jamie answered the phone after a few short rings.

'Hey, wee man.'

'Alasdair? Is that you?'

'Yeah. How was school? How did you get on at Chess club today?'

'I won both matches, so now I'm in the final. I don't think I'll win because Artur is Russian. Also, he can practice every evening with his father, who is a chess master. Dad isn't home tonight, and I don't know where he is, Alasdair.'

'Did he come home after work? Maybe he's got some overtime?' He stopped to saw his bottom jaw left to right seven times, punctuating his speech with the nervous tic. 'Are you okay, Jamie? Did he leave you something to eat?'

'I don't know. I haven't looked. A man was here. He was looking for you, and he was driving your car, so I opened the door. It was definitely the wrong thing to do.'

'It's okay, Jamie, you didn't do anything wrong. Has he gone away now?'

'Yes. He went away quite quickly. I said you didn't live here anymore and that he wouldn't find you unless he went to your house. He was quite unpleasant. Why was he driving your car? Did he steal it?'

'No, it's not my car anymore. I don't have a phone anymore either, so you should just wait until I call you for the next couple of days. I'll get a new one really soon.'

'I've done my homework, so I think I'll go upstairs to read soon. I got a new book from the library today.'

'Find something to eat first. And lock the door, okay? Dad will have his own key. Don't open the door again unless it's Dad or me, please.'

'I definitely won't open the door again. What he said made no sense.'

'What did he say?'

'He said, 'I will let you into a secret, Jamie. I think you're going to be even prettier than your big brother.' It's possible that he was drunk, as that makes people say nonsensical things.'

'Possibly. Just ignore it. And don't tell Dad about that when he gets home. Listen, I'm on my friend's phone so I can't talk for long tonight, but I'll phone you tomorrow.'

'Goodnight.'

'Goodnight, wee man.'

Of course, he should have known Scott would go there. He knew all the baggage, all the darkest fears he could exploit. With a fair degree of certainty, he could predict that his dad's job would be next, and now he himself wouldn't have much extra cash to replace the minimum hourly wage his dad earned to support him and Jamie.

'How old is Jamie now?' Chris asked when he went back into the living room.

Ally picked up his wine glass and the blankets and sank back down onto the sofa. 'He's almost thirteen, but he's sitting his Higher Maths and Physics this year. He's something else. Honestly, he's so bright it's unbelievable. The maths teachers can't keep up with him.'

'Like you then. You were like that at school, A's in everything.'

'No, I was never in his league.' He shrugged, needled by cravings. 'Scott's been there too, to my Dad's house. Jamie thought it was me because he was in my car, so he opened the door. He didn't do anything, but he made some creepy comment to Jamie. I knew he'd drag them into it somehow. Fuck's sake!'

Ally dug his fingernails into the palms of his hands, balling them up hard enough to leave white indents. Chris sat cross-legged in the armchair, finishing the last of the cheese and toast, occasionally glancing at the screen of his phone, which was balanced on the armrest.

'I have no idea what is going on. You'd better fill me in. It's got to be more entertaining than these Higher essays.'

Ally held the blanket protectively across his middle. 'The thing is... it's not like this happens all the time. Scott can be a dick, but he doesn't always act like this. Only since I signed up for the PGDE. He was so used to knowing where I was, and who I was with when I was working for Binnie. We had a legitimate excuse to see each other, and occasionally we would go away together and stuff like that. He realised when I had my uni interview that that was going to stop, and it pissed him off. I suppose it made me start looking for a way out, and he sussed that out really quickly.'

'So why doesn't anyone know about you and him? Is he married or something?' Chris asked.

'No, he's not married. He's engaged to Leisha Burnett. You know, the girl who reads the news on STV? She's based in Glasgow for work, so that helps. Mainly it's because of his folks, they're born-again Christians and he's shit scared of them finding out. His dad would disown him.'

Chris frowned and took his glasses off to dab at the lenses. 'I don't get how, in eight years, his fiancée has never suspected he's seeing you.'

'He hasn't known her that long, just since last year.' Ally drained his second glass of red wine.

'Eh? So, hang on... you've been with him for years, then he meets a girl and gets engaged, and you're okay with it?'

'No, not okay.' He stared into his empty glass. 'Really not okay.'

Chris leaned over and topped it up.

'There was a lot of stuff I wasn't okay with, Chris, but I was so in love with him I couldn't see past him. And yes, it does make me feel stupid, before you say it. Really fucking stupid.'

'Yeah.' Chris let the bottle drop on the table. 'Being in love with someone who doesn't feel the same will do that, eh?'

The comment hung in the air, making it glacial. Ally sighed heavily, fished out a cigarette and lighter and made to get up.

'It's snowing outside. Just stay there.' Chris got up and opened the window behind the sofa. 'You'd better stay here tonight. I'll take you back to yours in the morning to get ready for work. I don't know what we do about Scott Binnie, apart from keep you away from him until he calms down. Have you... I mean, have you told him you don't want to see him anymore? Like, spelled it out? If I remember him from school, he's not that bright.'

Ally tore at a flap of cuticle with his teeth, tasting blood. 'Yeah, I told him after what happened on Friday night, but he thinks I didn't know what I was saying because I was concussed. Anyway, he never listens if it's something he doesn't want to hear.'

'Did you know what you were saying? Did you mean it?'

Ally wavered, feeling a telling heat on his cheekbones. 'I think so.'

'You think so,' Chris said, shaking his head. 'Oh, well, that's okay then.'

Ally stared into his wine glass, tapping the end of his cigarette on a dirty coffee mug. 'Give me a break... I already feel like shit.'

Chris switched on his laptop and googled a photo of Leisha Burnett. The search returned several pictures, one of which was of her at a function with Scott Binnie. She was tall and slim with huge dark eyes, long auburn hair and perfect teeth. They looked revoltingly good together, Scott buff and clean-shaven in his kilt outfit and Leisha in a turquoise evening dress and heels.

'Does he actually sleep with her, or is she just cover, then?' Chris frowned over the laptop screen. 'She is pretty stunning.'

'No, he sleeps with her. He definitely sleeps with her.'

Chris clicked on the photo and studied it more closely. Scott had one arm around her tiny waist, and her fingers were wrapped around her clutch in a way that displayed her ostentatious engagement ring.

'Does she know Scott likes boys too?'

'I think I'm the only one who knows that.'

'Do you know her? I mean, have you met her?'

Ally took a deep drag on his cigarette and shook his head, exhaling slowly. He'd never made himself think about these things, and, in the moment, he hated Chris for asking them.

'STV's Leisha Burnett with her fiancé, Scott Binnie of the Binnie Homes Group, attend the North Scotland Business Awards at the exclusive Seacrags Hotel,' Chris read out loud.

'Tonight he told me that he'd finished with her. For me.'

Chris looked up from the screen. 'At the school, you mean? When I saw him? Why did he come to tell you that?'

'He said... he said he wanted me to know he really loves me, so he's finished with her and is going to tell his mum and dad about us, so we can move in together.'

'Do you believe him?'

'I don't know.'

'Do you want to believe him?' Chris asked gently.

Ally took a long time to answer. 'I want to be an English teacher. I want to finish this placement and pass. I want to start reading books again. I want to be able to afford my wee house. I want my dad to have a job and keep it together so that Jamie is okay now that Mum's moved away. I don't want to be alone all the time.'

Chris puzzled for a moment. 'Is that why you want to believe him?'

Ally looked at him, shrugged and bit his lip. As though recognising his desperation, Chris backed down.

'Why did you say you wanted to start reading again?' he asked.

Ally was relieved at the new line of questioning. 'I stopped reading a few years ago. I mean, I still read, but not much. Not like I used to... like we used to. I took work home, then I was tired, I watched crap on TV. I was always checking my phone, texting him every ten minutes if we couldn't see each other. He did buy me a Kindle, but I hate it. I don't know why, really.'

'I'm not reading either,' Chris said. 'I can't concentrate. It's since I started having trouble sleeping. I used to read for hours every night, but now I just get this horrible feeling when I realise I've got the whole evening ahead of me. Maybe it's because I'm always so tired.'

Ally hunched forward over his wine glass and studied the photo Chris had left open on his laptop. He could remember when Scott was invited to that event. Leisha had been staying at his apartment, so they couldn't see each other for a few days before and after. This provoked much frantic sexting. Scott booked two astronomically expensive rooms at opposite ends of the five-star Seacrags, and once Leisha was safely champagne-drunk and snoring, he'd left her alone in one of them. He'd smuggled Ally into the other one via a staff entrance and an enormous bribe to the harassed Front of House.

He'd woken Ally at about three a.m., carrying a bottle of Grey Goose in his hand and a wrap of cocaine, condoms and lube in his sporran. They didn't speak. He climbed onto the bed and pushed Ally backwards onto the plush pillows, straddling him so he could feel his hard-on. His breath tasted alcoholic, and he was sweating from the heat of the ballroom and the heavy fabric of the kilt material. Ally started to unbutton Scott's dress shirt and pull off his tie, but Scott stopped him to kiss the inside of his wrists and the sensitive crease of his elbow before taking his fingers into his mouth. Ally struggled free and continued undressing him until Scott sat astride him naked from the waist up, his gym-perfected abs and chest and arms shining with sweat. Ally broke the silence.

'I thought you were never coming.'

Scott shushed him, kissing him hard before going to cut the cocaine with his credit card on the bedside table. They both did a line. Scott took a long pull on the bottle of vodka and urgently pushed Ally's head down towards his lap.

'Ally?' Chris sounded irritated, impatient. He must have felt vulnerable after admitting to the reading thing, and now Ally wasn't listening.

'Sorry, I... yeah, I know. Have you tried anything, you know, that would help you sleep? Have you seen anyone about it?'

Chris drained his first glass of wine. There was a small amount left in the bottle, so he splashed a little into Ally's and the rest into the bottom of his own glass. 'Elaine... Elaine at work. Well, she strongly suggested that I make a doctor's appointment because, well, she and Eilidh talk. This morning Elaine even handed me the phone and waited until I'd called. I've been a bit shit at work. It's so hard when you're so tired you can't think straight. I've made a few stupid mistakes, like I forgot about Parent's Evening two weeks ago. I keep forgetting stuff, missing deadlines. She kept saying I should take time off. It's like she thinks they'd be better off without me.'

He got up and took himself to the kitchen, and Ally heard the clink of a second bottle of wine being opened. While he was gone, Ally pulled the laptop across the coffee table and lifted it onto his lap. Scott looked so sexy in the photo. So perfect. He had to close it, switch it off. He replaced the laptop on the coffee table and lit a second cigarette.

'You're a really good teacher,' he called to Chris. 'Your classes think you're amazing.'

From the kitchen, Chris mumbled something self-deprecating. Ally's head began to swim. He hadn't eaten since lunch, so he picked up the last bit of toast from the plate on the coffee table.

'You make it look really easy,' he said. 'You're so calm and you always know what to say. There wasn't anyone like you at Cairnhill. No wonder you're a PT already.'

Chris came back through with the open bottle and a big bag of crisps, which he tossed to Ally. He'd removed his glasses, which made Ally do a double take. It made him look younger, but the charcoal shadows under his eyes were more pronounced.

'Just an acting PT.' He settled himself back into the tatty chair. 'It's a good school—not all the kids are easy, but the staff are great. It's a good place to have a placement. Eilidh had her placement there and then came back for her probation year last year.'

'Is that how you met her?' Ally tore open the crisps.

Chris nodded.

Ally glanced around the flat. 'Do you have a picture of her?'

'Em... here.' Chris picked up the laptop and moved to the space on the sofa next to Ally. He clicked on his Facebook wall and brought up her photo.

Ally studied her profile picture, a full-length shot that looked like it had been taken at a wedding. The first thing that struck him was that she was overweight, made obvious by the pale, clingy dress she wore. She had long dark-brown hair and her face was freckly and sweet but not beautiful. She was no Leisha Burnett. Scott would have said she was fat, believing girls above a size twelve were fair game for ridicule.

'She's pretty,' Ally said.

Chris smiled. 'She hates having her photo taken, so she hasn't got that many on her page, and I don't have any on my phone. I did some sketches of her this weekend.'

'Can I see them, or are they not that kind of sketches?'

Chris pulled his sketch pad out from under the coffee table and passed it to Ally. They were mostly of her snub-nosed profile and her large, heavily lashed eyes. Small studies. He'd sketched her fingers curled around an apple showing the detail of her neatly shaped fingernails. On the last page, she was hugging her knees, looking down with her hair falling halfway across her face. It was her, but as Chris saw her, precious and sexy.

A sadness swelled in Ally's throat. He handed the sketch pad back to Chris, who smiled again as he traced his fingertip over his sketches.

'Chris? Remember when you drew me that time?'

'Huh?' Chris looked up, startled.

'You drew me when I was sleeping.'

Chris nodded, stiff-backed.

'I still have it,' Ally admitted.

Chris put the sketch pad down and picked up his full wine glass. 'No, Ally. I don't remember.' Then he stood up and left the room, shutting the bedroom door.

Ally listened to him moving around. He leant forward, cradling the wound on his head with his right hand. *You fucking idiot*, he berated himself. *You fucking moron*.

When Chris reappeared, he was pale and unsmiling. 'I changed the bed. You sleep through there.'

'I can't take your room, Chris! I'll sleep here. It's fine,' Ally protested.

'I don't sleep anyway.' Chris dropped a pile of blankets on the arm of the sofa. 'Go on.'

Ally obeyed; it seemed like days since he'd slept. Stripping off and folding his clothes neatly, he curled between the strange bed's cold sheets and inhaled Chris's familiar mint-and-sage smell. Despite himself, he fell asleep in minutes.

CHAPTER FOURTEEN

TUESDAY

After a long night with only scattered minutes of sleep on the sofa, I stand under the shower knowing I must face Ally and another day at work. Eilidh texted last night, but it just said, 'Back now.' She isn't answering her phone. Despair is starting to claw at my guts.

Outside, a dusting of snow has fallen, and the sky is still black and heavy. It's very early. I wrap myself in a towel and go silently into my bedroom to gather some clothes. It's too cold in the flat to sit marking jotters without several layers on. The room is dark save a grey outline around the window and the glow of the digital alarm clock.

Ally is breathing heavily in his sleep, so I reach for the small lamp beside the bed. Ally doesn't stir as it softly illuminates the room. He's sleeping with the quilt tangled around his lower legs. Compelled, I study the pale hairs on his arms, his lightly freckled shoulders, the expanse of naked skin from the nape of his neck to the back of his thighs, and his face, half-buried in the pillow, protected by his cupped hand. His arms and neck are splashed with livid bruises, and septic burns the size of a fag end. I scoop up some clothes and reach across to switch off the light again.

'Chris?'

I take a step back towards the door.

'Don't go.' Ally sits up and pulls the quilt around him. 'I'll go next door if you want to get dressed.'

I pull my T-shirt over my head and secure the towel around my waist. 'Look at the state of you. What happened to you on Friday night? '

Ally hugs himself, shaking his head. 'I don't remember.'

'It looks awful. What did he do to you?'

I'm not prepared for his volcanic reaction. 'Fuck off, Chris! Jesus, why is it okay for you to get all shitty about what you will and won't talk about, but you can expect me to spill my guts just because you ask me? You know I need a friend right now, so stop sitting on the fence, feeling pleased with yourself for helping me while staying judgemental and disapproving. It's been years, Chris, fucking years! Why is it still such a big deal for you?'

'So, you don't want to tell me what happened then? Are you embarrassed about what Scott gets off on doing to you?'

'Fuck you! Why would I tell you anything? So you can make me suffer for stuff that happened a decade ago?' Ally's knuckles are white as he grips the quilt defensively over his middle. 'You've always been so fucking uptight.'

I'm shaking. How fucking *dare* he talk to me this way?

'I can see how you'd go for someone like him,' I say. 'Someone who just sees you as a commodity. He doesn't respect you enough to disapprove of anything you do! Being the victim is so much easier though, isn't it? And you fucking love the drama, and the attention. You haven't changed.'

'That's not fair!' Ally's voice splits with anger. 'That's totally fucking out of order.'

'You'll have a nice scar when your face heals; probably make you even more attractive to the next rich, sadistic and unavailable fuckwit who comes along.'

Ally pulls the quilt further up his chest. 'When did you become such a vindictive cunt?'

'Oh, so I'm vindictive? He smashes your face off a table and whatever the fuck those other marks are, but you're saying *I'm* vindictive? You don't want to hear what I have to say, that's all. If someone treats you that way, you have a choice. It must be great having a nice car and all the perks, but, seriously, the money can't be worth putting up with that. You're not stupid; you've got a first-class honours degree, and if you had bothered to do something with that, then you wouldn't be here now.'

'You're fucking jealous, that's your problem!' Ally explodes, and I can see the tears coming.

My anger feels like heartburn, makes me sick. 'Yeah, that's right, pal, I'm really jealous of you. Everything about you right now is so enviable. You must think I'm as fucking shallow as you are if you think I'd be jealous of all the material shit you got yourself because you've been Scott Binnie's fuck buddy for all this time. Get over yourself!'

'No, you're jealous because I was... you're jealous because of Scott. You know full well I don't give a shit about money. It just pisses you off that I love him, well, that I'— now he starts crying—'that I loved him. You know what, Chris? You didn't know what you wanted. What makes you think you can still hold it against me now?'

'Because you humiliated me and made me feel like a total fucking idiot. You were meant to be my friend.'

'Yeah, but we weren't friends, were we?' Ally sobs. 'It was a mess.' He's crying so hard he drags the back of his hand across his snotty nose like a kid. I can't bear to look at him.

'You made it a mess," I say. "It was straightforward for me.'

'Yeah, because you were totally clueless and naive, Chris. You still are. You live in some uptight parallel universe.'

'For fucks sake, stop crying! You still love a bit of drama, eh? You know why you want to be with someone who pushes you around? It's because you have no self-respect and you'll do anything for a bit of attention. That's why you screwed around at uni.'

'I slept around because I was a fucking normal student! Not everyone locks themselves in their garret and pours their bleeding heart out on paper while refusing to sully their pure ideal of love by actually having sex, you know. It's like that Medieval Studies option we had to do in Third Year; you know Lancelot and Guinevere and all that courtly love bollocks. 'I love you Ally, but just the idea of you, though. Your very existence makes me a better person, but for fuck's sake don't touch me.' He forces a bitter laugh between the heaving sobs. 'I do still have all your letters, though. I put them all in a Lever Arch, so they read like a book.'

This catches me unawares and gives him time to forge on.

'Anyway, you probably won't have to work with me for much longer. I reckon when Dr. Laurenson opens his emails this morning he'll have a wee home video courtesy of Scott, starring yours truly, and that'll be that.'

He trails the back of his hand across his stained face again and goes to get out of bed. I stop him with a hand on his wrist. The unexpected touch makes Ally flinch and exhale. He expects me to hurt him, and this blindsides me. My temper is subsiding, but his tears are not. Eilidh left a packet of wipes on the bedside table, and I pluck one out and press it into Ally's fingers.

'Hey, wipe your face, stop crying.' I catch a fat, rolling tear with my thumb, shocked by the heat coming from the injured side of Ally's face. 'Shit, maybe you need some antibiotics for that?'

Ally's fingers close on my wrist—they're hot too—and he folds himself against my chest. I feel the damp of his face through the thin fabric of my T-shirt and drape my arm over Ally's back.

'I'm sorry,' I say. 'I shouldn't have said all that.'

I inhale stale smoke and sharp sweat and a faint menthol scent, like a trace of medicated shampoo. His fingers are still wrapped around my wrist. Gently pulling it free, I rest my fingers over Ally's, and his shoulders drop in a kind of relief. Minutes pass, and Ally's breathing slows. I let my free hand move very slightly. It's resting just below a shoulder blade. My thumb is barely tracing a tiny arc across the bumps of a vertebra. My body is sending my brain maddening white noise. *Your very existence makes me a better person, but for fuck's sake don't touch me...*

I am frozen. Ally is leaning heavily against me, clasping my hand and breathing into my chest. There is nothing I can do.

CHAPTER FIFTEEN

Ally opened his eyes again, alone, disorientated. Chris must have pulled the covers over him, leaving him to sleep on. He reached for his phone to check the time, then remembered he didn't have a phone. Did he cry himself to sleep in front of Chris? Did that happen? He rubbed his face and shuddered.

He found Chris working on his laptop in the living room, dressed and ready to leave. 'What time is it? Do we have time to go to my house, so I can get changed?' he yawned.

Chris nodded. 'It's half seven. We can if we go now.' He shut the laptop and picked up his bag of marking. He patiently passed Ally a thermal mug of coffee and his coat.

'You should have woken me earlier. Sorry.'

There had been a covering of snow overnight, and it was still dark and sub-zero outside. Traffic was building earlier than normal, and it was nearly eight when they got to Ally's house.

'I'll be five minutes.'

'It's okay, as long as we're in by quarter to.'

Ally climbed out of the car, desperate for his first cigarette of the morning. It was too cold to drive with the window down.

'Do you want to come in?' he asked Chris.

'It's okay; I'll stay and keep the heater going.'

When Ally appeared fifteen minutes later, he was showered and shaved and breathless with the effort of doing it all at speed. Wheezing, he folded himself into the passenger seat. The hot, dry air inside the car started him coughing.

As Chris pulled away, Ally put on his seatbelt and opened the padded envelope that he'd found lying on the doormat. There was no writing on the front. When he slid his finger along the glued edge and opened it, his mobile phone fell out, along with a folded sheet of Binnie Homes stationery that had Scott's spidery writing on both sides.

I went through all the messages on your phone and I read all your emails too. I was so sure you'd been seeing someone else, but I couldn't find anything, so now I feel even worse. Every single text in the last three weeks is to me, and all your emails are work ones. So now I don't know what to think. I know you think what happened was my fault and you're upset with me, but I know we can work all that out if you let me explain. You have no idea how shit I feel. I told Leisha I was in love with someone else, and I've told Mum and Dad that I'm in love with you. You need to stay out of their way though, I don't know what they'll do. Serena has known about us for a while. I can't believe you dumped the car and all the stuff I gave you. It's all yours; I don't want it back. I'm sitting in your car now, writing this, and it's fucking killing me. It was all I could do for you, Ally, all I could do was buy you stuff. So please take your phone back. At least then I know if you want to call me you can. I told Mum and Dad we're moving in together and I don't care who knows anymore. I've got some money put away where they can't touch it. I can't think about anything but getting you back, you've no idea. Please just call me soon so I know you're okay. I've been here for hours, I went back to your school and I went to your dad's house too. When you get this, just text me, please, anything. I'm fucked without you, I miss you, and I need you.

'He's sent your phone back?'

'Yeah,' Ally smoothed the note on his lap. 'He's told his family about us.'

'Fucking hell. They'll take a contract out on you.'

Chris put his foot down a little as they hit the main road again. Grey, sludgy light streaked the sky now.

'Jesus,' Ally said. 'What did he think would happen?'

'Is he trying to prove that he's serious about you? To get you back?'

Ally didn't hear Chris's question; he was reading and re-reading the letter.

Tuesday was a full day on Ally's student timetable, and because they arrived only ten minutes before the bell, he had to pull together final preparations for periods one and two while the others had registration class. Callum rolled up as the bell was ringing and, knowing that Ally was taking his first-period class, made himself a coffee.

The morning passed in a blur, and at lunchtime Ally worked at the computer in the base while Callum and Chris despaired about whose Second-Year students had written the stupidest answers in the end-of-unit test. Louise came in about one thirty, returning from her probationer training at the council offices. She'd come via the baker's and laid out various cakes on grease-slicked paper bags.

'What are you having, Ally? Donut or a custard slice? Do you want a coffee?' she called.

He wanted a cigarette, but without a car to hide in, it was too tricky to smoke discretely. 'Black coffee, one sugar, and a donut, thanks,' he said as Louise boiled the kettle and Chris asked her how boring her training day had been this time. Ally noted how he joked with the others, the warmth in his tone.

Louise brought the mugs across to where he was working. Sugar from the donut dusted the skirt of her black shift dress. 'All sorted for Higher this afternoon?'

'Hmm, I think so. Does this look okay?' He showed her his lesson plan and the discussion questions he'd prepared on *Macbeth*.

She took her time reading over what he'd typed and made a few suggestions. 'Guess what?' She sipped her coffee, smiling at him, 'I spoke to the Art probationer today.'

'Eh?'

'The Art probationer, remember? So fit it's ridiculous?!'

'Were we talking about this on Friday night? Because I was half-cut, and it's all a bit of a blank,' he said, still half focussed on the screen.

'Oh, never mind. All you need to know is that he's criminally attractive. He spoke to me at the CPD thing. He's never taken me on before. Guess what he said.'

He glanced sideways to see if Callum and Chris were paying any attention to their hushed exchange. They didn't seem to be. 'What?'

'Yeah, so, even though he's never acknowledged my existence before, he comes across at coffee time, casual as you like, and asks how our student is getting on,' she whispered.

'So? It was just an excuse to talk to you.'

'I don't think so. He asked your name, where you're from, what uni you're at. I said he should come to the pub with us on Friday and meet you.' She nudged him.

'Louise! That's really not cool.'

'Why not? Wait till you see him, he's gorgeous. His name's Luca, and he's half-Italian.'

Luca, like the Suzanne Vega song, but Louise was too young to get the reference.

'He was chatting you up,' Ally insisted.

'No. Honestly. I think this time, my gaydar was exact.' She laughed, making Chris and Callum turn around.

'What are you two lovebirds giggling about?' Callum said. 'Did you know these two left together after a few sherries on Friday night, Chris? He's a smooth-talking bastard, that Mr. McClay.'

'Oh my God, Callum, you're such a twat,' Louise said. 'You're not funny!'

'My wife thinks I'm hilarious,' he said drily. 'Says she just looks at me and can't stop laughing.'

Ally gauged Chris's reaction. He just shook his head and rolled his eyes in mock despair.

At the end of period six, Ally settled down in the English base and began planning Wednesday's lessons. The day had gone well, except that Jordan Franks kicked off again. This time Chris didn't intervene when Ally asked Jordan to step outside and calm down. The boy's animosity was searing, and he was well versed at hitting raw nerves.

'Who are you anyway? You're not a proper teacher, so why should I do what you say? You can't handle our class. If Mr. Elliot wasn't in the room you wouldn't know what to do.'

'Jordan, this isn't about me. If you act this way it holds everyone back, including you.'

'Don't care.'

'You wouldn't make such an issue of things if you didn't care.'

'Don't.'

'Okay, whatever. This needs to stop, otherwise...'

The minute hesitation was all the encouragement Jordan needed. 'Or what? You can't tell me what to do; you're not even a teacher. No one cares what you say, that's why no one's listening to you in there.'

The click of heels coming along the corridor silenced Jordan, who heard Elaine approaching before Ally did.

'Jordan Franks, come with me please,' she ordered. Muttering under his breath he followed her, shoulders slouched and hands in pockets.

'We've all been there,' Chris said. 'Everyone has a kid like Jordan who gets right under their skin. They don't hate you, they just hate school in general. You can't take it personally.'

'How do you always know what to say to him?' Ally drew blood round a ragged nail.

'Well... it's just variations on a script of positive requests, like a stuck record: 'Do this, Jordan, thank you' or 'Sit down, Jordan, thank you.' Instead of keeping on telling him what he's doing wrong and getting his back up even more, just remind him what he needs to do to be in the right.'

'Don't you get pissed off with him? It must be so hard not to just... lose it sometimes.' Ally frowned.

'Oh, God yeah! He made Louise cry last term and, literally, I could have punched him. She's pretty, and that usually snake charms the Third-Year boys a bit. They want to impress her, so they behave for her. Not him, though— Jordan took his phone out in class, threw his book on the floor and took a photo up her skirt when she bent over to pick it up. She held it together really well until the end of the lesson, but she was so upset afterwards I didn't know what to do. I called his parents, but they just thought it was funny.'

'Fucking hell.' Ally shook his head in disbelief. 'Did he get excluded?'

Chris laughed cynically. 'No, because apparently, that would look terrible for the school; we have the lowest rate of exclusions in the region. Basically, he got a day off-timetable and a letter home to his parents, who didn't give a shit anyway, and that's the end of it. We pretend we're promoting inclusion and positive behaviour. Great, isn't it?!'

'Poor Louise. Is that why you teach that class now?'

'Yeah, but don't tell her that. I made up some story about changing her timetable because of her needing experience teaching senior classes, but yeah, really, I didn't want her to get completely put off teaching. The problem is, she'll get a permanent job next year, and no doubt they'll pile all the shitty classes on her. There are plenty of schools much worse than here.'

'I suppose I saw that on my last placement.'

'Yeah, I wouldn't like to work at Cairnhill. Was it awful?'

'Not awful, but I, um, I had a pretty bad time with one class there too.' Ally chewed at a snag on his thumbnail. 'Is that normal? That one class just hates you? Won't do anything for you?'

'Yeah, pretty much, especially until they get to know you. Sometimes it takes months to win them over. I got ripped to shreds my first placement as well,' said Chris. 'I remember this Fourth-Year girl kicked off at me for asking her to move seats. She just sat back with her arms folded and said, 'Fucking make me, you specky cunt.'

Ally laughed, guarding his own anecdotes about things students said to him. *D'you fancy Mr. Welsh or Mr. Jackson? What are you looking at, his arse? Do you top or bottom, Mr.*

McClay? He had Scott's words echoing in his head, too. *If they find out you're gay, then you're toast.*

'Did stuff like that happen when we were at school?' he asked Chris. 'I don't remember it being that bad, do you?'

'Yeah, well, we were total geeks at school. I think the most rebellious thing I ever did was leave my homework on the bus, and all the teachers loved you. You never got in trouble.'

'That's not true!' Ally said. 'I was always getting in trouble for chatting in class, forgetting to do stuff on time. I got demerits for being late unless your mum drove us to school.'

Chris raised an eyebrow. 'Yeah, but you always charm your way out of shit, eh?'

He turned his back on Ally and began typing again.

Ally bit his nails to the quick over what to do with the Third-Year class. He was shifting the S3 pupils around on a seating plan like a kind of human Rubik's cube when Callum came in to the base and noisily shut the door. He'd taken his Second-Year class up to the library and had borrowed the evening paper from the librarian.

'Fucking Audi drivers, eh, Ally?' He spread the front page of the local paper across Ally's keyboard. The photo on the cover was of Scott with Leisha, plus a smaller one of the red A3 taken through the gates of Kirkton House with the plate blurred out.

Police Stop Businessman in Possession of Class A Drugs: Shame of Wealthy Local Family.

Local magnate Scott Binnie, 28, was arrested in the early hours of this morning after police pulled him over in an Audi A3 owned by Binnie Homes Group. Binnie, who is engaged to STV star Leisha Burnett, was found to be in possession of

Class A drugs. Reports that he was under the influence at the time of his arrest have yet to be confirmed. Mr. Binnie's father, Campbell Binnie, MBE, gave a short statement this morning, requesting privacy to allow his family to support his son at a difficult time. His fiancée, Miss Burnett, 25, was unavailable for comment.

Ally shrugged and handed him back the paper.

'Isn't that who you work for?' Callum asked.

'Worked for.'

'What a tosser, eh? If I had his kind of money I wouldn't be snorting it up my nose. And I wouldn't be driving a shitty A3. No offence, Ally,' Callum said as he scooped his planner from where he'd dumped it earlier on the tatty seats by the window.

'None taken.' Ally coughed to disguise the shock warping his voice.

'These guys live in a different world, eh?' Callum dropped the paper on the coffee table and wandered off.

Ally tried to refocus on his seating plan, but his pulse thundered in his neck, drowning out his thoughts. He pulled at his tie and sipped some water. Unable to settle, he went to find his phone, which he'd left in the pocket of the coat he'd slung on the back of the chair beside Chris's desk. Chris's classroom door was closed but he was working at his computer, so Ally let himself in.

'You okay?' Chris asked.

Ally scrambled in his coat pockets until he found the phone and walked out of the room again, switching it on. Distracted, he didn't hear Chris's voice. The phone lit up, still having a little battery. He shut the door of the English base, huddled on the window seats and tapped on Scott's number. It went straight to voicemail.

He tried again repeatedly, frantically, until he became aware that Chris was sitting next to him, speaking to him, his voice insistent but unintelligible through the white noise in his mind. Chris took the phone gently out of his hands and placed it on the table. Then he passed him a bottle of water, which Ally sipped obediently. He still couldn't process anything that Chris was saying. Chris picked up the newspaper from where Callum had dumped it among the dirty coffee mugs and cake crumbs that covered the low table. He seemed to take forever reading the short article.

I'm fucked without you. I miss you, I need you.

'Maybe I'm not cut out for this,' Ally said through clenched teeth,

'Ally, you're so cut out for it, it makes me sick. You're good at everything, you always fucking were.'

'Why do you think he's not answering his phone?'

'Well, either because he can't, or because he doesn't want to talk to you,' Chris said. 'He gave you the phone back, so he knows that he can get hold of you.'

'It's my fault this happened.'

'No, it's not. You know it's not. Come on, I'll drive you home.'

Ally barely spoke in the car. There was no need to, because Chris was wired and uncharacteristically talkative. As he smoked his last cigarette, he wished Chris would stop asking him questions.

'Are you sure you're okay?' he asked Ally when they were by the shop where Ally normally bought cigarettes.

'Mm-hmm. I'll just get out here.'

'I'll pick you up at half seven tomorrow, okay?'

Ally was checking his phone, biting his bottom lip.

'Ally?'

'What?'

'I'll pick you up usual time tomorrow, eh?'

Ally nodded, folding himself out of Chris's car and into the murky evening.

CHAPTER SIXTEEN

Dr. Rae is female, about my age, and excruciatingly attractive. She has a dainty stripe of freckles across her nose.

'It's mostly that I can't sleep. I mean, not more than an hour or two at a time.'

She leans forward at that, her fitted floral blouse gaping at the front. 'When did this start?'

'A few months ago. It wasn't so bad in the summer.'

'How are you feeling?'

I haven't slept for four months—I feel like shit.

'I'm just tired all the time. I forget stuff and make stupid mistakes. I suppose it's starting to get me down a bit.'

'Okay, so is there anything that's stressing you out at the moment apart from not being able to sleep? What kind of work do you do?'

'I'm an English teacher.'

She laughs, sympathetic. 'Teaching is a stressful job. Do you work long hours? Or is that a stupid question?'

'I suppose I do. It's quite full-on. I'm Head of Department just now so there's a lot of extra work.'

'And how are things at home?'

The question blindsides me with its implication that a thirty-year-old professional like me might have a home filled with a significant other, pets, possibly children, and not a shitty rented flat with the same furniture I had as a student, and where I sleep alone among sticky Kleenex and live off crisps and takeaways.

'I live on my own.' I rub my clammy palms together, staring at the floor. 'I do have a girlfriend, but she's living abroad. I suppose that gets me down a bit too.'

'When you say that it gets you down, what do you mean by that? Are you feeling quite negative a lot of the time?'

'I feel useless, like I keep getting things wrong, forgetting things.'

'Do you have trouble concentrating?'

'Yeah, I can't read anymore.' I despair at how stupid I sound. 'I mean of course I can read, I'm an English teacher, but I can't concentrate on a book anymore. I used to read all the time. It was sort of... what I did.'

She nods. 'What do you enjoy doing apart from reading?'

It sounds like an awkward question during a bad date. 'I don't really have much time after work. I do a bit of drawing, I play the guitar, or well, I used to. I'm too tired all the time to do anything much.'

'Have you got family close by? What about friends? Who do you talk to?'

I'm sweating under the hot strip light. The room stinks of carpet glue and disinfectant as the articulate young woman keeps asking me question after mortifying question, so patient and concerned.

'Have you talked to your girlfriend about how you're feeling?' she asks.

I've not spoken to her in days, she's ignoring my calls. No, I don't. I can't speak to her and I can't speak to you.

I just shake my head dumbly. I never imagined it would be this hard. I almost wish she'd tell me to man up and get a grip. It would be easier.

'Take your time, Chris. It's not easy to talk about these things.'

I wish I were dead. I can't believe that thought just tore its way out. Everything I'm fighting to contain is oozing from the cracks in my composure. Eilidh sees it, and it repels her; Ally sees it, and it provokes him. I'm mired in this malignant sadness. There's a shadow forming between me and the world, and it's harder and harder to push through it.

'Have you thought that you might be depressed?' she asks softly, leaning forward again in her chair.

I nod and swallow over the congestion in my throat. 'I'm drinking too much, I don't eat properly, I can't relax. I thought I was maybe just a bit stressed out with the new job, but it's starting to feel like everything takes just the biggest effort ever. I'm so tired...' I have an appalling urge to stop fighting and cry, but I bite down hard on the inside of my cheek and dig my fingernails into the flesh of my arm.

Dr. Rae touches the same arm very lightly. 'I'm going to ask you this question because I have to, and it's important that I know, but have you ever had any thoughts of harming yourself?'

I shake my head and shrug. 'I'd be no great loss. I just let people down. My stepdad doesn't talk to me. I know deep down it isn't going anywhere with Eilidh, and I can't sort stuff out in my head that happened ten years ago. I'm useless.'

'That's evidently not true, Chris. You're holding down a very responsible job and are well educated, presentable, and articulate. You feel like this because you're depressed, so you've done the right thing in coming here. It will get better—you will feel better, believe me. We just need to sort out what the best way forward is for you.'

She prints out a couple of prescriptions—sleeping pills for a week and antidepressants for longer—and gives me some standard advice about what to do if I feel worse. 'I need to see you again in a fortnight, so can you make another appointment on your way out, please? If you need to see me before then, that's absolutely fine too.'

She stands up, indicating that the appointment is over. Flayed and vulnerable, the idea of stepping back out into the busy waiting room paralyses me. I just look at her in despair.

CHAPTER SEVENTEEN

WEDNESDAY

Ally stopped to get some shopping for Jamie and to stock up on cigarettes and custard creams, his current staples. He bought as much as he could carry home from the arcade of shops beside the bus stop. Not having a car was an infuriating hassle, and the crappy November weather made it even more so. His hair curled in the damp, and his fingers were chilled and sliced by the handles of the overladen bags.

The streets in his parents' estate were named after promising oilfields of the seventies: Piper, Thistle, Claymore. Jamie's bike lay abandoned on the overgrown, litter-clogged front grass, and light from the kitchen filtered through the greasy slatted blinds.

He let himself in without knocking. 'Jamie, it's me. Where are you?' He pushed the kitchen door open and was assailed with the smell of bins and chip fat. He wrinkled his nose and put the carrier bags on the sticky table. 'Jamie?'

'I have one more sentence to complete,' came a muffled voice from the living room. Jamie lay on the floor writing in an A4 jotter, the muted TV providing the only light in the room.

'How can you see to write anything? It's so dark in here.' Ally flicked the switch on the standard lamp as Jamie continued writing without looking up. 'Is Dad home?' He found the remote under a sofa cushion and switched the TV off.

'I've finished my geography homework now.' Jamie looked up and made a startled sound before scrambling to his feet. 'What has happened to you? Why is your face like that?'

'I tripped and hit the corner of a table. It's okay. I'm fine. Look—it's not that bad.'

Jamie came close, smelling of teenage skin and unwashed clothes, clearly both fascinated and horrified by the damage to the side of Ally's face. 'Is it painful? Did you have to go to hospital to get those stitches?'

'Yeah, I did. It's not too bad. Not like when you fell off your bike, eh?'

'Now I have a cycling helmet and I always wear it. It's very important. Will you do my English homework for me, please?'

Ally laughed and snatched up the jotter his brother had been writing in, flicking through the pages. 'No, I will not do it for you. That's cheating. What is it you have to do?'

'I have to write about a significant memory, but I don't think I have any *significant* memories,' Jamie said.

'Oh my God! Have you got Mrs. Stewart? I did that same homework fifteen years ago!'

'Yes, Mrs. Stewart calls me 'Alasdair's brother' when she forgets my name, which is quite often. She's quite an old lady, so that is why she forgets everything. What significant memory did you write about for Mrs Stewart?'

'It was such a significant memory that I've completely forgotten what it was.'

In truth, Ally remembered what he'd written about with chilling clarity, and he also remembered the excruciating chat with his guidance teacher that followed it. Maybe Mrs. Stewart remembered it too.

*My dad is called David McClay. My significant memory
is the day he lost his job at Aberdeen Journals. That was a
bad day, because since then he's not a journalist. He's not
anything anymore, and he's not like my dad.*

Jamie must not write anything similar for her.

'Are you hungry?' Ally asked. 'I got some shopping.'

'Yes, can you make me an omelette and help me do my
homework, please?' Jamie was still eyeing Ally's injury.

There were no clean plates or pans to be found, so
Ally filled the sink to do some washing up. Jamie spread
his homework across the kitchen table and methodically
sharpened his pencils, laying them out in order of size.

'Is Dad on the late shift tonight?' Ally asked over his
shoulder.

'He's home. He's upstairs. Alasdair, what should I
write about?'

'I don't know, wee man. It's your memory, not mine.
What's significant to you isn't necessarily significant to
anyone else.' He buttoned back his shirtsleeves to keep
them out of the dishwater, watching Jamie in the dark
reflection in the kitchen window.

'I don't know what's significant to me,' Jamie puzzled
unhappily. 'I wish this was physics homework.'

Ally tried to encourage him. 'Think about, um... think
about something you remember that was really important
to you at the time.'

'Like when Mum moved out? Is that a significant
memory? Could I write about that?'

Ally closed his eyes for a moment and sighed. 'It might
be better to write about something positive,' he suggested.
'Did you say Dad is upstairs?'

'The door has been closed all afternoon. I don't go in to his bedroom if the door's been closed. Dad's not in a good mood. I'm not allowed to phone Mum tonight, so I'm glad you're here.'

'Why aren't you allowed to call her? What's been happening, Jamie?' Ally lowered his voice.

Jamie shrugged and began copying his title and underlining it in his jotter.

After shaking his hands dry and wiping them on the backs of his trousers, Ally left Jamie at the kitchen table and shouted up the stairs. 'Dad? You there?' He climbed the stairs, stepping over several piles of washing and an abandoned plate and mug.

'Dad?' He knocked on the bedroom door. 'It's Ally. Can I come in?'

There was an unintelligible grunt and the sound of the bed springs complaining as someone moved. The door opened grudgingly. Inside the room it was dark and smoky, and the flickering TV gave out an unhealthy orange light. An unmistakable smell oozed from Ally's father, sickeningly strong.

'Jesus, what happened to you?' David McClay asked.

'Just fell. It's nothing.'

'I didn't hear your car.'

'It's... are you coming downstairs or what? I'm making Jamie something to eat.'

His dad yawned. 'What time is it?'

'It's half seven.' Ally hovered at the door, getting nowhere. 'Dad, what's happening, eh? Scott said you got a warning at work last week because you've been off a few times, been late a lot.'

Ally's father drew back in distaste. 'Yeah, your pal Scott, eh? All of twenty-eight years old and he's done fuck all to earn the millions he's sitting on. He'll get his wrist slapped for doing drugs and then straight back to living the high life. Not fair, is it? You with your Dux medal and all your Highers and nothing much to show for it.'

'You been drinking, then? Jamie's hungry. Have you looked near him today?'

'Jamie's fine. There's nothing coming over our Jamie. Do you want a fag?' Unsteadily, his dad he moved towards the dresser and shook a couple of cigarettes out of the packet.

'You're smoking in the house now?'

'It's my house.'

'Won't be if you lose your job again,' Ally said. 'Jamie wants to stay with you, fuck knows why, but you could at least make an effort for him.'

'You look more like your mother every time I see you, Alasdair. You bitch and moan like her too.'

Tentative footsteps on the stairs cut Ally short as Jamie called out, 'Please, can you come back downstairs now, Alasdair? I'm quite hungry now, and you did say you would make me an omelette and help me with my essay.'

'Dad could help you with it, Jamie. Dad's really good at writing,' he said through his teeth before turning his back to go downstairs.

After getting Jamie started on his assignment and doing enough dishes to make supper, they heard irregular footsteps coming down the stairs. Jamie glanced up at the door and then determinedly refocussed on his English jotter.

'Hey, sunshine.' David ruffled Jamie's hair and pulled out the chair next to him.

'It's very important that I concentrate on this homework. I need to complete it before Alasdair goes home so that he can correct it for me.' Jamie continued printing and underlining his title.

'He's not an English teacher yet, pal.'

'This kitchen's disgusting.' Ally dropped a mouldy tomato into the overflowing bin under the sink.

'My son, the domestic goddess,' David wheezed and then laughed at his own joke. 'You'll make somebody a great wife one day, Alasdair.'

Ally ignored him and carried on grating cheddar while the pan warmed up.

'What did you do to your face then? It's a mess.'

'Tripped and fell against the coffee table.'

'When?'

'Friday night.'

'Had you been drinking?'

Ally said nothing, keeping his back turned as he cracked the eggs and speared the yolks.

'I heard you put in your notice at Binnie,' his dad continued.

'Yeah, that's right. I did.'

'Scott take your car back? Jamie said he came here looking for you. He must be pissed off.'

Ally took a deep breath and bit his lip, laying down the fork he was holding. 'I'm on placement just now. I can't keep up with everything, so yeah, I put in my notice.'

'I suppose you must be alright for money these days? You'll manage a few months living off your savings. Remember, teachers don't earn the kind of money you're used to making at Binnie. No bonuses or company car anymore. You'll be taking a fair cut in your salary.'

Ally turned on his heel, seething. 'Are you actually advising me on money, Dad? Really? Or are you just worried I won't be able to sub for you the next few months? If so, all the more reason for you to get your arse into work in the morning, eh?'

'You're a right obnoxious little shit, Alasdair McClay.'

Ally looked over at Jamie, who was adept at zoning out of confrontations, and he bit back his response, composing himself as he waited for the omelette to cook.

'This is almost ready, Jamie. How are you getting on with your essay?'

'I have a friend now,' Jamie said, looking up from his English jotter. 'At school. I have a friend that I made by going to Chess Club in the library at lunchtime. It can be hard for me to make friends, and I haven't really had any friends since starting at the Academy. When you took me for fish and chips at the beach, I told you about how I had found a place behind the recycling bins to hide at lunchtime because I get terribly anxious about people who I don't know bumping into me or trying to talk to me. It took me a long time to be able to go to Chess Club, and in the end Mrs. Forsyth took me there and sat with me the first time. I know that she did that because you phoned her, Alasdair, but that's okay, because now I have a friend. My friend is called Artur, and he's Russian and very good at chess. Sometimes we even talk about other things too, although he can't speak a lot of English yet. We go the library together every lunchtime now.'

He gave a rare hint of a smile without eye contact, but Ally knew the smile was for him.

'So, my significant memory is about fish and chips,' he said, and carried on writing.

Ally called Scott as he walked home from the bus stop. When he answered, his voice sounded lost and hesitant.

'I wanted to call you, babe. They wouldn't let me,' Scott said.

'I heard what happened,' Ally said.

There was the flick of Scott's lighter and a breathy pause. 'You don't know the half of it. They wouldn't let me talk to you—Dad and Serena took my phone. Dad could make sure that I don't lose my licence, if he wanted to, but he won't. He fucking hates me, Ally. Mum won't speak to me since I told them about us. She's crying and praying and all this bullshit. They're making me go to this place, like I'm some kind of junkie and all I did was a bit of coke. They're fucking clueless. I'm not going. They can't make me.'

'It's probably not such a bad idea,' Ally said. 'Better that than the police make an example of you.'

'No,' he said. 'That's bullshit. I'm not going through with it. I don't have a problem, everyone does coke. I was just unlucky to get caught.'

Ally heard Serena's voice in the background. She was there, monitoring their call.

'It's been all over the papers,' Ally said, 'so it looks better for you if you go. Anyway, it would do you good to get some space to think.

'Ally, I'm not going. They won't let me see you or speak to you. They're just doing it to keep us apart.'

'It's for the best.'

'What's for the best? Ally, seriously. If I could just... I can make this right, you know I can. We can sort it out.' Scott's voice was raw with desperation.

'It wasn't working, you know that. Your parents will never be okay with it and you'll lose everything.'

'I don't give a fuck anymore; I don't care. You're right to be pissed off with me, I was a dick to you, and I know that. Can't you see I'm really trying to make it right? Jesus, Ally. I love you, I'll do anything.' Scott began to cry, and Ally heard his sister hiss at him to get a grip and hang up.

'Scott?' Ally asked.

'I'm here, babe. I'm still here.'

'You should go. I think you should do the rehab thing, just to calm everyone down.'

'When I get back, you'll move in with me? We'll look for a place together?'

'We'll talk about it when you get back.'

'You don't mean it. I know you don't mean it.'

Ally sighed as he fumbled with the key to his front door. Serena was shouting at Scott now, and the line went dead.

Nothing seemed to help still his racing mind. He poured a massive gin and splashed in some token tonic, then lit up and tried to do some work on the laptop. Ally fought a nagging urge to speak to Chris, even though it seemed like only a memory of their friendship still existed. He thought of Tuesday morning, and how excruciating it was that he'd folded against Chris's unwilling shoulder to seek solace that he had no right to.

He hadn't pulled the plain, red folder of handwritten letters down from the high shelf of the wardrobe for a long time. Chris had always written like a teacher, not a misplaced apostrophe or spelling mistake to be found. Lots of the letters had appended sketches, and most included quotes from whatever Chris happened to be reading at the time. Ally had filed them chronologically, with a divider between each semester. The earliest ones, from the first angst-ridden term away from home, were hard to read. The final ones, impossibly so.

He carried the red folder back downstairs to where his drink and ashtray were and rested his heels on the edge of the sofa so that he could prop the folder open across his thighs.

Honestly, it never stops raining here. I'm looking out the window now, and literally everything is grey and dripping and miserable. I'm reading The Sun Also Rises *and thinking about Spain and how they must get tired of it being hot all the time. I hate my flatmate so much. Last night he brought his stupid loud girlfriend back, and the walls are so thin. They don't even bother to hide it. God, I miss you.*

I miss you so much. I can't believe I won't see you until December. I am making a few friends, but it's not the same. I hope it's better for you. At least, back home, you know people. I see and hear and read new things all the time, but I'm always wondering what you would think of them, or what you would say in that situation. You always know what to say.

I hope things are better for you at home now. It must be so hard trying to study when Jamie is up all through the night crying. Do you think your mum is getting better now? I'm glad she went to the doctor, because I've read it's quite common to feel like that after having a baby. I know you are working most nights, but if you get a chance, it'd be good to speak on the phone. I don't know about you, but this is not at all what I thought uni would be like. I love the courses, and I think I'm doing alright, but I didn't think I'd have so much time to feel homesick. I should probably have gone into halls for the first year like they suggested. It might have been easier to meet people. Making friends is bullshit, isn't it? I thought everyone would be like-minded and it'd be easy to talk to them, but it's just like school really. There are cliques and certain crowds, and unless you go out drinking all the time, you're sort of on the margins. I suppose it's not that easy for you to go out drinking either when you're living at home and working in the evenings?

Poor Chris. It had been easier for Ally to stay on his pedestal than to admit he was unworthy of it. At least it had been something to try and live up to. It was a long way to fall, when he inevitably did.

He flicked through the three years of letters, from the heartbroken hormonal muddle of Freshers' Week to the final weeks of that first year. By the second year, he'd started working at Binnie, where Chris would pick him up after work during the holidays. They'd go back to his pristine home and shut themselves in Chris's room. Chris absorbed him, to the point where Ally couldn't imagine why he screwed around during term. He was content to stay in their small world of books and records and cups of tea, frantic kisses and clumsy hand jobs. He felt adrift when Chris went back to Glasgow.

He was addicted to the feeling of being desired by strangers, and it was ridiculously easy to feed that addiction. Ally, the overachieving misfit, discovered that he had more than just his impressive Higher results when it came to attracting an exciting kind of attention. By the third year of university, he had lost control, and couldn't enjoy sex with strangers for more than a few climactic moments. When he spent any longer than necessary in someone's bed, it was only because he didn't want to go home to his own. He wasn't discreet; he didn't care what the bitchy circles he moved in were saying about him. Soon, he started sleeping with Scott behind Chris's back. He almost couldn't believe that Chris didn't know, couldn't taste the guilt when he kissed him. Surely Chris, of all people, could read between his lines?

CHAPTER EIGHTEEN

2001

I call Ally, feeling desperate, but his mum answers the phone. She's never sharp when I phone, just sounds varying degrees of harassed. Usually Jamie's screaming in the background and she shrieks at him to stop doing something. But this time it's late, after eleven, and there's no sound in the background save a TV turned up too loud.

'Is that you, Chris? No, he's not here. He's out again. He's never in these days.'

'Oh. It's okay. Sorry for phoning so late. I just... I just hadn't heard from him, you know, about this weekend? Could you ask him to call me when he gets a chance?'

'Where are you just now? Still down in Glasgow?' she asks.

'Yeah.'

'I'll leave a note for when he gets in.'

'Thank you.'

I hang up the phone and trudge back to my bedroom. The Anglepoise lamp burns over the flat-pack desk strewn with pens and lined A4. My hand hurts from writing, so I put the nibbled biro down and bite my lip hard. Not a word of what I write is for anyone to see. Later I'll shove it right to the bottom of the wheelie bin. Ally told me about Jamie's imaginary friend called Will, who he talks to for hours in a coded language. My A4 notebook serves a similar purpose for me.

It's one of those nights when I can't even listen to music, because every minor chord or wistful lyric is scalding. I can't cry, so I just sit on the squeaky single bed, gripping a pillow and digging my fingernails into the thin skin of my palms. I picture my bed at home, a double divan in a spacious first-floor room with a sloping ceiling and Velux windows. My guitar is on its stand, clothes are hanging on the back of an old chair, and untidy piles of books and CDs colonise every corner. Familiar sounds come from downstairs, and Mum is pushing the door open and letting the light flood in to wake me for school, putting a cup of sweet tea next to my bed.

Only kids get homesick. You're not a kid. Get a grip.

I get up, wash my face and make a cup of tea. The kitchen of the rented flat smells awful, of old fat and unwashed dishcloths and bins left too long. The cracked and bulging linoleum makes sucking noises beneath my feet. It's after midnight before the phone rings. I run to answer it.

'Hey, it's me. Mum said you phoned.' Ally sounds treacly and good-natured, as if he's been drinking.

'Yeah, it's... nothing important. I just wanted to speak to you, and I wondered if you'd thought any more about this weekend?'

'This weekend?'

I don't understand. Maybe he is drunk, because he can't have forgotten. We've always put a lot of thought into each other's birthdays. His was in July and I made him a meaningful mixtape and bought him a plain silver ring and a signed Iain Banks novel.

'I mean, it's fine if you can't manage. It's no big deal,' I say.

The silence on the end of the line confirms the latter suspicion.

'What did we say we'd do this weekend?'

I take a deep breath, try to keep my tone even. 'You said you might come down this weekend. For my birthday?'

Ally swears under his breath and apologises. 'Oh shit, yeah, of course! What have you got planned? Have you got people coming to yours or are you going out?'

How can it be that he doesn't understand me anymore? And if Ally doesn't understand me, then who does? I'm devastated.

'I... It doesn't matter. If you can't come, I might just get the train home to see Mum and Paul instead.' My voice betrays the kind of night I'm having, its loneliness, its hopelessness.

'Aw fuck, Chris! I'm sorry. I'll change my shifts at work. I'll come down. You sound miserable.'

'I wish I'd never come down here to uni. I miss you. You haven't written for ages; I was starting to think you don't—'

'I've shitloads of coursework just now, and I'm working thirty hours a week. And I've got Jamie to look after for Mum,' Ally protests.

'You always seem to be out drinking. Even your mum said that when I called earlier.'

I hear him sigh. 'I miss you too, Chris. I'm sorry. I'll text Scott and see if I can change my shift.'

'Scott?' I ask uneasily. 'As in Scott Binnie? Are you on first-name terms with him now?'

Ally grunts and changes the subject. 'What's the plan for this weekend anyway?'

'What do you mean?'

'For your birthday? Are we going out?'

'I wasn't really planning anything,' I say. In fact, I was planning on spending all weekend with Ally, being myself. Reading to each other, talking and touching, and lying next to him trying to tell him how I feel because I can't show it the way he wants me to.

'It's your twenty-first, you idiot. You have to do something!'

'I don't know. I haven't been going out much lately.' Not at all, if I'm truthful, except to lectures and the library and the twenty-four-hour corner shop for cider and instant noodles.

'I bet going out in Glasgow is much better than Aberdeen.'

'If you want to go out we can go out,' I say, without enthusiasm.

'Chris, I'm sorry I haven't written back.' Ally's voice drops. I picture him sitting on the bottom step in his house's small hallway, holding the phone against his ear with his shoulder. 'I love getting your letters, Chris. They're wee works of art. They're so good sometimes it puts me off replying. There's nothing I could write back that would measure up.'

'Don't be stupid. You're good at everything, and your writing's amazing.'

'Bollocks.'

'Where have you been tonight then?'

'I... I met up with a few friends from my course after work.' He hesitates, coughs. 'Chris, are you okay? You sound really down.'

'I miss you. I shouldn't have come here. I wish I weren't so far away from you.'

'I do miss you too, Chris. I know I'm a thoughtless dick, but I do. I miss you all the time.'

'I love you,' I whisper, almost hoping he doesn't hear me.

'Oh Chris, you know I... Me too.'

I put the phone against my chest, inhale, exhale and swallow everything back.

'Are you still there? Chris? Chris?'

'Uh-huh, I'm here. When will you know if you can change your shift?'

'It should be okay. They don't really care when I do the hours as long as I get through what I'm meant to. I'll send a quick text just now if you can hang on?'

'It's twenty to one in the morning, Ally. Maybe you shouldn't be texting right now?'

Ally was confident that he could text Scott Binnie any time and be sure of a prompt response. Still he felt a sickly mix of guilt and nerves, talking to Chris about Scott.

'It's okay, don't stress,' he told Chris.

Ally pictured the way Chris's bottom lip tensed and pulled sideways when he disapproved of something, and the way his hazel eyes narrowed.

My sweet, sexy Chris, he wanted to say. *Why can't we ever get it right? You write about how much you love me, but I can't make you see it's not love because love wouldn't be so scared and hung up. Love is trust, openness, freedom. I can't keep kissing your warm skin, breathing your breath, crushed up against you in agonies of frustration. I can't do it anymore.*

'Well, phone me when you get your train booked and I can meet you at Queen Street like last time. Are you working tomorrow?'

'Nah, I've got an essay due by Friday, so I'm going to try and get that done in time for once.'

Beside him, his mobile phone lit up with a text back from Scott.

Yeah okay but that's another blowjob you owe me

'Scott says it's okay, so we're on for this weekend,' Ally said, quickly texting back.

I get all the good jobs

'Well, if you're sure. Feels like ages since I last saw you.' Chris's tone warmed as Ally's phone blinked again.

You love it, my wee slut.

'Eh... yeah, I know.' He was typing and talking at the same time, his attention divided.

Get the boardroom keys this time

'I was thinking maybe we could go the Glasgow Film Theatre,' Chris said as another message pinged in from Scott. 'There's a film on this weekend I've wanted to see for ages, and I keep thinking you'd like it too, so we should go together.'

You can just get down on your knees in the stationery cupboard like the rest of them

'Uh-huh. It's your birthday,' Ally said as he fired back.

I'm sure none of this is in my contract, Mr. Binnie

Chris continued. 'If the weather's decent, we could get some beers and sit in the gardens. I've not been there in ages. I'm hardly ever outside. I feel like a vampire these days.'

I still want to fuck your brains out, blondie

Ally caught his breath. 'Uh...'

'I'm sorry, you're falling asleep listening to me. You should go to bed,' Chris said.

'No. I'm, yeah... I suppose I'm a bit sleepy. Can I call you back tomorrow?'

'Yeah, of course. Can't wait to see you.'

'Me neither. Night.'

'Night, Ally.'

Ally lay down on the sofa in the darkened living room and responded to Scott's text with an 'I'm so horny right now I might even let you' while sliding the fingers of his free hand under the waistband of his jeans. Scott texted back in seconds.

Cock-teasing bastard. You know I'm in London. When can I see you?

CHAPTER NINETEEN

FRIDAY

On Friday morning, I get an email from Ally's tutor, who's coming in to observe him next Wednesday. The times coincide with the S3 class with Jordan Franks, who has rallied a few of his more obnoxious classmates into doing their best to derail Ally's well-planned lessons and find a chink in his armour.

Ally hides it well until the bell goes, but he's becoming despondent about his abilities. He tries every strategy and suggestion that I throw at him, but he's at a disadvantage because he hasn't got my established rapport. The other classes on his timetable have been completely won over. He's fresh and funny, and his lessons hold the kids' attention. I overhear snippets of animated chatter in the corridor as classes file out, saying things like 'Have you got Mr McClay? He's a total legend, eh?'

I can grudgingly admit that Ally deserves this. He puts in hours of preparation and takes every piece of advice with almost overzealous gravity. Most importantly, he's genuine towards the pupils, straight-talking and supportive, and while his expectations can be naively high, it ends up working in his favour, as most pupils read it as a well-placed faith in their abilities. I stood there myself a few years back, and it was exhausting, soul-excavating stuff. No group of professionals could ever shrivel you with one muttered comment like a room full of thirty teenagers.

Like all trainees, he's not the complete package, but it's obvious he's committed. I can say all this about Mr. McClay from the back of the classroom because he is no one significant to me, not the way Ally is.

At break time, Elaine comes in to see me and shuts the classroom door behind her, which is never a good sign. Instead of perching on a desk, she pulls a chair over to sit beside me at my computer desk.

'I came to see how you are, Chris? How did you get on with the GP on Tuesday?'

'Fine. I got sleeping pills, just for a week.'

'Did you talk to her about how things have been?'

'Yeah, she gave me antidepressants. I suppose that'll help too.'

'I still think you should take some time off work.'

I fiddle with my glasses, pretending to clean them. 'No. I don't need time off.'

'Has Eilidh called you?'

I massage the pulsating pain above my left eyebrow. 'Not really, not since she left on Monday. I think she's avoiding me.'

Elaine's expression betrays her distaste. 'Well, she should have spoken to you. She spoke to me last night. She promised she would contact you. She's accepted a job in Argentina. She came home this weekend with the intention of telling you, but she thought you were in a bad way, so she didn't. The truth is, she felt she couldn't tell you.'

I exhale slowly. My fingers return to the pulsing in my temples, and I screw my eyes shut against the artificial light. 'I knew something was up. It's okay.'

'It's not okay, pal.' Elaine puts her hand on my arm. 'I'll cover your classes this afternoon if you want to go home.'

For a moment, I'm about to accept, but being in the flat alone is a bleak prospect. 'No, I'd rather stay. At least I know now. I mean, about Eilidh.'

'We can talk at the Rowan Tree tonight. Are you going?'

Yeah, I think we're all going after work.'

'You've a nice department, you know. They all think a lot of you, and your student's a lovely guy, isn't he? Seems really switched on, great with the kids. You've a lot of friends here, Chris,' Elaine says. She waits for a reaction from me, but when I haven't got anything, she adds, I'm glad to hear you're coming out after work. I'll buy you a drink.'

She pats me on the shoulder as she gets up to leave. Her heels sound on the linoleum.

Ally was talking to Louise in the base when Elaine let herself in and sank into one of the battered seats around the low table.

'You need to keep an eye on Chris. Don't let him sit in his room all lunchtime and make sure he does come to the Rowan tonight.' She helped herself to a biscuit from the packet on the table. 'He's not having a good time of it just now.'

Louise put down her phone. 'What's wrong?'

'He's just had some bad news. Don't say I mentioned it, but you know I worry about him.'

'Is it Eilidh?' Louise asked, glancing at Ally.

Elaine nodded because her mouth was full of chocolate digestive. 'Silly girl. He's such a nice lad.' She shook her head, dusting biscuit crumbs off her lap.

'Ally, did you know?' Louise asked. 'You guys are old friends and you've been car-sharing with him. I'd no idea. He never speaks to us about Eilidh.'

'Me neither. I didn't realise.' Ally looked at the floor, ashamed that he had failed Chris. 'He hasn't said anything.'

'Well, he really needs his friends right now, Ally, so you just keep an eye on him for me.' Elaine addressed him firmly, as if reminding him of a longstanding arrangement.

Luca, the Art probationer, arrived at the pub later than everyone else because of an extracurricular ceramics class. He'd changed out of his clay-spattered work clothes and wore a threadbare Blondie tee shirt over worn black jeans. He had a sleeve of tattoos, a pierced lip and artfully mussed dark hair.

Louise nudged Ally sharply in the ribs. 'Ridiculous, isn't it?' she whispered.

Luca met Ally's appraising glance with deep brown eyes, acknowledging him with a squinted smile.

'Definitely verging on the ridiculous,' he agreed. Ally tried to hide his fading black eye and his stitches with a coquettish sweep of his hair to one side as Louise called Luca over very unsubtly and pulled a chair up from a neighbouring table.

'What happened to you, pal?' Luca asked. His knee brushed against Ally's as he sat down.

'I had an argument with the edge of a table last weekend.'

'I'm Luca, I work in the art department.' He offered a hand, and Ally noticed his slim fingers, clay-stained nails, and a couple of plain, silver rings.

'Ally, English student. Do you want a drink?'

Louise stood up. 'It's my round. What do you want, Luca? Same again, Ally?'

'How's it going, then?' Luca asked when she'd disappeared. They made small talk, which Luca somehow made sound exotic. He was Glaswegian and second-generation Italian, not to mention attractive due to the sexy asymmetry of his lip ring. It minutely affected how he said certain words and threw the rest of his well-proportioned features into relief.

Luca monopolised Ally for the next two rounds. Louise was deep in conversation with Chris and Elaine but periodically caught Ally's eye with a smug wink or a smile. Elaine made her excuses at about eight o'clock, and then Ally was briefly aware of her not quite making it out the door because of some involved exchange with Chris. But Luca's flirting intensified, and he couldn't concentrate on anything else.

After the fourth round of drinks were cleared, Ally patted his pockets until he located his cigarettes and lighter and shrugged on his jacket. 'Do you smoke?' he asked Luca.

'Social smoker,' Luca said, smiling as he got up and followed him outside.

They sat down together on a bench at the side of the building, secluded from view of the bar. Luca sat close and leant in so that Ally could light his cigarette before catching his gaze and holding it. Ally felt his guts contract in a knot of desire; his eyes were compelling.

After a few more minutes of stilted conversation, Luca coughed and stubbed out his cigarette on the wall, turning to face Ally. 'I'm not reading this wrong, am I?' he asked. 'I don't know a lot of people up here, so I could be—'

'No,' Ally said. 'You're not reading it wrong.'

Luca's kiss was hesitant, with a brush of lips and a slight clash of teeth before he dared a gentle swipe of his tongue along the inside of Ally's bottom lip. Ally was unaccustomed to the scratching of the silver ring.

'You're gorgeous,' Luca said. 'Even with your shiner.' He fingered the cheekbone where the bruising stopped.

'You too, but I...' Ally fumbled for words. 'I know it sounds like total bullshit, but it's horrendous timing.'

'Why? Are you seeing someone?' Luca dropped his hand back to his side.

'Bad breakup,' he said. 'Honestly, you're so hot, but I couldn't...' Just the thought of going home with Luca made his throat dry with fear.

'Can I have your number then?' Luca asked.

'What?'

'Can I have your number? I don't know a lot of people here, and I like you.' He took out his phone.

Ally pressed a second gentle kiss on the side of Luca's mouth and gave him the number. 'Let's not go back in together, eh? Lou will wet herself with excitement.' He stubbed out his cigarette and stood up to go.

Luca smiled. 'Cool, okay. See you later, yeah?'

Louise was waiting for him just inside the door. She grabbed his arm. 'Did Chris find you?'

'Chris? No. Why? Where is he?'

'I don't know,' she said. 'He saw you go outside with Luca and he went quiet, said he needed to talk to you, and then he disappeared. I thought he was with you two.'

'No, he wasn't with us.' Ally bit his lip. 'Have you tried phoning him?'

'He's not answering. Why would he just walk off like that? Remember what Elaine said? What if he's not okay?'

She was shaking with cold and panic, so he hugged her. 'Shh. It's okay. I'll find him.'

'I'll come with you.' She clung to his arm.

'It's okay. I'll find him, and I'll text you, okay? Don't worry.' He tried to pry her fingers off his arm, feeling sick; Chris must have seen him kiss Luca. 'When did he leave? How long ago?'

'Just after you went outside—maybe ten minutes ago?'

'And he didn't say anything?'

'No, he just walked off. He hasn't even got his jacket!'

Out of the corner of his eye he saw Luca emerge from the gents. 'I'd better go.'

It was a clear, cold night, and Ally could see his breath crystallising in front of him as he sprinted down the first couple of streets. Soon, however, his smoker's lungs pulled him up short, making him wheeze for breath. He knew Aberlayne moderately well, but if Chris had taken anything but the most obvious route home, he wouldn't catch him. It was a dark and uninviting Friday night, still a week from payday, and the town was deserted. His mobile vibrated in his coat pocket.

Was it something I said?! Luca x

He stuffed it back in his pocket and picked up his pace again. Sweat gathered between his shoulder blades and trickled icily down the small of his back. What if Chris wasn't going home?

A few minutes from Chris's block of flats, Ally made out his hunched figure in the distance. He vaulted the railings of a small playground to cut off a corner. The grass was damp, and the smooth soles of his work shoes made him slip and grab for the ladder of the climbing frame before stumbling across the dark expanse and hopping over the lower fence on the other side. Crossing the street at a run, he was close enough to call out now, but he was too breathless. Chris slowed a little, fishing his keys out of the pocket of his suit trousers as he neared the car park in front of the flats.

Suddenly, Chris looked back, and even in the dark, across the fifty feet or so that separated them, Ally sensed he wasn't welcome.

'Wait,' he called as Chris began to walk away.

'I don't know why you followed me, but just go back.' Although Chris was only in his shirtsleeves, he didn't seem cold.

'No. I'm not going. I'm not leaving you alone. I'm so sorry, I just keep fucking up.'

'Leave me alone.'

'You didn't tell me about Eilidh.'

'Ally, go away. I don't want to talk to anyone. I especially don't want to talk to you.' His voice was a monotone.

As he opened the front door, Ally pushed past him and made his way to the first-floor landing, but Chris walked by him blindly to unlock the flat, switch on the light and go to the kitchen. Ally heard him pouring a glass of something and a chair scraping across tiles. Ally made himself walk in to the kitchen. It was neat vodka in the glass, and Chris necked it quickly, like water.

'I know you don't want me here,' Ally said, 'but I don't want you to be on your own.'

No reaction.

'I didn't know what was happening,' Ally continued. 'I have been a pathetic friend and I lied to you, so why would you trust me? I trust you though. I've never met anyone I trust like I do you, or anyone I could speak to the way we used to. If you can't stand me now, I'll take that on the chin, because I deserve it. But I will always care about you, even if I have the absolute shittiest way of showing it.'

Chris still stared blankly ahead.

'Louise said you came outside to find me, but I didn't see you. Luca's sexy, and up for it, and I'm human. You probably don't give a shit what I do or don't do these days. It's just that I'm wrapped up in myself and didn't realise you were having a bad time. Chris, are you even listening? Because you're scaring me.'

Chris inclined his head slightly.

'Chris, I know I screwed around and lied about it. I just couldn't handle the way things were. It wasn't enough for me, and you knew it wasn't enough for me. I couldn't understand why you weren't as frustrated as I was. You're straight, and we should never have gone there.'

Chris slowly pushed the chair back and stood, tipping a second large measure of vodka down his throat. Then he picked up the bottle and a small tin from the window ledge and went down the hall. Ally listened as the toilet flushed and the bedroom door shut.

The flat was deathly silent. Ally went to perch on the sofa, straining to hear any noise from Chris's bedroom over the sound of his thumping heart. Lighting a cigarette, he sent Louise a brief text because he'd promised he would.

Ten long minutes passed. He stubbed out the cigarette and went back into the kitchen to fill a glass of water. His throat burned with nicotine and exertion. Running the cold tap, he remembered the tobacco tin Chris had picked up from the window sill and carried with him to the bedroom. He spat his mouthful of water back into the sink, dropped the glass and shouted Chris's name as he stumbled to the bedroom door.

Chris had arranged the contents of the foil blister packs into a neat pile on the duvet cover. His tie and trousers off, he was sitting cross-legged, his shirt unbuttoned, on the bed behind them, hugging the vodka bottle in the crook of one arm. He didn't react as Ally burst in, just continued extracting the pills one by one from their blister pack and adding them to the pile.

'Chris, for fuck's sake!' Ally scrambled onto the bed and sent the white tablets flying across the faded, blue-checked duvet cover. He knelt in front of Chris, removed the tobacco tin and the vodka bottle from his reach, and gripped his arms. Chris didn't struggle, and his pinched face was set like plaster.

'What the fuck?' Ally's voice cracked. 'What the fuck, Chris?' He shook him, gripped him tighter, pushing for a reaction. 'Please say something. I don't know what to do!'

Chris's eyes were downcast. He exhaled painfully. Even through the clammy shirt, Ally could feel the thud of his friend's pulse as he gripped onto his forearms.

'I'm so tired,' Chris whispered. 'I'm so tired, Ally.' He folded himself up on the bed, foetal, and screwed his eyes shut.

CHAPTER TWENTY

SATURDAY

Ally waited as Chris's breathing slowly gave way to something resembling that of sleep. He swept the scattered mess of loose pills back into the tobacco tin and gathered those that had rolled under Chris's body. Then he wrapped them in a wad of paper and flushed them all down the toilet.

He picked up clothes from the bedroom floor, pulled the curtains, aligned the dusty pile of books on the bedside table. Then he pulled a book from the top of the pile, heeled off his own shoes and propped himself upright on the far side of the bed, setting watch over Chris.

Trying to get comfortable, he removed the phone he'd uncomfortably wedged in his pocket. He replied to Luca's text with a brief, vague promise. Laying the phone down beside him, he ran his thumb over the book's front cover. It was an Iain Banks novel, one he hadn't read. A memory surfaced of buying a crisp new copy of *The Crow Road* for Chris's nineteenth birthday, their meaningful exchange of books as gifts. An urge to wash his hands, to scrub himself with scalding water, overwhelmed him. The scum of memories felt foul and scaly.

Asleep, Chris looked like his teenage friend of memory. His hair was shorter and neater now, but his face hadn't changed, at least in the gentle light. He had a shadow of dark stubble, and only the ghosts of his summer freckles were detectable. A small, silver scar marked his top lip from when he fell off a bike as he raced his brother down the steep ramp leading into the leisure centre car park. There was another scar too, from an appendectomy at aged sixteen. Ally's fingers recalled its texture.

Worried that the cool air would wake him, Ally worked the quilt out from under Chris's legs and arranged it over his sleeping friend before creeping out of the room to smoke out the open window. Although the flat was in a new development, it looked neglected. On the wall beside the bookshelf, his old *Paris, Texas* poster hung dog-eared and faded, and his Jackson Pollock print was tacked on the back of the kitchen door. Pinned to the fridge were a couple of photos: a younger Chris with his arm wrapped protectively around his mum at his brother's wedding, and a holiday snap of his small, freckly niece and nephew.

One Thursday evening during the summer vacation, Chris's stepdad, Paul, had come home from offshore unexpectedly and popped his head in his stepson's bedroom to say goodnight. Chris was in bed, stripped to the waist, with Ally lying on top of him. His knee was wedged between Chris's legs and they were kissing, Chris's hand wedged under Ally's waistband. Chris saw Paul across the room and froze. It marked the beginning of the end. After Paul's tirade, Ally lost the sanctuary of a place where he could be alone with Chris.

Losing himself in the Iain Banks book, the night began to wear on, an hour passed, then two. It had been so long since he'd picked up a book and started to read, a bewildering estrangement. Reading had always been his safe place, his escape. At the worst times, the best place to be was in someone else's writing.

Ally felt a movement beside him as Chris's eyes fluttered open and shut.

'You're still here,' he groaned, creating a barrier between them with a pillow.

'Yeah, go back to sleep.'

Ally went back to the book, plumping up the pillow propping him against the headboard. At three a.m., a tiny movement started him. The bed was shaking slightly, rhythmically.

'Shh, it's okay,' Ally said as he edged closer to Chris, who was sobbing behind his clenched fists. When Ally tried to touch his arm, Chris recoiled, so Ally just continued to soothe him, crouching close as if sheltering him from invisible elements.

Nearly forty minutes later, exhaustion extinguished the sobs and Chris lay limp and sweaty, his face obscured in the folds of the quilt and pillows. Ally made two mugs of tea, sweetened Chris's and carried them back to the bedroom. Putting it down on the side table, he waited to see if Chris reacted.

'Tea if you want it.'

Nothing.

Ally went back to his Iain Banks book, sipping from his own mug. He checked his phone when he'd drained the last of his tea. There were a couple of lengthy messages from Scott, begging him to call, meaning Serena must have relented and given him back his mobile. He must be feeling remorseful, locked up at his parent's house.

Ally was used to complying. He'd reduced his horizons to being whatever Scott wanted them to be. For a moment, he felt familiar need, and then frozen by the unbearable thought of being alone. He began to reply to Scott's message, the book slipping out of his left hand as he typed.

Chris pushed himself up on his elbows and reached for the lukewarm mug of tea. Ally let the phone drop and recovered the novel, his message unsent. The tea had cooled enough for Chris to drain in a couple of swallows before lying back and staring at the ceiling.

'Just go home,' he whispered. His face was marked with pillow creases and his eyes were raw and gummy.

'No, I'm staying. Do you want more tea?'

Chris shook his head and fell silent again. Ally crossed his legs and leant forward over the pages of the book. He read and read until about six a.m., when he turned the final page and let himself doze off. Chris's eyes had closed, and his breathing had steadied.

About half past seven, a shorter episode of Chris's wracking sobs stirred him, and he sleepily draped an arm over Chris's back, ignoring his flinches of protest. When Chris shrugged off his arm and inched further away, Ally got up, used Chris's bathroom, showered and helped himself to clean underwear and a T-shirt he found drying on the radiator in the hallway. After quickly checking on Chris as he passed the bedroom, he went to see what he could find in the kitchen. The bacon in the fridge was still in date, and the bread wasn't mouldy. There was plenty milk for coffee, and some butter, too. Outside, it was a grey and grudging winter morning. The cold lino sucked at his bare feet.

The silence in the flat made Ally edgy so he switched on the digital radio on the window ledge, reassured to hear other voices in the still air of the flat. Swilling tea as he cooked the bacon, he dredged up old daydreams about making breakfast for Scott. He'd had multiple fantasies where they had more than sex—this included waking up together, eating at restaurants and shopping together, but mostly they were about holding hands.

Scott had never once held his hand, and it had become a slight fetish for him: fingers curled in fingers, the heat generated between palms and pink, sweaty creases, the jigsaw fit of slotting knuckles. Scott's hands were beautiful like the rest of him, his nails well kept, his nail beds flat and pale. His fingers had soft, fat tips and dark hairs below the knuckle, and his palms were broad and smooth. Ally had felt them on him and in him and around him so many times, but he'd never slid his own fingers between those knuckles, closed his hand and squeezed gently.

Fuck it, he'd have to wait until his hard-on subsided before carrying the mugs to the bedroom. Although the disembodied images turned him on, the idea of having sex turned his stomach. He was avoiding any thought of last week. The hospital staff had tried to show him, and then to tell him, what the bruises and the pooling blood meant, but he detached himself from its meaning. Flirting with Luca last night had compromised that. It would still be there when the bleeding stopped, and the bruises faded.

You know the name for it, you know what it was. Blame the drugs? You're not innocent either—you've got a dirty wee kink for him taking over. He just got carried away.

Erection well and truly wilted, he carried Chris's bacon sandwich and tea to the bedroom and swept the remaining books off the bedside table so that he could put them down. Chris squinted at him, his eyes garishly bloodshot. He got up, pushed past Ally and stumbled to the bathroom.

Ally hovered in the hallway, feeling grubby as he listened to Chris have a long, noisy piss. He darted back into the bedroom when he heard the toilet flush. When Chris came back, it was without the shirt he'd slept in, and he scooped a T-shirt off the bedroom floor and pulled it over his head.

'That's mine,' he said, indicating the T-shirt Ally had helped himself to.

Ally nodded. 'I know. I've got your pants on too.'

Chris muttered something and flopped back on the bed, massaging his temples. 'What are you still doing here? Why can't you just fuck off?"

Ally picked up a second book, a James Robertson novel this time. Sipping his tea, he checked his phone again, listening to the music from the radio coming through the wall from the kitchen. Chris sank back onto the pillow again, still and staring. Ally began reading *The Testament of Gideon Mack* as Chris's bacon sandwich went cold, as did his tea. The feeble winter light was snaking in through the gaps around the curtains.

CHAPTER TWENTY-ONE

It must be around lunchtime when Ally finally puts down the book he's reading and shuffles off the bed, probably heading to the window for a smoke. I study the paperback resting in the indent left by Ally's body. The book is one Eilidh gave me, one of many I never could start reading. I resent the smell of smoke, the heat and noise of another body in my tiny bedroom. I wait for the end of Ally's suffocating vigil, but it never comes.

Beside me on the bedside table sits a cup of tea gone cold and cloudy and a bacon roll, unwanted like every other attention. When Ally returns, he puts down a fresh mug of tea and perches on the edge of the bed. 'Try and drink some, eh?'

Even if I wanted to drink, I've no more energy or motivation to move. I don't think I could even lift the cup.

Ally clears his throat, a tarry rasp. 'Chris, what can I do? Don't say fuck off, because I won't.'

I want him to shut up, to go away. I clamp my hands over my ears.

'Maybe it would help if you called Eilidh?'

I curl tighter into a foetal position beneath the quilt, shielding my face. How can he sit there telling me to call her?

'I can't leave you alone, Chris. Are you listening?' Ally's voice rises in a bossy crescendo.

I lift the cover and squint out at him. He's not going to leave. 'There's just... nothing to say.' My eyes feel raw.

The fear and vulnerability that comes from looking at him makes me retreat again.

'This is an amazing book.' Ally picks up the James Robertson novel. 'I'm going to read it to you.'

Hour after hour in the dingy light of my room, Ally reads aloud from *The Testament of Gideon Mack*. A few chapters in, I roll onto my side, facing toward Ally's voice. With every word he reads, my dull senses begin to respond. Detached from his body, Ally's voice is soothing instead of antagonising, and I see a faint path leading out of the bleakness of my thoughts.

As it grows dark again, Ally stops reading.

'I'm starving. I'm going to phone for a pizza,' he says, laying down the book.

I push myself up to a seated position, yawn and sigh, disappointed. I'm impatient to hear him read more. This is the magic that I thought had deserted me: the magic of hearing your own pain, your own hope, in someone else's words. It's eroding the hard shell that has crystallised around me, cut me off. That is the way out, the light of words and thoughts, all renewed by Ally's voice. Love and faith and loyalty and pain are no longer concentrated like a sunbeam coming through a glass to incinerate me; instead it's deflected, shared and connected with humanity.

'Ally,' I call to him, but my voice has atrophied. Ally has picked up the house phone and left his mobile on the duvet cover. The screen lights up; someone has been calling him repeatedly. Five missed calls. 'Ally?' I call again. 'Your phone.'

Ally returns with the pizza and a fresh waft of smoke. He drops the book in the centre of my bed. I leaf through the pages he's read so far.

'Your phone keeps ringing,' I tell him.

He looks at me, right at me. 'I'm ignoring it. Come on, help me eat some of this. It cost a fortune.'

'No wonder. It's enormous.'

I unwillingly pick up a slice, eying it like a kind of challenge. It turns gluey in my throat, and it's an effort to swallow. I persist, even though my stomach is vacillating between hunger and nausea.

Ally eats most of the pizza himself, then picks up *The Testament of Gideon Mack* and begins where he left off. After a few paragraphs, I interrupt him.

'I don't think he's mad,' I whisper.

'You mean Gideon?' Ally asks. 'No, maybe not.'

'He's only mad if you take it all literally, which is what faith means, more or less. So, really, he's the sane one because he doesn't really believe what he's told. If you *don't* question how things appear, if you take them at face value, then that's a kind of madness.'

Ally seems to take this personally. 'I suppose it could be naivety, but I don't think it's madness to believe some of what you're told. If you question everything, then you've got no solid ground. There has to be something that you don't doubt,' Ally says, smoothing the page down.

'So, you believe that he met the Devil?' I ask.

'No, of course I don't, but *he* believes that he did.'

'Does he? Does he believe anything? And don't you think that makes him mad?'

'I think it's meant to make you question his sanity. But is it any crazier to believe you met the Devil than it is to believe in God? Like you say, he's lost his faith in God, so he wants to believe in something.'

'If you lose your faith and you don't know what to believe in anymore, and the things you used to take for granted disintegrate, then you're going to meet the devil like he did. I don't think he's insane.' I don't know why I feel so impassioned about this character.

'I think he's lonely, though, and kind of... lost in his own head.'

'Yeah.' My mind is off on a tangent, pawing over something Ally said. 'Ally... you know when you said there has to be something that you don't doubt? What do you mean? What can there really be that we don't doubt?'

'Love,' Ally says without hesitation. 'I mean, of course you can doubt that someone loves you, but you can't doubt love itself—that it exists and that it's what makes life worth living.'

I turn inwards, sealing myself under the duvet and clutching my stomach.

Ally begins to read again. His voice is less expressive, but the words compensate, banishing the constant interference in my head.

After a couple of hours, he begins to smudge his sentences together with tiredness. I notice his eyes are heavy, so I take the novel out of his hand, fold down the corner of the page, and lay it on the bedside table.

'I'll go and sleep on the sofa,' Ally yawns, but then makes no move to go. I watch him give in to the weight of his eyelids and witness the instant when the tiniest muscles around his eyes and mouth relent. Just like I used to, I watch Ally giving in to sleep. His lips part slightly to reveal his distinctively neat and gappy teeth, and his long eyelashes settle on the tight, grey skin under his eyes. He makes it look so easy, when I battle to sleep at all.

It's so straightforward for you, you know. You make friends easily, and girls and boys want to sleep with you. You excel without working for it, and you're good at everything. You make me sick sometimes. And yet I am drawn to you too, like the pathetic idiot I am.

I am drawn to you, and here you are again. At the worst possible time, when I feel there's just no point to anything anymore. I feel like no one would miss me if I were gone, like it would be a relief to go to sleep and not wake up. I loved you, but I held you back, and I did the same to Eilidh. I'm just a dead weight, disposable. I just get in the way.

Why are you here? Why would you take all this time and trouble to read to me like I'm blind or in a coma? You know, don't you? You know exactly what it means to me, and how it's the one thing that would help. And only you would know that...

CHAPTER TWENTY-TWO

MONDAY

Even dressed for work, Luca is irritatingly hip with his skinny black tie and shiny black hair. He sets my teeth on edge when he casually drops by the English base and pretends to make friendly conversation with Louise; he's looking for Ally, of course, but he's way too cool to say so.

Studiously ignoring him, I finish my coffee and send the email I'm typing so that I can return to my classroom. Ally's already there, putting jotters and question papers out on the desk for the next class.

It's my fault—I insisted on coming in to work, even though I have a broken valve inside and it's bleeding me dry. I can't move my face into any kind of expression as I hover beside my desk, trying to remember what it was I came here to do. Ally stops what he's doing and frowns at me.

'Chris, maybe you should—'

'What was I doing again? Was there something I was meant to do for you?' A tension headache gnaws behind my right eye. I sit down at my desk and rummage for painkillers. Distracted, I don't catch Ally's reply.

When I look up from my desk drawer, Ally's crouching beside me, checking what I'm swallowing. 'Nurofen.' I show him the packet. 'I've got a headache.'

'Maybe you should have stayed at home?'

'Teachers don't take time off, Ally. You'll learn.'

'You look awful.'

'Thanks.'

'I mean you look ill.'

'I know what you mean!' I snap at him. 'If you need some eye candy, go next door and see Luca. He's hanging around the base looking sharp in his best suit hoping to impress you.'

'I saw him earlier.'

'I bet you did. What was I thinking?'

Ally turns away and starts setting up the interactive whiteboard for the class coming in. I pretend to mark jotters, but I can't focus, and now I'm fighting the prickling tears of frustration. *I can't go on like this.*

Ally forced me to call and make an appointment with Dr. Rae. He even offered to come along and explain why he flushed my medication down the toilet on Friday night. I know he slipped off to talk to Elaine this morning, which means she'll know what happened. I feel exposed and humiliated and annoyed. Louise is particularly saccharine this morning. Thank God Callum is his usual blunt, insensitive self.

There's a timid knock on the classroom door, and Katia lets herself in.

'Mr. Elliot?'

'Hi, Katia, come in.'

She notices Ally at the back of the room and shrinks back.

'It's okay—Mr. McClay is just setting up for your class.'

'I'll go,' Ally offers, but Katia hurries forward to my desk.

'This is your book. I've read it now. Thank you.' She looks uncomfortable as she hands me back my cherished copy of *The Pearl* in a thick plastic wallet. A couple of sheets of Hello Kitty notepaper are tucked inside. 'My Dad says not enough just to read, and I have to write extra essay for you, improve my English more. Also, please can I have other books and I write you more essays?'

I assume that this is also a paternal request. I skim over her writing on *The Pearl*. She has retold the story in her own stilted and pedestrian words.

'What did you think of it, Katia? Did you enjoy reading it?' I ask.

'Was very difficult. Hard to understand sometimes.'

'Did you really think the language was hard to understand? Or did you just not understand what the pearl was meant to be?'

She looks at me, with a nervous grimace.

'Can you go and think about that? This time you need to write about what the pearl symbolised, what the moral of the story was. You know what I mean by that? I know the story; I've read it about a thousand times. I want you to tell me what you make of it, what your reaction to it is, why you think the characters become like that, why it's written the way it is, what it says about the way people are.'

She pulls her homework diary out of her rucksack and makes a note in Polish. 'I'm sorry was not good essay first time. I have to practice more.'

'It's fine. I'll look out for something else you can read once you bring this back.'

'Thank you, Mr. Elliot.'

'You're welcome. See you next period.'

She looks puzzled. 'Will Mr. McClay not teach us next period?'

Of course, she wouldn't realise that I stay at the back of the classroom when Ally teaches. She's always focussed on him, or on the pages in front of her.

'I did also extra homework for you, Mr. McClay—I wrote about two characters from *Of Mice and Men*, not just one.'

She grins, then blushes—she can't talk to Ally without blushing. She passes him her homework jotter, and Ally smiles over her neat, pink handwriting and double-underlined headings.

'Oh, well done, Katia. You've been busy this weekend. Thank you.' When she closes the door, he says, 'Aw, she's lovely, eh?'

I shrug, thinking how naive he can be. 'A bit of a worry is what she is. Her dad is pushy, and she doesn't have many friends. She comes by here all the time, so she doesn't have to hang around alone. She does all this extra work, but it's usually pretty dire.'

'She's no trouble though, is she? Just works away quietly and answers every question you ask.'

'Can't you tell that she's unhappy? She looks lost. The girls she sits with are all prettier, or cooler, or brighter than she is.'

'If you say so.' Ally frowns and shrugs. 'You know them better than me.'

Ally left Chris's room before his Second Years arrived and went along the corridor to Louise's room. Her classroom was much more organised than Chris's, with colourfully labelled plastic boxes and walls that she'd covered in inspirational quotes and pupil's work painstakingly displayed with backing paper and borders.

'Hey, are you busy?' He closed the door behind him.

'It's okay. I'm just sorting out some Media Studies stuff. How's Chris now?'

'Not great.'

'I can't believe you sat with him all weekend. You must have been so worried about him.' Louise tucked a strand of black hair behind her ear and motioned to him to pull up a seat.

'He's going to let me drive him to the doctor after work.'

'My sister takes antidepressants. She was a bit like Chris is now.'

Ally nodded. 'He's embarrassed about it, which makes it worse. He doesn't want to stay off work either. I think it's work that's keeping him going.'

'It's so lucky you were placed here, Ally. Chris doesn't seem to have a lot of friends outside of work. He'll be so glad to have you around.'

'I don't think he's that bothered.' Ally gnawed at the skin on the side of his thumbnail.

'I can't believe Eilidh did that to him. You know, I tried to like Eilidh, but she was a bossy wee cow.'

'You didn't like her?'

'We were quite friendly at first. She did her probation year here too. The awful thing is, she knew... God, this is so embarrassing. She asked me how I was getting on the first week, and I said, 'I've landed on my feet, it's a nice department, and my PT is *lovely*.' She asked what I meant by *lovely*, and I said he's kind and supportive and... well, cute and single.' Louise bit down on her bottom lip. 'Then Eilidh gave me this big lecture about how unprofessional it would be to flirt with someone I work with, especially someone promoted like him. I was mortified I'd ever mentioned it. Then, a few months later they were going out, and I realised why she'd been like that. I felt a right idiot.' She was peeking through her fingers at Ally, her face pink.

'Maybe it would cheer Chris up to know he has a secret admirer?' Ally squeezed her shoulder.

'Oh God, *please* don't say anything! I will actually kill you!'

'I think he'd be really flattered.'

She gave him a withering look. 'Seriously, though, what should we do? I tried to speak to him this morning. I didn't want him to think I was just pretending I didn't know what happened.'

'What were you talking about before he left the pub on Friday?'

'He wasn't talking much at all. He was just listening to Elaine—I think she was trying to give him a bit of a boost. I think he really wanted to talk to you, but you and Luca were getting on so well that he couldn't get a word in.'

'Did he say he wanted to talk to me?' Ally frowned.

'No, but he was glancing across at you and sort of fidgeting, like he wasn't really listening to Elaine either. What happened with Luca anyway? You didn't tell me!'

'Nothing happened.'

'You went outside together. I bet something did happen!'

'Okay, maybe I gave him my number.'

'Oh my God! How exciting! Has he called? Texted you?'

'Yeah, I think we're going out for something to eat on Wednesday night after my Crit lesson. Just as friends, Lou, so please don't get too excited.'

'Why just as friends?' she asked. 'Does Luca think it's just as friends? Does he know that?'

He got the feeling that Luca and Louise had already had this conversation, and his heart sank. 'I've just split up with someone. Plus, Eilidh had a point about sleeping with people you work with. It's not good, believe me. I have years of experience.'

'But clearly you fancy each other. Won't it be weird just being friends?'

'No weirder than working with Mr. Elliot is for you.'

'Touché,' Louise said. 'Did you kiss him?'

He groaned theatrically. 'What did he say?

Her smug grin said enough.

'Well, next time you're invading my privacy, try and be a bit subtler about it.' He kissed her cheek. 'See, I kiss all my friends, nothing in it.'

'What about we drag Chris out for coffee and a sandwich at lunchtime? Would that be a good idea?' she suggested.

'We can try. He's teaching just now, but I'll ask him at the end of the period.'

As he opened Louise's classroom door, an unusual level of noise was coming from the pupils in Chris's room. He peered in through the small window to see that the class was unsupervised. Chairs were overturned, books had fallen on the floor and balls of scrunched-up paper were being batted back and forth across the room. As Ally opened the door, only the most biddable pupils fell silent; the rest didn't notice him at all. For the first time, he had to raise his voice to get their attention.

'You're Mr. Elliot's class? Yeah?'

'He just walked out, sir. Are you teaching us now?' This from the only pupil he recognised, a loud, scruffy boy who sat on his own at the front.

'Sam, can you take this to Miss Macari, please?'

Ally scribbled a note to Louise and gave it to the boy, who was obviously chuffed to be selected for the task. He barked a few orders at the others to straighten the tables, pick up the books and put the paper missiles in the bin. Incredibly, they complied. He asked a confident-looking girl with glasses what they had been working on. She showed him her jotter, and from there it was easy to get the class back on track until Louise arrived. 'You go and find him,' Louise whispered. 'I'll watch these guys.'

I don't know what's happening to me. I can't think, my pulse is racing, and I feel cold. The staffroom is deserted, I try to sip water, but it hits my stomach like lead. The more I pressure myself to get it together, the worse I feel.

I'm scared, but I don't know what of. I just walked out. I just left my class. I should go back, but I can't move.

The door opens, and I know it will be him. Why won't he leave me alone? Ally sits beside me, waits for me to speak. I crumple the plastic cup in my fist.

'You can go back,' I say. 'It's fine.'

'Louise has got your class. Are you okay?' Ally asks.

No, I'm not okay, because you're always here and you always make things worse.

'I've had enough,' I say. 'I can't do this.'

Ally tries to touch my arm, but I flinch away like he's rabid. He shakes his head at me. 'Chris, stop feeling sorry for yourself.'

This is the last straw. 'Fuck you, Ally! What are you doing here? Why are you always there, everywhere I go? Haven't you got friends to win and people to influence elsewhere?'

'Stop acting like you don't know why I came here, Chris. It's not a coincidence. I asked to be placed here. I phoned Dr. Laurenson myself, and I pestered my tutor until I got my own way,'

'Sounds like you. Why, though?'

'I knew you worked here.'

'And?'

'I'm here because of you. Despite what you think, I don't have anyone else, and I don't know what else to do. I know you have every reason to hate me, but I don't believe that you do.'

'Honestly, Ally, I don't care about you enough to hate you,'

Ally wavers but doesn't shut up. 'I do understand how you're feeling, but you can't give in like this.'

'Ally, you haven't a fucking clue what you're talking about.'

'But I do. I'm here because of you, because I didn't just want to give in to it. I was really scared about what was happening to me, and I needed help. I needed someone I could trust, and... you still feel like a safe place to me.'

'Don't,' I warn him. 'I honestly can't take this right now.'

'You don't really hate me, Chris, you...'

'Shut up, Ally! I don't want you here. You're not helping. Just fuck off and leave me alone.'

I expect him to cry. It's his go-to avoidance technique. He doesn't. He turns and walks away. It's me who cries, horrible, wrenching sobs, and I'm not even certain why.

CHAPTER TWENTY-THREE

Ally stopped only once to light a cigarette as he left
Aberlayne Academy and headed for the charity shops and
pound stores, bookies and bars that overran the bleak town
centre. He walked until the pavement ended on the other
side of River Layne Bridge, which crossed to the stark new
industrial estate. There was no shelter from the wind off
the river, and he was frozen now, his feet cold and wet. The
inevitable formed in his mind. Leaning on the bridge, he
sent the message.

I miss you. I'm sorry.

Ally kept walking for another forty minutes, following the
B road out of town. The rain came on hard and sharp, and
he waited under a dilapidated bus shelter as several lorries
sprayed him with filthy water. Struggling to light a soggy
cigarette with his numb fingers, he felt his phone vibrate.

'Can you come and get me?' he asked.

Waiting in the bus shelter, his every muscle tightened
against the rivulets of sleety rain snaking down his back.
Although it was the middle of the day, the cars that passed
had their headlights on. The road was lined with ancient,
dripping beech trees and the scraggy remnants of hedges.
Higher up, a Georgian farmhouse was set back from
the road.

Ally waited for around an hour before beginning to
wonder if he would really appear, and what he might do if
he didn't. Twenty minutes later, the Range Rover stopped
at the side of the road and the door opened.

'Jesus Christ! Look at the state of you. Hurry up and get in.'

Scott didn't remove his superfluous shades. He drove, aggressively, in the direction of Bridge of Layne. After several miles he turned up the car heaters, irritated by Ally's chattering teeth and his clothes dripping on the tan leather.

Scott's apartment was in a redeveloped baronial granite building with brass plaques, wrought-iron railings and other caricatures of expensive taste. There was a neat space for the Range Rover at right angles to a high fence. Looking over his shoulder to reverse into the space, Scott removed the sunglasses. Ally stared through the rain-smeared glass until the engine stopped.

The high-ceilinged Victorian rooms had been modernised with no expense spared. Thick, tweedy, oatmeal carpets and enormous leather sofas were arranged around a flat-screen TV and a minimal fireplace with a glowing wood-burning stove. The open-plan kitchen was understated, with sparkling granite worktops, a Scandinavian fridge, and multiple gadgets with German-sounding labels.

Scott dropped his keys on the kitchen table, laid down his designer sunglasses and left Ally standing in the entryway, muddy and dishevelled. He watched as Scott laid out the makings of two gin and tonics.

'Can I borrow some dry clothes?' Ally asked.

Scott put down the knife he was using to slice the lemon, stepped around the breakfast bar and draped his arms around Ally's shoulders. 'Yeah, I'll look something out for you. Go and run a bath and I'll bring your drink.'

Ally stripped off his damp clothes, dropping them on the marble floor, and laid his phone down beside the freestanding bath. The water seemed golden against the chalky-white tub. In the living room, he heard Scott switch on the TV and flick through the channels, leaving it on a rerun of a car show. The water was so hot it was only just bearable as Ally slipped in, dipping his head under then pushing his wet hair back off his face. The wound at his temple smarted in the water. Scott came through carrying two glasses and perched on the edge of the bath, passing one to him.

'Bet that feels good, baby.' Scott trailed his fingers in the bath water.

'It does.' The ice clinked and jostled with the lemon and lime for place.

Scott tipped down the toilet seat and settled there with his drink. 'So, tell me I was right all along then.'

'No... It's just that I don't think I can go back to Aberlayne. I've fucked up there, but I haven't given up.'

'You're a regular disaster area, eh?'

'You're in a worse mess than me, Scott, and it's all over the paper and the internet!'

'Oh, relax! You're just touchy because you've realised I was right all along. You're a clueless little fucker, you always were.' He downed most of his gin and tonic and knelt beside the bathtub, pushing his hand under the hot water to clamp it around Ally's wrist. With his other hand, Scott tipped Ally's chin up with an index finger.

Ally saw the faint white dusting on the dark, fine nostril hairs. Scott nuzzled and kissed around the cut on Ally's face.

He flinched. 'Stop it!'

'Stop what? Stop touching you? You don't want to be touched anymore, is that it? That's a first.' Scott pulled at him. 'Who is it then? Just tell me. It's killing me.'

'What are you talking about?'

'Who else are you fucking, Ally?'

'No one. There's no one.'

'You're a pathetic liar, you know. I'm a fucking mug dropping everything for you, eh?'

Ally nodded dumbly. Scott's fingers raked downward through damp, tousled hair to fondle Ally's cock. He was encouraged by its reliable response.

Ally blanched, and his throat tightened. 'I can't,' he said, scrambling out of the tub. He combed his fingers through his wet hair and wrapped a towel around his middle.

Scott mocked him, shaking his head. In search of more alcohol, Ally went back to the kitchen, splashing disproportionate amounts of gin into his tonic. When Scott joined him, he was pink from the steam of the bath. He pressed Ally against the fridge and plied his mouth with kisses until Ally softened to his insistent tongue.

Later, while Scott cooked them an elaborate meal, Ally watched in hazy fascination, drinking steadily. Scott was as confident and efficient in the kitchen as he was in bed. He'd pulled on a tight T-shirt and gym shorts, and Ally's thoughts were saturated in sex. After three huge gins, the main course was ready, and his head was swimming. Scott took a bottle of white wine out of the fridge. He talked fast and without pausing for responses, as if he'd saved up everything he wanted to say over the last ten days. Or done a shitload of coke.

'Where do you want to live? When we live together, I mean?'

'Huh?' In the barrage of words, Ally had only been half listening.

'Where do you want us to live?'

Scott was busy plating the meal. As he laid the white plate in front of Ally, he straightened it fussily and poured him a glass of Chablis.

'This place is in my name. I'll sell it, add it to the money I have safe so, and we can buy someplace nice together. We could rent your place out maybe. It probably wouldn't make much if you put it on the market. I know I can get a job with our competitors easily; I've already made some calls. It just depends where you want to go.'

'I don't know. I haven't thought about it.'

'What about your teaching course?' Scott asked.

Ally hid his face in his hands and sighed through his fingers. 'I can't go back to Aberlayne.'

'But can you still pass your course if you don't finish this placement?'

'I'd have to repeat a placement next session, and I don't have the money. I need to graduate and get a job.'

Scott reached across the table and laid his hand over Ally's. 'Don't be stupid, babe. I've got plenty of money, and if that's what you want to do, just get on and do it.'

Ally looked up warily into his eyes. 'Really?'

'Yeah, of course. I suppose teaching's at least the sort of job you can do anywhere, eh? We could even live abroad.'

He must have done another line in the bathroom. Ally ate slowly and drank quickly.

'What about your family? What will they do if we move in together?'

'I told them I don't give a fuck. They accept it, they don't accept it... I don't care either way. Of course, we're burning in hell and all that shit, but they can't stop me.'

'But they can make our lives really difficult.'

'Then we move away.'

'I have a family too.'

Scott suppressed a snort of laughter.

'What's so funny?'

'If I were you, I'd be happy to move as far as way as possible from your old man. He's an absolute menace. And what's the deal with your wee brother? You never said he had that Rain Man syndrome or whatever it's called.'

'Fuck you, Scott! Like your family are the fucking Waltons?' He pushed his chair back and got up from the table.

'You off in a sulk?'

'No, I need a smoke.'

'Sit down, finish your food and stop being so... gay.'

'You're not funny.' He sat down and knocked back more Chablis.

'Easy tiger,' Scott said. 'That's too expensive to neck like that. Plus, you get into all sorts of trouble when you drink too much.'

Ally rocked back in his seat and hugged his stomach.

Scott cleared the plates away and put an ashtray in the middle of the table. He lit up, then neatly lined up his full pack of cigarettes and lighter with his coffee cup. With a provocative grin, he waited for Ally to ask. Ally topped up both wine glasses and tried not to react. Scott blew his first lungful back across the table at him.

Standing unsteadily, he went to the bathroom, tapping the pockets of his discarded work trousers to find his battered pack of fags. There was only one left. He let one or two furious tears escape in the privacy of the bathroom, splashed his face clean, and went back and lit his last cigarette with Scott's lighter. As a petty protest, he picked up his wine glass and moved to the plush sofa, where he smoked, nursed the full glass and pretended to watch the muted TV.

Scott laughed at him but didn't move. He took his time and finished his glass of wine before stubbing out his cigarette and moving over to where Ally sat, kneeling on the floor in front of him. 'I love winding you up. You're so fucking sexy when you sulk, with that wee pout. Look at those pretty lips.' He forced a kiss. 'Do a line with me and then I'll take you to bed, baby.'

Ally knocked back his wine and slid down off the sofa so that he straddled Scott. Wrapping one arm around the back of his neck, he kissed him aggressively. The other arm dragged at the neck of his T-shirt until it tore, and he pushed and scratched at the skin below until Scott winced. All down his neck and shoulders, he sank his teeth into skin. Scott reached for him, trying to undress him, but he slapped his fingers away, forcing them behind his back. Caught off guard, Scott was unable to resist.

'Don't you think I want to top, sometimes?' he asked, tugging Scott's shorts out of the way and gripping him as he pushed the two fingers of his free hand into Scott's open mouth, moistening them.

Scott just watched him for a moment, seemingly stunned to silence. 'I don't do that, baby.'

'If you really love me so much, you'd do it for me.' Ally pushed him back onto the carpet, hooking his knees up, surprised he could manoeuvre Scott so easily. Kissing down the inside of his thigh, he touched and licked and began to press gently. Scott lashed out and pulled away.

'Stop, Ally! Fuck's sake! I said no!'

Ally sat up, taking a moment to enjoy seeing Scott so toyed with. He got up and went back to the table to refill his glass again.

'You said no, eh? Right enough, you said no.' Ally's voice blistered with sarcasm.

'What the fuck was all that about?' Scott sat up and wrapped his arms around himself. 'You're drunk. You'll end up like your dad.'

'Did you say something about doing a line?' Ally glanced at the small plastic bag on the coffee table and then drained the last of the white wine.

Scott watched him as he looked in the fridge for another bottle. 'They say alcoholism runs in families.'

Ally smiled unevenly and hunted for a corkscrew. 'Says the cokehead.'

'Hanging up beside the fridge,' Scott prompted, getting up and pulling his shorts back on.

'You're such a good lay.' Ally looked him up and down.

'Shut up, Ally. You're being a dick.'

'No, it's true. You're fucking beautiful. It's like a drug. I just think about fucking you all the time. I should be happy. So why am I so very fucking miserable, Scott?'

'Because you drink too much, and you're an idiot. You're half cut, and you're speaking shit. Go and sleep it off.' Scott leaned over the breakfast bar, smoking and frowning.

'You don't make me happy. I keep coming back to you. It's been years, and I'm so stupid, I never get it. Nothing ever changes. You're never the answer.'

Scott grabbed at his wrists. 'What are you talking about? You said this afternoon that you'd made a mistake.'

'I make a lot of mistakes. You said so yourself. Come on, you want to do some coke and fuck me. You'll do it anyway. That's what you did before.'

Scott backed him up against the exposed-stone wall. It was cold and uncomfortable against his naked back. 'Seriously, Ally! Stop fucking with my head! What are you saying? Don't you want to be with me?'

Ally laughed involuntarily, anxiety and alcohol churning his stomach. 'I think I want it, but then you're... I mean, we're not equal, are we? You buy me off or keep me hanging on. It's never been equal and it's never going to be.'

'Jesus, you're always the fucking victim, aren't you? I dropped everything to pick you up this afternoon. You make it sound like everything's my fault. You're so ungrateful! What more do you want?'

'Want?' Ally turned away. 'Nothing. Just leave me alone.'

'Listen!' Scott cupped Ally's face in his hot hands. 'Things are really shit just now, for both of us. We shouldn't be bitching at each other. I need you right now, and you need me. Hey, are you listening?'

Ally nodded, eyes downcast.

'I think if we just... if we just stick together, get through this, then we can have everything you said you wanted. I've told Mum and Dad now, so you can move in here until we get sorted with our own place. Look at me! Why aren't you looking at me?'

Ally wrenched away when Scott gripped harder. 'You've told *your* parents. We move into *your* place. What about me? I've been dropping everything for you for years. I can't do it anymore!'

'It won't be like that. Listen to me. You'll be here, with me, all the time. You'll have whatever you want.'

'No, I won't,' Ally said through his teeth. *Honestly, I don't care about you enough to hate you.*

'Listen, Ally, I need you. How can I convince you that I'm serious? If you want something, you just ask me. You know, I don't think you've ever really asked me for anything. None of the shit that mattered to Leisha ever matters to you.'

Ally shoved him backwards. 'Yeah, so I'm low-maintenance. Thanks! Handy for you that I didn't want a Porsche or an account at Chanel or a Tiffany engagement ring. But you never thought I was fucking perishing jealous of you and her? You never thought I might want that commitment? Rubbing that in my face was the single shittiest thing you could do to me.'

'Oh God, sorry. I shouldn't have mentioned Leisha.' Scott crowded back in until he was pressing heavily on Ally's chest. 'You know that I had my reasons. You know how things are with my folks. I just don't believe you'd have stayed with me all this time if you thought I didn't care about you.' He raked his fingers through Ally's hair and pressed a kiss on his forehead.

'This is pointless.' Ally slumped against the wall. 'I don't want this anymore. I don't love you.'

Scott stared at him, open-mouthed. 'Fuck sake, Ally! You blow hot and cold at the best of times, and now you've had too much to drink. Let's go to bed and talk in the morning.'

'I want to sleep on my own.'

Scott hesitated, stunned by the unprecedented rejection. 'Why?'

'I don't even know what I'm doing here.' He shouldered past Scott to the guest bedroom, shut the door and crawled under the cool quilt in the darkness.

CHAPTER TWENTY-FOUR

'Can't you call him?' Louise asks. 'He probably went home.'

She'd found me crying like a stupid kid in the staffroom. She hid me in the sickbay and dabbed my face dry, then gave me sips of water until I could speak again. Then she asked me where Ally has gone.

'I don't have his number,' I tell her. 'I was a dick to him. He wouldn't answer his phone if it he saw it was me anyway.'

'Why, what happened? What did you say?'

'I was feeling sorry for myself and I took it out on him.'

Louise puts her arm around my shoulders. I'm humiliated that, of all my colleagues, it's her who found me like this.

'You don't know that. He had other stuff going on.'

'I know! He was trying to talk to me, but I haven't been able to think straight about anything. Could you call him, please?'

Louise tries, but she only reaches his voicemail and leaves a brief message. I watch as she cups the phone against her chin with slim, shellacked fingers. Her thick foundation leaves a film on the screen of her phone.

'Did you say you had to be somewhere at half four, Chris?'

'Uh, yes. I've got a doctor's appointment.'

'Oh, that's good. Ally said you had a bad weekend.' She keeps trying to make eye contact, trying to reach me, but I'm just wishing I were anywhere but here. In fact, I wish I were dead, unable to feel any pain.

'Listen, what are you doing after your appointment? I just thought maybe we could have dinner together? There's no point sitting in different places worrying about the same thing, is there?'

I look at the pretty and straight-talking Louise. If I go home alone tonight I will do something stupid. I should accept her offer. 'That'd be good, thanks,' I whisper.

She seems relieved. 'I live near the Surgery. Come to mine after and I'll have something ready.'

'I'd better go. Can you text me your address?'

I shrug on my rain jacket and crouch down to rummage for my car keys in my rucksack.

'They're here,' Louise says, passing them to me. I already looked them out and laid them on the desk just moments ago.

Dr. Rae keeps me for a full half hour. The more I talk, the more self-loathing seeps out of me like pus. Yes, I tell her, if Ally hadn't come in to my room I would have taken all the tablets, washed them down with the vodka and happily gone to sleep. Yes, I really wanted to be dead then. No, I'm not so sure now. I feel like I might be needed, but I really do hate myself, everything about myself.

She asks me about Ally and a tear runs downs my cheek. Then another. I can't even say his name.

'Sounds like a really good friend. You would call him if you felt that way again?'

I dig at my eyes with the heel of my hand. She passes me a tissue, which I crush in my fist.

'I'm sorry to hear about your girlfriend, but long-distance relationships do tend to be difficult. Had you been together long?'

We weren't together, I just imagined we were. I missed her, and I still do, but I was nothing to her. I'm humiliated. I shake my head and mouth 'no' for Dr. Rae.

'I really think I should sign you off work for a few weeks.'

'No, I feel a bit better when I'm at work. I think that now a couple of my colleagues know how things have been... They understand why I'm not myself. I like the people I work with, so it gives me a bit of a boost.'

She nods and turns away to start typing. 'How's the sleeping now? I suppose you haven't really had the benefit of the sleeping tablets yet.'

'I'm still not sleeping much. I got A—my friend to drive into work this morning because I felt so exhausted.'

'Try taking the tablets at the same time each night for three days to help you break the cycle of not getting off to sleep. You'll be amazed how much better you'll feel once you start getting a bit more sleep.'

I nod, feeling numb.

'You'll have bad days, that's normal. Just make sure you have a plan for them. Keep that appointment you made for next week. I know it doesn't feel like it, but you are doing well. It will get better, I promise.'

I don't believe her, but I get up and leave anyway.

Louise's tiny flat is on the ground floor of an old granite block. She's changed out of her work clothes and it's strange seeing her dressed casually. She looks even younger wearing skinny jeans, ballet pumps and a black sweater. She's layered on more foundation until it's mask-like over her delicate features and clipped her short black hair behind her ears. Her perfume smells like Parma violets and cocoa.

The kitchen is a tiny galley off the living room, where she's set up a folding table. 'Do you want a glass of wine? There's red or white.'

I follow her to the doorway of the kitchen. The cooking smells remind me I haven't eaten all day. "I'd better not. Can I have a glass of water?'

'Of course. I'm just making lasagne—I hope that's okay?'

'More than okay. Thanks so much.'

She pours me a tumbler of water and passes it to me, returning to the cooker.

'I still haven't heard anything. Have you?' I ask.

'No, nothing. I called again but still just his voicemail.'

'I drove across to Bridgend before I came here. He's not at home either.'

'He's got family in Bridge of Layne, hasn't he?'

'I know where his dad lives, but I think it's more likely he's with Scott.'

'Is Scott his ex-boyfriend?' Louise asks over her shoulder.

I'm taken aback. 'I didn't realise you knew he was gay. He doesn't really tell anyone.'

Louise turns back towards the cooker. 'I got the wrong end of the stick the weekend before last. He asked to share my taxi home, and well, I thought... anyway, it's fine now. We had a laugh about it. Today we were chatting just before he came to find you. I was kind of teasing him about Luca and how they're meant to be going on a date on Wednesday and he said he'd just broken up with someone. He didn't go into details, though.'

I refill my glass because my mouth has gone dry and sticky. 'Did he really say he was going on a date with Luca?'

'No, not really. He said they were hanging out as friends, but they obviously fancy each other. You saw them on Friday, didn't you? They were all over each other.'

'Don't encourage him, Louise! Ally really doesn't need to be screwing around while he's here.'

She stirs intently, her back turned to me.

'I'm sorry, Louise.' My voice is shaky, my throat tight. 'It's just there's so much you don't know, and I know you've made friends with Ally. He charms everyone. There's so much going on, and I don't know how I feel about you getting dragged into it. I don't know...'

She turns around and leans against the kitchen unit, her dainty fingers tucking her hair behind her ear. 'You don't have to be here, and I don't have to have you here, so maybe that makes us friends. You are likeable too, Chris. You've always been so kind with me at work, and I know you're worried about Ally. If it helps you to tell me, then tell me.'

I turn away, pretending to go and look out her living room window. The smell of her cooking and the tidy, grown-up warmth of her little home embarrass me. I don't know how much I want to tell her. Some stupid little scenario is forming in my imagination. As a colleague, Louise is uncomplicated and hard-working. As a twenty-two-year-old girl in skinny jeans with huge brown eyes and too much makeup, she puts me on edge.

If she wasn't my trainee and eight years younger than me, I would want to sleep with her. Maybe I do want to sleep with her, and there's a remote possibility that it might happen. After all, we're alone together and she's cooking me dinner. Am I kidding myself that it might be on her mind too? What kinds of avenues am I shutting off by opening up to her? And here I go, imagining the relationship beyond the sex. Don't *normal* guys just think about fucking with as little complication as possible? Why does every crush I have inspire an involved future love story before I've even had the guts to say hello?

'Come and sit down. It'll be about half an hour,' she says, washing her hands.

I sit on the end of the sofa, not being stand-offish, but not being presumptuous either. She arranges herself on the floor, cross-legged and looking up at me with a glass of wine in the diamond of space she's created with her knees.

'Where do you want to start?'

'Okay, so Ally has been seeing this guy, Scott Binnie, for years, but in secret because... well, partly because Scott's quite well known.'

Louise nods. 'Yeah, he's Campbell Binnie's son, Binnie Homes? I thought he was engaged to Leisha Burnett from the telly.'

'You're right, he is. But he's been stringing Ally along for years. Ally has worked for Binnie Homes since he was at university. He was Dux of our school and he got a first at uni. He wouldn't tell you because he's not like that. Ally always wanted to teach, but he got that job at Binnie Homes then just stuck there.'

'You went to school with Ally? And uni, too?' she asks.

'No, I went to Glasgow while he stayed at home, went to Aberdeen. Anyway, Scott isn't happy about Ally doing teacher training. He's been giving him a hard time about it, trying to discourage him. He's very possessive, controlling. I think he realised Ally was distancing himself. Remember when he came into school that Monday and said he'd fallen? Well, he told me that Scott was waiting for him when he got in from the pub. They argued, Scott shoved him, and he fell. That's how he got hurt, and he... he said he'd had enough, told Scott it was over.'

I realise that now I'm raw and open. The tears stinging in my eyes are embellishing the story for me.

'Now Scott's saying that he loves Ally,' I continue, 'and wants to come out to everyone and move in with him. Ally's scared of him. He hid at mine on Monday night and I saw his... he was covered in fag burns and bruises.'

'Jesus!' Louise shakes her head. 'Ally doesn't want that, surely?'

'Ally's scared about what Scott will do if he breaks up with him. Ally's changed so much. He was confident before, self-assured, and now he just seems angry and scared. He's not who I remember.'

Louise shifts so that her legs are folded to one side. 'Who do you remember?'

I stop breathing to think. 'We were best friends at school, but I hadn't spoken to him for years when he came to Aberlayne.'

Sweat pools under my collar and slicks my eyelids. If I say it all out loud, I will acknowledge that it has never really gone away. I've reworked it interminably in my mind. It has a foetus-like possibility of its own, and letting it see daylight will be painful. I'll lose control of it.

Louise prompts me. 'Okay, so any idea why he disappeared from school this morning? What did he say to you?'

Now I look right at her, hoping she'll see me floundering, but instead she scrambles to her feet to check on the lasagne. When she returns, she sits on the sofa, leaving an unthreatening distance between us, with her back against the armrest and her legs crossed so she's facing me.

'I don't know where to start.' I stab each fingernail into the pad of my thumb, one by one.

'There's no hurry.'

'I didn't think I'd ever have to see him again, and it would've been okay with me if he'd never turned up at work. Today he admitted that he'd requested a placement at Aberlayne because he knew I was there. I just couldn't... it was too much; I couldn't deal with it. I've been feeling so low anyway, and he thinks he's helping, but if he'd just have left me alone...'

'When you were younger, I'm guessing you were more than friends?'

My hands hover around my stomach. 'Kind of.'

'What do you mean, kind of?' Louise doesn't even look surprised.

'I don't know how to explain it.'

'You were 'kind of' more than friends, which I'm imagining got complicated. That's why things are so awkward now?'

'More than friends in that... well, I was in love with him. But I'm not... I don't think I'm like he is. I don't know. We didn't have sex. I mean, we kissed and messed about all the time, and he'd sleep over. And we did daft things like holding hands when no one was looking. I wrote him love letters, every week, I wrote these... I don't know. I feel so stupid.'

'It's not stupid.' She smiles. 'Did Ally love you too?'

'Yeah, he said he did. I was a total bore. I'm seriously uncool. I wrote about a million love letters to him when I was away at uni. I used to send him poems and sketches and quotes from everything I read that reminded me of him. It was before decent mobiles. He wrote back, but never as much as I did. Then we were inseparable during the holidays. When he wasn't working, he'd always stay at mine because his mum and dad had another baby. His mum got postnatal depression, and his dad drinks so they don't get on. I think my mum knew about us, but she never said anything. My stepdad works offshore so he was away a lot. It was me... I did want to, but I don't know...'

I take a deep breath. Louise is watching me, and I know I'm shaking and sweating.

'Then we got drunk one night. We were in my room and I'd kind of hinted that I was up for giving it a go, so we were in bed. But then my fucking stepdad walked in because he'd come home early and heard a noise. He got an eyeful and went apeshit. I felt so guilty and mixed-up about it anyway, and then Paul let rip about how upset my mum would be if she knew. So yeah, that was the last of Ally staying over at mine, and then it just got... impossible. He would come through some weekends and stay with me in Glasgow during term time. I thought everything was okay. What a fucking idiot I am, honestly.'

I'm getting flustered, disgusted at myself.

'Anyway, I missed him so much. I didn't make any friends because I was pining for him. I was home one weekend, and we went out with some friends of his that he'd met at uni. He was acting like he wanted to show me off to them, but I could tell something wasn't right. The way they talked about him, it was like they were talking about someone else. The drunker everyone got, the more side-lined I felt. They were doing drugs, which he knows I hate, and I knew they were talking about me. I asked Ally if we could just go home, make up some excuse. I suppose I was clingy and

I kept nagging him. I just wanted to have him to myself. We were pretty drunk, but even then, I felt funny kissing him where other people could see us. He was annoyed with me, and we fell out a bit... you know, just a few angry words because he thought I was ashamed of being with him. Then he disappeared to the bathroom. This guy Ally seemed friendly with came and sat next to me and said, 'I feel sorry for you, Chris, so I'm suggesting you go after your boyfriend.' I said I didn't know what he was talking about. He just shrugged and said, 'Follow Ally into the gents. Go now.' So, I did.'

Louise seems to know what's coming and reaches for my hand.

'I found him going down on some random guy. He saw me, but I just walked away. I don't remember getting home, and I couldn't eat or speak to anyone for a week. It felt like my guts had been ripped out. I only talked to him once after that. We met up after we both graduated, but it didn't go very well because he admitted that he slept around loads at uni. I was so angry, and now that I think about it, he must have started seeing Scott by then. He said, 'I did love you, but all we did was kiss and fumble about and it wasn't enough.'

'Did you try and explain why you couldn't go through with it?' Louise asks, playing with my fingers.

'Yeah, I did. I tried. I knew that I loved him, and I told him that, but he's known forever that he's gay. I didn't know what the fuck was going on with me. It's so hard to explain. I think I just absolutely worshipped him, to the point where I felt like I couldn't even be myself—and you know I wasn't that sure at seventeen what 'being myself' really meant. I'd had sex with girls, and I knew I wanted to have sex with Ally,

but the thought of it... I don't know. I was terrified it would
be the wrong thing. I suppose I thought sex would let him see
right through me, see that I wasn't really like him, and then
I'd lose what we had.'

Louise lets go of my hand and sits back. 'Maybe he did
really love you, but the no-sex thing was a deal breaker? Sex
is a big deal. You can definitely have sex without love, but I
can't imagine falling in love and not having sex.'

I'm nodding, but my mind is shadowy with unwelcome
thoughts. 'So, if I didn't have sex with you, you'd think I didn't
love you?'

Louise cracks up at this, and we both laugh at my idiocy.

'Oh my God, I didn't mean it like that!' I'm more
embarrassed than she is. 'I get everything back to front, don't I?'

'No, it's refreshing.' She smiles.

'You mean I'm a freak, not a normal red-blooded guy?'

'I think you must have been quite naive. That explains why
you got so hurt.'

'I'm still pretty clueless. I'd no idea about Eilidh. My last
girlfriend went travelling and met someone else. I don't see
the signs. I feel like I haven't learned anything.'

'Well, you've learned to protect yourself a bit more, I hope?'

I rest my chin in my hand and study her. 'You're so...
together, Louise.'

'I put on a good show,' she deflects. 'Do you still love Ally?'

Her question knocks the words out of me. She feels my
hands shaking and she lets them go again.

'It's okay, it's none of my business. I need to take that
lasagne out of the oven now. I think you should have a glass
of wine.'

She goes to get it and gives me the space I need.

CHAPTER TWENTY-FIVE

TUESDAY

Ally woke to the sensation of a weight settling on the edge of the bed, followed by cool fingertips on his cheek.

'Morning, baby. It's half ten'

'Mm,' he said, forcing his gluey eyes open.

'I'm going for a run, then I'll make you breakfast.'

Ally pushed himself up on one elbow. 'You're going out running?'

'Yeah, I brought you a coffee.'

It was pale and milky; he took his coffee black and sweet.

Scott smoothed his thick fingers through Ally's fair hair, rearranging it crudely. 'I always do 10k on Tuesdays.'

'Okay.'

'Sore head?'

'No.'

'I love you. You're not still sulking with me?'

'I want to go home.'

'Why? What's wrong?'

'Nothing. Just go, Scott.' He gave him a shove towards the door

'Are you crying?'

Ally shook his head and hid under the covers until he heard the front door shut and the key turn. He raked his knuckles across his eyes and swung his legs out of bed. He was still wearing Scott's sweatshirt and jersey shorts, too big and familiar-smelling. Leaving the white coffee to go cold, he wandered into the open- plan living room and kitchen. November drizzle choked the winter sun, suffusing the room with grey light. All that was visible through the streaming glass was Scott's Range Rover, a frost-ravaged patio and some empty planters.

He put the kettle on the hob and helped himself to one of Scott's cigarettes from the pack left on the breakfast bar. His laptop sat there charging beside his mobile. Remembering the scheduled Crit visit the next day, he sat down with the coffee and the ashtray and opened his Hotmail to let his lecturer know he wouldn't be there. There was a subject less email from 'chris.james. elliot@btinternet' flagged as sent at 4.17 a.m. earlier that morning.

Ally,

Everyone at school is worried about you. Louise suggested I should try emailing you since you're not answering your phone. I'd hate to think you won't come back and finish your placement, especially if it's even partly because of me. I've been thinking so much about what you said this morning, and you know I prefer writing things to saying them.

Even though I find it hard to be around you, I've missed you. I think you saved my life by reading me that book this weekend. I feel so lost right now. You said I still feel like a safe place to you, and I am trying to understand what you mean. You still terrify me—that's why I went on the defensive by saying I don't care. If you need me, then I will try to help. I know how you act on impulse and then regret it, and you know how I never act on mine, and then also regret it. You don't need to go back to him. You don't need anyone. You are the single most magnetic person in the world.

*Please let me know you are okay, and if you need me, I
will try to be there.*
Chris

Ally let himself cry until he tasted tears in his dry mouth.
He pressed reply and cancel about twenty times.

Chris,

*I've always needed you. I don't know what I'm doing. Give
me a day or two. I'm so sorry.*

Ally

He pressed send without giving himself time to revise
anything and quickly closed the window. Like a trapped
bird flapping against a window pane, he paced across the
oatmeal carpet, a cigarette and a coffee mug busying his
hands. He went to fetch the mobile phone he abandoned
in the bathroom only to find it gone. Scott's bed was neat
and untouched. Ally picked up his discarded clothes from
around the sofa, mindlessly smoothing and folding them.
His wallet fell out on the floor with some keys and condoms.
His lighter weighed dully in the other pocket of his worn
in jeans.

He tried the front door again. It was just after eleven
a.m., break time at school. Would Chris take out his phone
and pick up his message? How would he explain Ally's
absence? He went back to the laptop and typed a brief
message to his tutor asking if he could rearrange his Crit
visit. He copied Chris on his email to his tutor.

After that he washed last night's dishes and glasses,
trying to stop the panic threatening to get a stranglehold
on him. Eventually he heard feet on the gravel outside and
the key turn in the front door. Scott's breathing slowly
returned to normal as he heeled off his muddy trainers on

the porch, and he discarded his sweaty T-shirt on the way to the living room, his chest hair matted and glistening, his legs spattered with mud and his face pink.

He leaned on the wall. 'You're up.'

Ally nodded, taking a quick hit of his sweaty semi-nakedness.

'Hey, come here.' Scott crossed the room, crouching down next to him and tugging at his fingers.

'What?'

'Come with me.'

He obeyed the slippery heat of Scott's hand on the small of his back. The master bedroom had a clinical white wet room, which Scott pushed him inside before locking the door behind them.

'What are you—'

'Shh.' Scott kissed his mouth shut.

He tugged Ally's T-shirt over his head and tossed it into the corner, nudging him over to where the shower rose hung. The water was cool but harsh, making him yelp as Scott pushed him under.

'Shut your slutty wee mouth until I tell you to open it for me.'

Scott slipped his own shorts down and dropped them in the corner, then took a firm handful of Ally's wet hair in one hand, pulling his head back so his neck was exposed. Ally tensed, thinking teeth would leave an obvious mark there.

'Why are you flinching? I won't hurt you! Not any more than you want me to, anyway.'

Putting his arms around Ally's hunched shoulders, Scott let the water soak them both, rinsing away the sweat and mud from his run. Their eyes were level, and Ally tried to read Scott's while hoping Scott couldn't read his.

'I know I went too far last time. I know I did.' His voice was almost lost in the noise of the running water.

Although the water was warm now, Ally shivered.

'I'm sorry, Ally.' Scott pulled at Ally's arms, forcing him closer. 'I am really sorry.'

Ally had worked diligently over the years to suppress his fantasies about Chris. And yet as Scott pressed against him, aroused and insistent, all he heard was Chris's voice, all he felt was Chris's skin. Scott kissed down Ally's neck, nuzzling his collarbone before following the line of darkening hair below his belly button. He dropped to one knee as the shower ran.

As Scott took him in his mouth, Ally screwed his eyes shut and supported himself against the wall, letting the well-worn images of Chris merge with the sensation of Scott's mouth and tongue. Chris's sage smell; the scar on his lip; the blond down on his earlobes; the freckles spilling over his wiry forearms; his sweet and earnest kisses. Ally thought of them all as he pushed rhythmically against Scott, his fingers curled in wet, dark hair.

You are the single most magnetic person in the world.

Fuck your stupid hyperbole, Chris Elliot. Are you saying that you want me?

He groaned softly as Scott added a hand to his efforts, snuffling insistently below him.

I've always needed you.

'I'm going to come.'

Scott removed his lips hastily, but kept his hand sliding firmly as Ally folded into him, clinging on through his orgasm with jerky shudders.

'Good boy,' Scott whispered. 'Come here, baby.' Scott half led, half carried him, damp and breathless, into the bedroom.

After Scott sat on the edge of the bed, Ally knelt on the floor and numbly and efficiently reciprocated. It didn't take long. Dragging the back of his hand across his mouth, he picked up the discarded towel and roughly wiped himself clean. Caught by a strangling nausea, he staggered to his feet and went back into the bathroom to clean his teeth.

Scott called out sleepily from the bed. The instinct to obey met with a wall of repulsion, and Ally started to cry. Clinging to the edge of the sink, he turned so that he couldn't see his miserable reflection.

Sighing impatiently, Scott got up and opened the door. 'What are you doing?

What's wrong?'

Ally couldn't say anything that made any sense.

'Hey, stop it. Come on.' Scott tugged at his wrist, but Ally was rooted to the spot, his breathing ragged. 'Come on out of here. Put this on. You're shaking.'

He let Scott drape a robe around him and nudge him back into the bedroom.

'Stop it.' Scott shook him by the shoulders. 'I can't handle you crying. Just tell me what's wrong.'

'I don't know what's wrong.'

'For fuck's sake, Ally! Stop it! My parents have disowned me and I'm getting packed off to rehab, but I'm not crying about it.'

Ally didn't know what was left to say. There were no books on the cabinet beside Scott's expansive bed. There were no books anywhere in his apartment. What was left now that the sex terrified him? There was no point saying anything. There was only one person he wanted to talk to.

'I want to go home.'

Scott was pawing at Ally's arm, bewildered. 'I'll take you home later, baby. Go and make us some coffee, eh? I got you more fags. Calm down.'

'I just want to go home.' Ally curled up on the bed, hiding his face.

'Stop this, babe. Stop crying now.' He pressed a kiss onto Ally's clammy forehead and squeezed his fingers clumsily.

'Please don't touch me.' Ally gagged, tucking his head between his knees.

CHAPTER TWENTY-SIX

WEDNESDAY

The long dawn hours ebb away. Although sleep hasn't been even a vague possibility, I'm strangely functional. The dismal fog hanging over me is clearing, but my mind is feverish. I go looking for the book Ally read to me. It's still abandoned on my bedroom floor. I haven't changed the bed since Ally slept in it, so there's a lingering scent of his aftershave and stale cigarette smoke.

I pick up the pillow and carefully pluck off a strand of fair hair, tucking it inside the cover of *The Testament of Gideon Mack*—the testament of a faithless minister who meets the Devil. If I were ready to read again I'd devour it. The book is a signpost on the road where I've been lost, a rumour of a path out of the wood. It's Ally's voice I hear reading it.

Last night, Louise persuaded me to try calling Eilidh one last time.

'Go and do it now,' she said, 'You can go through to my bedroom. And don't just give up if she doesn't answer. Leave her a message and guilt-trip her.'

Louise's bedroom was cluttered and smelled powdery-sweet. I stepped over discarded clothes, including a dainty pink bra and tangled knickers ravelled in a slither of tights. The bed was unmade, and I couldn't sit on it because it felt like an intrusion.

I called Eilidh, my mind a white-noise blur of humiliation. It went to voicemail. I hung up, kicking the skirting board in frustration. After preparing a couple of sentences in my head, I dialled again, ready to recite them on to the voicemail.

'Hello?'

Even the prepared sentences were lost at the sound of her voice.

'Chris?'

'Yeah, why haven't you called me?'

'I meant to.'

She sounded so composed. Anger sharpened my thoughts.

'You meant to? But you didn't,' I said.

'Elaine said she told you... about my new job?'

'Yeah, Elaine told me. You knew, though. You knew when you were here last weekend, and you didn't tell me.'

'I was going to. You just seemed really... fragile. I didn't know what to say.' She sounded unrepentant.

I dragged my fingernails back and forth across the woodchip. 'That's bullshit. You just needed to tell me what was going on. You spent the whole weekend acting like we were okay.'

'God, you just don't get it, Chris! You wouldn't accept that I never wanted anything serious. I've always wanted to live abroad, and I *did* tell you that. I was trying to tell you this weekend, but you didn't want to know.'

I felt a weary exasperation, like the one that comes from reprimanding the same boringly teenage behaviour in class.

'Well, you didn't try very hard, Eilidh. You could've saved yourself the airfare. It can't have been worth the money just to mess with my head for a couple of days.'

'That's not fair, Chris. I came back to talk to you; it's not my fault that you seem to be in a tailspin.'

A splinter from the woodchip buried itself viciously under my fingernail. 'So it was easier just to let me think everything was fine? You thought it'd really help my state of mind if you ignored me and let me find out from Elaine at work?'

Eilidh huffed impatiently. 'As far as I was concerned, everything was fine! I thought we were friends, and that you'd understand why I don't want a relationship while I'm working abroad. But because we were sleeping together, you got the wrong idea.'

'No, Eilidh, you got the wrong idea. It's not okay to get other people to do your dirty work, especially not my fucking line manager! It's not okay to mislead me for months and then make it sound like it's my fault for being naive. If we were friends, you would have been straight with me, about everything, right from the start.'

'I was straight with you! You're just a bit too... intense sometimes, Chris. Honestly, I think you just hear what you want to hear because you're so desperate not to be alone.'

Winded by this, I bit down on my bottom lip. 'You know what, Eilidh? The only thing I didn't get these last few months is that you're a vacuous bitch.' I hung up before she could respond, swaying against the wall as the anger rapidly receded to a shivery numbness.

Later, I tried to excuse her behaviour to Louise. 'It wasn't a big deal for her, it wasn't serious.'

'But was it serious to you?' Louise asked.

'Everything's serious to me. Everything's a big deal.'

'She thought it was just sex, but you're not very good at just sex.'

I pretended to be offended, but Louise just laughed.

'Thanks, you're doing my ego the world of good tonight,' I said.

'Aw, you know what I mean. You're an inverse of the average guy. He wants meaningless sex, whereas you want the meaningful stuff and aren't so bothered about the sex.'

'Yeah, but I really am bothered about it! Everyone is. Aren't you?'

'I like to think I can separate love and sex. A lot of my girlfriends say, 'Oh, I could never have a one-night stand.' They have this prehistoric idea it's not cool, not classy or whatever, but the way I see it is, it's a need, a function. Sometimes I just want sex—not intimacy, not love, not a relationship. I just want to have sex with a hot guy, or, more likely, whoever I end up with at two a.m. when Ritzy's is closing. You should work much harder for love. It must be more fulfilling, so it must be worth it.'

'You don't sound very sure that it's worth it.'

'I'm not, because I've never fallen in love. I've had a couple of boyfriends, but ultimately I'm not ready to put in the effort.'

'It's not an effort!' I was shocked that she thinks this way at age twenty-two. 'You make it sound grim. I don't think it's a case of being ready. Either you love someone, or you don't.'

She laughed at me again. 'You're so sweet, honestly.'

'I think... I mean, I have this theory that, well, you know *The Pearl* by John Steinbeck? It's a parable. The pearl corrupts the couple who find it. I think sex is like the pearl,' I tried to explain.

'No, you idiot! The pearl symbolises wealth, and how greed dehumanises us. You're meant to be an English teacher!'

I smiled at her indulgently. 'Okay, Miss Macari, bear with me. I mean, you start with something innocent and good and worthwhile. You understand each other, and there's trust and there's loyalty. Then there's this thing you can't resist, it's not rational, and it just takes over, and it changes every—'

'You're talking about Ally.'

'No... well, yes.'

'You loved him so much you couldn't bear to defile and corrupt your feelings. You are an absolute basket case, Chris Elliot. Do you know that?'

'Yeah, I know.' I shrugged. 'I'm an idiot.'

'I don't see why everyone you have feelings for has to be put up on a pedestal. We're all flawed, we all screw up, and underneath we're all animals following our baser instincts. You know full well that love and sex aren't mutually exclusive. You're just scared of getting hurt. Did you love Eilidh?'

'I don't know.'

'So, your theory is bullshit, isn't it? You didn't start with pure, untainted mutual adoration and throw it all away when you took her pants off, did you?'

'No, but it was pointless, wasn't it? I could have been anyone to her, like you said. If it's just sex, then I could be any random she picked up. It is like *The Pearl*! It makes you greedy for something that hollows you out and hurts other people.'

'Oh, dear God, Chris. If you weren't my boss, I'd be saying you just need to get drunk and get laid more.'

'Ally says I'm uptight too.'

'He's right. You need to chill the fuck out.'

She'd had a few glasses of wine now. The empty plates had been cleared and I was nursing a second coffee, wishing it were wine.

'Okay, sorry if I'm out of line asking this, but do you think you'd feel differently if Ally were a girl? I mean, is the issue that you're not cool with fancying boys?'

I could never be that direct with myself. My mouth opened, but nothing comes out.

'It's okay. I'll shut up,' she said.

'No, don't. I've never spoken to anyone about it. I've had it in my head for years and it's never gone away, and I think it's part of the reason I get so low. If I start talking about Ally, I won't be able to stop, and then I'm forced to admit to myself there's still... something. I'm thirty now. I want to fall in love and get married and have kids. I really, seriously need to move on, but I don't seem to be able to.'

'You don't want to be in love with a man. Is the whole *Pearl* theory basically because you're squeamish about gay sex and it's nice and comfy in the closet?'

'No!'

'Well, how would you know if you haven't tried it? I'm assuming you haven't tried it?'

'No... It's only... I can't talk about this anymore.' I get up, pace to the window.

'If you know you still feel like this, then why can't you have this conversation with Ally?'

'I can't talk to Ally about sex, it's the elephant in the room. We talked about everything, but not that. Now we can barely look at each other. I still wake up thinking about Paul walking in on us, or me finding Ally with that guy in the toilets, and I feel sick.'

'Well, then you're fucked, aren't you? Or not, as the case may be.'

Louise winked at me, cutting through my self-pity. Then she stood up, walked around the small folding table and hugged me. Her hair brushed my cheek and one small breast brushed against my arm. It seemed like a come-on, so I reached up and pulled her down onto my lap. Her huge, dark eyes widened, then she nuzzled my neck and laughed again.

'Ouch! Here was I thinking you must be dead from the waist down.' She shifted on my lap away from the rapid swell of my cock. 'You're just a typical man after all.'

I was mortified, felt like a total creep. 'Oh God, I'm so sorry. We've been sitting talking about sex and—See! It's bad news, Lou!'

'Yeah, because I can't possibly be your friend now we've had a cuddle and you got a semi over it,' she said, shifting back to her seat. 'Lighten up, honestly!' Louise checked her mobile which was propped up on the table like a third guest. 'Luca texted back, hang on. No, he's not heard from him either. He says he's going to try texting him too.'

I studied my hands. *Ally seeing Luca is bad news.* 'If he's with Scott, it's probably not a good idea that Luca tries to contact him.'

'Do you really think he's with Scott then?'

'I don't know where else he could be. Like I said, he's been kind of brainwashed by Scott.'

'What if they've just decided to make a go of it?'

'They won't... I mean, he can't.'

'But he might. People do,' she said, quickly typing a response to Luca's text. Then she looked up from the screen of her phone. 'Are you jealous, Chris?'

'Of whom?'

'Well, Luca for a start. You were vile to him at the pub on Friday.'

'No, I wasn't, Lou. I didn't speak to him because he was too busy chatting Ally up to notice anyone else. I haven't got a problem with Luca, but Ally's like a kid in a sweetshop with someone like him. He can't help himself.'

'And what about Scott?'

'Scott Binnie is an absolute tosser. He's narcissistic and brain-dead.'

'The thing is, though, he's hot.' Louise fanned herself, exhaling through pursed lips.

'You know he's had new teeth and a nose job, don't you? And he was fat at school.'

'So, what? He was an ugly duckling? He's a *very* pretty boy now,' she said. 'You *are* jealous, Mr. Elliot!'

'I'm not jealous of Scott Binnie. I just think he's a dick.'

'They've been together since Uni? That's a long time,'

'It isn't like that. They're not a couple. They've just been fuck buddies. Scott treats him like—'

'Like a rent boy? Your precious Ally? He flashes his cash around and Ally drops his pants for him. Sordid, isn't it?'

'But Ally's not into the money thing,'

'Hmm. He must really love him then, after all. What do you think?'

'Stop it, Lou. It's hard enough.'

'Well it was when I sat on your knee.'

'Oh, fuck off.' I squirmed. 'Okay, I'm jealous. I don't want Ally sleeping with Luca, and I fucking hate Scott Binnie. Now will you shut up about it?'

'Okay, okay,' she said. 'I thought so. You need to go home anyway. It's after eleven and I'll turn into a pumpkin soon.'

'Oh God, sorry. And thank you for dinner. For everything.'
'Any time,' she said, and we hugged, and it felt great.

Back home I open a bottle of wine, and after two hours of composing and editing an email to Ally, I eventually send it. Lying on the sofa, I stalk Eilidh's Facebook page for anything enlightening and draw a blank. Louise's page is candid and entertaining, like her. I flick through her photos, peeved with myself. I really do find her attractive. Now that we've spent an evening chatting, I know I'll develop a silly crush that will make me awkward and extinguish any interest she ever had in being friends. But we must be friends now, because she knows what no one else does. She made it real, by letting me say it out loud and truly hearing it when I did.

CHAPTER TWENTY-SEVEN

During interval, Katia politely knocks on my classroom door and waits to be invited in. After she closes the door behind her, I instinctively pull out a chair from behind one of the desks for her to sit on.

'Yesterday I miss English, and I'm come to see if I can have the work I have missed?' she says, hovering by my desk before perching on the proffered seat, twisting her fingers and unable to look at me.

"Mr. McClay isn't here today, Katia, but you can take a note from the homework board. Are you feeling better now?'

She doesn't look well. Her enduring cold sore is raw and weeping, her hair looks greasy, and she has a fragile look I haven't noticed before.

'Mr. Elliot, I want to tell you something, but please you can't tell anyone else.'

My heart sinks. I reach for a pen. 'I can't promise that, Katia. It depends what it is.'

'Is at home. At home is very bad.' Her English deteriorates as she dissolves into tears. 'My uncle is staying with us, from Poland. He come to live here too but has no home yet. He sleeps in my room, in my little sister's bed because we have only two bedrooms. I'm very frightened the things he is say to me, and he say if I tell my dad, then he says to him what a bad girl I am. I know my dad believe him. My mum is not here, is in Poland visiting my grandmother.'

'What is he saying to you, Katia?' I keep my expression and tone neutral.

'I can't say those things, Mr. Elliot.' Her acned cheeks are scarlet. 'Bad things he want to do to me. I don't want him in my bedroom. I don't want to go home.'

Scribbling in shorthand as I listen, I focus on the wording of each question I ask her. 'What are you frightened of?'

'Frightened he touch me, frightened he do bad things to me. Then my dad know I'm a bad girl. He believe my uncle I'm a bad girl.'

'A bad girl because...?'

'My Dad think I'm lazy and always talking to boys, not doing my schoolwork, not studying enough. Is why I can't have mobile phone or computer like my friends. I can't go out, he's very strict with me. I tell you because you know is not true, Mr. Elliot, you know I am working hard for you and doing extra study. I'm never talking in class. You can tell him!'

I tug at my shirt collar with two clumsy fingers. 'Katia, please try not to get so upset. Try to stay calm.' I find her a tissue in my desk drawer. After letting her cry a little more and blow her nose, I say, 'You said he is saying things that scare you. Does he do anything to you that you don't like?'

Is that question too leading? How I want to act and how I am obligated to act as a professional are so at odds that I wish she'd chosen another trusted adult.

'Only looking at me, all the time looking at me. And then he come in at night and say what he will do to me.' Sweat is beading on her face, a drop breaks on her collarbone.

'Do you feel safe at home?'

'No.' She sniffs. 'Not when my mum is away. I don't want to go home. My sister only seven years old. Yesterday I stayed at home and miss school because she in bed sick, and I didn't want her alone with my uncle.'

'Have you thought about talking to your dad about what's happening?'

She shakes her head sadly, and I see it's an impossibility for her.

'Katia, I can't... I can't keep this a secret, do you understand? I'm worried about you, and I need to tell somebody else who can make sure you are safe from now on. It's part of my job to do that. I'll have to talk to Mrs. Curran, and your guidance teacher, okay? They need to know so they can help you.'

She nods tearfully. 'Thank you, Mr. Elliot, I'm so sorry,'

'You don't need to be sorry. You did the right thing by telling someone.' I produce an encouraging smile for her.

'What will happen now? You have to tell Mrs. Curran?'

'Maybe you could wait here while I go and find her. Is that okay?'

'What about my homework? For Mr. McClay? He's back tomorrow?'

I get a painful lurch somewhere under my ribcage. 'I think so. If you want to just copy down the homework, I'll be back really soon.' I take my notepad with me.

Elaine is on the phone but waves me in the door when she sees me hovering in the corridor. I wait, fidgeting, for her to finish her call, something about a Stage Two meeting.

'Sorry, Chris,' she says when she eventually hangs up. 'How are you?'

'I'm okay, thanks. I've got Katia Kamisky in my room, and I need your help, because it sounds like Child Protection stuff, and I've never... I don't know what to do now.'

'Is she still there?'

I nod.

'Did you write everything down? Even what you asked her?'

'Yeah, I mean, in scribbles, shorthand. It's here—I'd need to finish it off for it to make any sense.'

'And does she know you are telling me this right now?'

'Yeah, I remembered to say I couldn't keep it secret. I said you'd need to know.'

'Good, well done. What has she told you?'

'She has an uncle staying, and he's sleeping in her room with her. He's started making suggestive comments, well, kind of stronger than that. She's scared, and her mum isn't around just now. She's also frightened for her seven-year-old sister, so she truanted yesterday to look after her, because she doesn't want her alone with the creepy uncle. And you've met her dad...'

'Yeah, he's a bit odd. Why do you think she disclosed to you? Do you teach her?'

'Usually, but Ally's had that class lately.'

'Okay. Where's he today? Off sick? I noticed he wasn't there at break time.'

I say nothing because it's easier.

'I'll come back with you and talk to her, but can you keep making notes for me? Have you got a class that needs covered?'

'I can ask Louise; we share that class anyway. Should be okay.'

Elaine lays her fingers on my elbow. 'I know you could do without this just now, Chris. How've things been?'

I shrug wearily, looking at the floor, drained and stuck for words.

CHAPTER TWENTY-EIGHT

Ally woke in Scott's bed and struggled to open his eyes. Frustrated with his crying, Scott had brought him two pills and a glass of orange juice and told him to go and lie down with the lights off. That had been about midday on Tuesday. The clock beside the bed said it was evening, nearly half past eight.

Weakly sitting up, he looked around the bedroom; it was dark and stuffy, the only light coming from the small bedside lamp. There were no personal touches. It could have been any suite in a very expensive hotel: neutral, expensive and minimalist.

His throat sticky with thirst, Ally got out of bed and helped himself to a pair of Scott's jeans and a T-shirt, which were hanging on the back of the leather armchair. They smelled of smoke and Chanel aftershave. Opening the bedroom door, he called for Scott again.

After sinking two tumblers of cold water in the kitchen, he checked the other rooms and found he was alone. Beside the front door, on the console table, he found a bunch of keys, his iPhone and an envelope with his name written in Scott's untidy scrawl. Carrying them all back to the living room, he sat down at the breakfast bar and opened the envelope to find a folded piece of lined paper and a wedge of twenty-pound notes.

Ally baby,

Dad and Serena came for me. They're making me go up north tomorrow and I'd no choice. Call me when you get this.

Your car is in the garage, and I've left the keys for it and my house keys too. Stay here, eh? I'm sorry I couldn't say bye; I didn't want them knowing you were here. I wish I knew why you were in such a state. I really do love you. Scott x

Altogether, Scott had left five hundred pounds. Campbell Binnie had put a stop to his part-time wages. He sipped the water, rereading the note and feeling a kind of relief. His phone showed several missed calls and messages—mostly from Louise, but a few from Luca, who he'd unintentionally stood up. Nothing from Chris.

He left the car keys and all the money save twenty pounds for taxi fare. He took the phone and the note, and after setting the alarm and locking the door, he dropped Scott's keys back through the letterbox.

The taxi picked up next to the small shop where he could buy cigarettes. Once inside, he called Louise.

'Where are you?' she asked. 'Are you okay?'

'Yeah, I'm okay. I'm sorry. I fucked up.'

'Where are you?'

'I'm heading home. It's a long story, but I'm okay.'

'You're coming back to Aberlayne, aren't you?'

'I don't think so.'

'Ally! Listen, come round here now. I've got the bag you left at work and Chris found your keys in it.'

'I can't stay long, Lou. I really need to get home.'

When he rang her buzzer, Louise greeted him with a hug, which made his throat thicken. The TV was on, and she was dressed in fleecy pyjamas while doing some marking on the tiny living room floor.

'I'm sorry if you were worried about me. Everyone at school must be so pissed off.'

'No one's pissed off. Just concerned.'

Louise brought him a glass of wine and asked if he was hungry. 'I've got leftover lasagne. I was entertaining last night.' She winked. 'I'll go and heat you up some.'

'Who were you entertaining?' he called.

'I can't tell you. You'd be raging jealous.'

While she was in the kitchen, he dialled Scott, who answered before the second ring. 'I got your note. Your house is locked and the alarm's on, and I put the keys back through the letterbox for when you get back.'

Scott seemed taken aback by his business-like tone. 'Feeling better, then?'

'Uh-huh. You?'

'Where are you?' Scott's voice was gravelly with restraint.

'I can't speak right now.'

'Where are you, Ally? Who are you with?'

'I'll call you later,' he said as Louise came back into the room.

'Don't hang up on me!'

'I'll call you later. I can't talk right now.'

After he ended the call, he stared at the blank display.

Louise sat on the carpet in front of him and passed him the warm plate of pasta and a fork. 'Who was that?'

He began to eat; it smelled delicious, and it at least it was something else to focus on. 'This is really good, thanks.'

'There's plenty more. Who were you talking to?'

'To Scott.'

'That's what Chris thought, that you had gone to him. What's going on with you and Scott?'

'I don't know.'

'Are you getting back together?'

'No. No, we're not. Is it okay if we don't talk about him?'

'What about Chris? Have you spoken to him?'

'No, but he sent me an email. Has he... did he say anything about me?'

Louise topped up his wine glass. He stopped eating and balanced the plate on his knees.

'Yes, he did. Chris said quite a lot about you, Ally.'

'Oh... okay. Was he angry? What did he say?'

'You know that you need to talk to him, Ally.'

Ally shook his head. 'I tried. He went apeshit. It's better if I don't.'

'You're not serious about dropping out, are you? Chris thinks you're doing well. He called the uni today and said you weren't up for your Crit this week for personal reasons, but you would be next week. He told them that you could do extra days with us at the end to make up any hours. You're so close to passing.'

Ally shrugged and pushed what was left on the plate to one side, putting down his fork. Louise picked up her phone and started typing a message. When she'd finished, she stood up and took his plate away.

'You need to have some tiramisu. I made heaps.'

'Twist my arm then.'

This time she brought back two bowls, both heaped with dessert, and tucked into one herself. Her phone lit up and began to ring. She finished her mouthful of pudding and answered it.

'Hiya. Yes, he's here. Uh-uh. No. Okay.' She passed her phone across to him. 'It's Chris.'

He shook his head.

'Don't be a dick. Talk to him.' She dropped the phone in his lap and left the room.

"Are you okay?' Chris asked.

'Not really. Everything's a mess.' They were talking over each other as if there was a delay.

'Did you get my email?'

"Yes, I did. I got it.'

'I can pick you up for work tomorrow, usual time,' Chris said. 'Unless—'

'I can't come back tomorrow. I mean, I think it's best if I don't come back.'

'Don't be a fuckwit. I'll pick you up at eight. How are you getting home from Louise's tonight?' He talked in the tone he used with pupils, cool and direct.

'Uh...'

'You know what, I'm on my way now. I'll come to Lou's to pick you up and I'll drive you home. We need to talk anyway.'

'No, Chris, please don't. I just need some time. My head's a mess.'

'I'll be there in ten minutes. Stay where you are.' He hung up abruptly.

I smell of Scott and I'm wearing his clothes. This morning I gave him a blowjob and I haven't washed since he came all over me. I'm disgusting, and you're too good to be near me. Let me go home and rot alone.

Louise found him with his head in his hands. She settled beside him on the sofa and put a gentle hand in the small of his back.

'Hey, what did he say?'

'He's on his way over here,' he whispered into his fingers. 'I can't see him. I need to go.' He pushed himself off the sofa and shrugged on the borrowed coat.

'Ally! What's wrong with you?'

'You don't understand. Honestly, it's for the best. He doesn't want to know.'

She placed herself between him and the door of her flat. 'That's pathetic. You owe him an explanation at least. What are you running away from?'

'You're right. I am pathetic. You and Chris need to stop trying to see the best in everyone, because some of us are just total cunts.'

'Ally, this is bullshit!'

'Bye.' He shut the door a fraction too hard.

CHAPTER TWENTY-NINE

My car headlights rise and dip over a speed bump. I see him, and I know he's seen me. I pull over to the side of the road and get out, leaving the engine running.

Ally lets me take him by the elbow and waits while I open the passenger door. He slumps into the seat and lights up without a word. He won't look at me. I can't talk. When he's finished, Ally flicks his fag end out and winds up the window. There's an air freshener on the dashboard that I stuck on to hide the smoke smell lingering in my car.

I turn onto Ally's cul-de-sac and park in front of his house.

'Thanks,' Ally says, getting out of the car.

'I'm coming in with you.'

Ally tugs his work bag out of the car and finds his house keys. Inside it's cold. I wait while he adjusts the thermostat and locks the door.

Ally's living room is tidy and grown-up. There are shelves laden with books and photos lining one wall, ceiling to floor. The kitchen is through the door at the opposite end of the living room, and I go to make tea. Ally's disappeared upstairs, and I can hear the shower running.

I take ages to find everything in the shiny kitchen. The biscuits in the cupboard are custard creams. Ally lived on custard creams when we were at school. It's kind of reassuring that his adolescent addiction endures. Laying the mugs on coasters on the light-wood coffee table, I sink into the leather sofa and switch on the TV, settling in to drink my tea. Ally appears ten minutes later in pyjama bottoms and a sweater, his face scraped pink and hair still wet from the shower. A deep flush runs up his throat like a red wine stain, and a medicated citrus smell comes from his damp skin.

I hand him the mug of tea and put the packet of biscuits between us on the sofa. Ally takes a handful and stacks them on his knee. He twists the top layer off, dips the plain biscuit in the mug and eats it, then scrapes the filling off the bottom layer with his teeth, swilling it down with a mouthful of tea before finishing off the final layer.

I watch Ally process the biscuits one by one.

'I went back to him,' he says after the fourth custard cream.

'Why?'

'I didn't know what else to do.'

'What do you mean?' I study the rim of my mug.

'I don't know. He won't listen to me.'

'What do you really want?'

Ally hugs his knees, letting biscuit crumbs fall as he stares at the floor.

'I can't be around him anymore.'

'Well... don't.'

'I'm scared, Chris. I don't know what else he'll do.'

I wait for him to expand, but he doesn't. 'What are you scared of?'

Ally swallows and his knuckles tighten, beginning to show white as they clasp around his knees. He indicates the scar above his eye. 'He's been... God, something really bad happened after, well... I think something happened, but I...' Trying to talk is making Ally gag and choke.

I inch closer to him on the sofa. 'I saw your bruises, remember?'

Ally nods, staring ahead. 'When he pushed me, I fell and hit my head on the corner of this table,' he says. 'I blacked out on the floor. I don't think I remember anything much, but when I opened my eyes I was in bed, undressed. I was in a mess—bleeding, throwing up—so I didn't realise 'til he made me get dressed that something was far wrong.'

'What do you mean? You didn't realise you'd hurt your head?'

'No, I was so worried about that, I didn't realise... The nurse at A & E, when she was finishing the stitches on my face she saw bloodstains on my jeans, and she asked what had happened to me. She brought this other doctor and a counsellor through, and they were all looking at me, asking all these personal questions: has someone hurt you, was it someone you know, did you consent, do you normally bleed after anal sex. They asked all this stuff, and I said I've been out with friends from work. They just looked at each other. They asked why there were marks round my neck and fag burns on my arms. I couldn't tell them, even if I did know. I just wanted to get out of there. They made a bit of scene, but I walked out. Scott says I don't remember because I was drunk, and I like it when he... I was drunk, and it wasn't the first time... so I can't expect any—'

'Ally,' I stop him, chilled. 'You're telling me Scott raped you?'

'I don't know. Something happened. I don't remember saying no to him.' He shakily dissects a fifth custard cream and leaves it uneaten on the arm of the sofa.

'You don't remember anything because you were unconscious!'

'I don't really know what I said, or what he did or didn't do. Louise and I had a lot to drink that night.'

'It doesn't matter whether you'd had a drink or not. What if Louise had been raped? Would you say it was her fault because she'd been drinking?'

Ally shakes his head. His clean skin is starting to sweat, and he dabs at his forehead with the sleeve he's pulled over the heel of his hand.

'Jesus, Ally,' I exhale, tensely. 'Stay away from him. Please!'

Ally reaches for his cigarettes and the lighter on the coffee table. His grim focus on lighting up and getting to the first deep drag makes me wince.

'I need you to help me.'

'Huh?'

'I need you to help me, Chris.'

I look at Ally. The scarlet flush on his neck has paled, and his hair is drying unevenly, silvery blonde in some parts and darker through the damp lengths on top. 'What do you mean?'

Ally reaches for the ashtray. 'What a stupid question. As if you don't know.'

I can't make eye contact, and my skin is burning. 'I don't.'

'Chris, whatever happened back then, I'm still me, and you are still you. I don't have anyone else. I've lost touch with everyone because of Scott. It's been great coming to Aberlayne because I've had company and conversations that he's not checking up on every fifteen minutes, but I came there because of you. Thing is, Scott was right about a lot of stuff about me. You'd agree with him. I'm impulsive, I can't be trusted... I'm slutty.'

'I would never say that.'

'No, you wouldn't put it that way, but it's what you think of me. What he thinks of me.' Ally drags bitterly on his cigarette and turns away to exhale.

'Don't tell me what I think, Ally, and don't compare me with him.'

Ally coughs, dropping ash on the sofa. 'No, you're right, you're nothing like him. Not everyone is as... *good* as you, Chris. You judge other people by your standards and they fall short, because your standards are insane. That's why you're driving yourself nuts trying to live up to them. But there's no one like you, Chris. I don't have anyone else.'

I can't answer. My throat is tight. While reaching for my mug of tea my hand brushes Ally's on its way to the ashtray. I try to ignore it, but my skin is singing with pain.

Ally has wide, frightened eyes. 'I need you, Chris.'

I understand, and I take his hand, still holding him at a safe distance. The silence is there for us to fill, but we can't. Ally sits cross-legged, facing me. His eyes, his skin and his lips all look drained of colour, overexposed like an old Polaroid.

'When Scott and Leisha got engaged I heard about it through someone else's Facebook page. I was heartbroken. I kept thinking... well, hoping he'd make a proper go of it with me once he got his head around things. It was really stupid and naive, I know. I suppose it never occurred to me that he'd expect me to go along with it, with him and Leisha. That's when things really started getting fucked up. When I said that I wanted to end it, I knew I'd lose my job. But Scott has so much stuff on me, pictures and videos. I know I was an idiot to let him, but it was just the kind of stupid shit we got up to. I'm not out, because of him. If he put any of that stuff out there it would fuck everything up for me.'

'He thinks he's entitled to his money's worth.'

Ally tucks a cushion over his stomach as if to protect it from a blow. 'You think it's about money, don't you? Because you know what it was like for me at home, you think I'd do anything to be well-off. Scott did give me stuff, luxuries I could never have paid for myself. But I worked for my salary, I made payments on my student loans and debts, and I bought my own house. I haven't sponged off him, and I wasn't with him because he's rich.'

'No, obviously, it was his caring and considerate personality that did it for you, and all the things you had in common.'

There's a brooding pause while Ally reaches for another cigarette and lights up again. 'Do you ever feel like you're not happy because you don't deserve to be happy?' Ally asks.

'Yeah, I do. Like I haven't worked hard enough to earn it. Or I just... yeah, don't deserve it.'

'I told myself I was lucky to have what I had, and it would be greedy to push for more.'

'Of course you deserve more, you fucking idiot.'

'Don't you think it's karma or whatever? For what I did to you?' He lapses into a coughing fit before I can reply. It gives me time to think.

'That's bullshit. It's been a long time.'

Ally turns away from me, and the healing wound glares from his temple. It looks septic. He'll scar.

'There's no point in me trying to defend myself. I just thought you were doing the same as me, since we were in different cities. It was easy for me to think it wouldn't matter to you, and that you'd meet someone else. We were only eighteen when you moved away. Who the fuck knows what they want at eighteen?'

'I would have done anything for you, Ally.'

'Anything except fuck me. You wouldn't do that. Just because you're not okay with it, you had to make me feel shit for wanting it. I hated that you couldn't accept that part of me, that part of us.'

I dig my fingernails into the palms of my hands. 'I loved you, Ally. You made yourself feel shit. No, I wasn't okay with it. I wasn't dealing with it, but that doesn't excuse what you did to me.'

Ally sighs and rubs his forehead with the heel of his hand. 'Jesus, Chris! You know that Louise... she really likes you. She fancies you.'

'What?'

'Louise fancies you.'

'You're full of shit!'

'I'm not. She told me. Don't you like her?'

'Oh my God, are we back in high school? I like her, she's gorgeous. Why are we even talking about this?'

'Well... we're talking about deserving to be happy. You're a catch, so if you're straight, then get a hot girlfriend who's into you. What were you even thinking, shagging Miss Piggy's wee sister?'

'Firstly, don't say that about Eilidh. Secondly, you'd be the last person on Earth I'd go to for relationship advice, so you can fuck right off!'

I didn't mean to lash out. I expect him to cry, but he doesn't.

'God, I'm so glad you're here.' Ally lowers his eyes and his voice. 'I was trying to tell you in the staffroom that I engineered the placement myself because I wanted to see you again. I knew you'd make me feel safe, and I knew something bad was going to happen with Scott. I could see him losing the plot, doing more and more coke and other stuff. I need you, I need you back, the way things were. You always made stuff feel okay when my dad went off the rails on stupid benders and scared us all shitless. It was arrogant of me to think you'd be okay with me turning up again like this. I never thought.'

I'm twisting and pulling at my fingers in agonies of indecision. 'It's pathetic, but I feel... the same as before. I haven't moved on and it fucking terrifies me. I'm still not okay with it, but I'm still completely smitten.'

Ally stares at me until his cigarette ash falls on his thigh and burns him, jolting him out of it. 'What are you talking about? Smitten with who?'

I want to scream at him, but it comes out as a hiss. 'Jesus Christ, Ally. You, you fucking idiot!'

Ally runs his fingers though his hair and stubs out his cigarette. I grip his yellow-tinged fingers. He reads my fear and moves close to me, burying his face in my shirt. I rest a hand on the back of his neck.

'You still smell the same. I love the way you smell,' he says.

'You stink of smoke.'

'Ouch. Thanks a lot.' He nuzzles against my collar bone and sighs. I feel his hot breath on my skin.

'What is it you want me to do?' I lace his fingers between my own and soften a little against him.

'I don't trust myself.'

'I don't trust you either,' I say, with only a hint of humour, 'but for some fucked-up reason, I'd still do anything for you.' I press a tender kiss onto Ally's hair, shocked and soothed at how familiar it feels.

Ally closes his eyes and inhales again. My skin is prickling wherever it touches his. My mind has stilled. We sit in dazed silence until I need to move, releasing Ally's hand.

'Where's your bathroom?'

'On your right as you come in the front door.'

I study my tired face in the bathroom mirror, take my glasses off to splash it with cool water. I feel warmth low on my abdomen, and a buzz of expectation. Smoothing my hair with damp fingers, I become shy as I step back out into the living room. Ally is doubled over his phone, scrolling through the messages.

'Can't you block his number?'

Ally puts it down and looks at me. 'It's his phone. The contract's in his name.'

'Tomorrow after work we can go into town and get you sorted with your own phone. Has he got keys for here?'

'No.'

'That's good then. How did you leave things?'

Ally gets up, and I follow him into the kitchen, where he shows me the note from Scott. I wish that he hadn't.

'Tell me what happened when you left work. Everything,'

'You want a G & T first?' Ally suggests hopefully.

I want a drink badly but know I shouldn't. 'I can't really drink just now, with those pills I'm on.'

Ally pulls out a chair and sits at the table, waiting for me to join him. 'I wasn't thinking straight. I just walked and walked for ages, then remembered I'd left my house keys at school. It was sleeting. I felt so sorry for myself that I texted Scott, and he came for me. I knew the moment he pulled up I'd fucked up again. I realised how scared of him I am now, how there's really nothing left... well, except that I still fancy him, which is pathetic. We went back to his, and he was really pleased with himself because he'd been right all along about how I wouldn't stick it out.'

'Did you sleep with him? You did, didn't you?'

Ally reddens and studies his fingernails. 'He tried, asked me to do some coke with him. I panicked. I've been in so much pain, there's no way... well, you can imagine.'

I shift in my seat. 'You do coke as well?' He knows I disapprove.

'Yeah, sometimes. Not like Scott, but yes, I do a bit of coke. It's hard to avoid it.'

'But you didn't have sex with him?'

'I... He didn't fuck me.'

I can't hold these images in my brain. 'What aren't you telling me?'

'He was acting like he never heard any of the stuff I said. That's what he does. He doesn't care what I say. So, he starts kissing me in the shower and says he's sorry for what he did to me, and then... well, he gave me a blowjob and I—'

'Okay.' I put my hand up defensively. 'Don't tell me anymore.'

'I'm so sorry, Chris. I realised I'd just stopped caring what happened to me. He didn't even get why I was upset. He got pissed off with me crying and slipped me out a couple of Valium to shut me up.'

'For fuck's sake.' I screw my eyes shut. 'Ally, if you see him again... I can't help you. Don't call him, don't text him, just stay the fuck away from him! He doesn't give a shit whether you love him anymore. He's just getting off on controlling you because he feels entitled to you.'

Ally gets up and makes himself a drink. I watch the tremors through his back and shoulders as he fights tears with his back turned. He shuffles sideways to get ice from the freezer.

I can't watch him cry, so I cross the kitchen. Ally takes a slug of his G & T and rests his forearms on the worktop. I circle his waist with my arms and pull him close, resting my chin on his shoulder. I can feel the slight heaves of his distress, and the tension as he fights it, but I don't let go.

I give in and have a few drinks with him. We talk about work, avoiding anything else. We're both brittle and shell-shocked. After midnight Ally asks if I'm staying over. 'I've a spare room,' he says.

'If you really don't mind, I'll just sleep here. I don't sleep much. Sofa suits me.'

Ally lets me shower and undress while he smokes his last cigarette of the night. When I come downstairs, I'm tongue-tied as I try to say goodnight. He thanks me, though I don't know why, and goes upstairs.

I listen carefully to every sound from upstairs, Ally brushing his teeth, flushing the toilet, his footsteps across the landing. The lights go out, but a sliver of light from his bedroom plays on the wall halfway up the stairs. The house grows silent, but the strip of yellow light remains, and I can't focus on anything else. Time trickles by as I watch for the light to go out.

I think over this evening, the warmth of a body leaning against me, the frail connection of our interlaced fingers, my lips brushing the pale, damp gold of Ally's hair. My doubt is receding, a new belief is taking root. I fold up the duvet, get off the sofa and quietly climb the stairs. The light is still on, and I knock and push the door open. 'You're not sleeping either? Can I come in?'

Ally flips the duvet back on the other side of the bed.

'Yeah, I can't sleep. We can watch a film if you like.'

I climb into the warm bed and roll onto my side, right next to Ally. I push my hand under his T-shirt and it rests on his hip bone. Heart thudding, I press a tentative kiss on the side of his mouth, which Ally turns to catch, open-mouthed. I wrap my fingers around the back of Ally's neck and drag a deep kiss from him, encouraged by the way his lips part so easily, giving way to the press of his tongue through those sweetly gappy teeth. When I pull away and look at him, he's everything I want, and I wrap my hands around his waist and drag him nearer.

'Chris.' Ally grips the small of my back. He can understand me now that sex scares him too.

'I'm here. It's okay.' I cradle him, feeling infinite comfort and no fear.

'Do you want—?'

'It's me, Ally. I don't want anything from you.' I cup Ally's chin in my hand, running my thumb along the moist curve of his bottom lip.

CHAPTER THIRTY

THURSDAY

About three a.m., Ally drops off, his head on my chest. We've exhausted ourselves kissing and talking. I'm dozing on and off, waking with every noise the house makes or any slight movement from Ally. The combined heat of our bodies is uncomfortable, but I can't let him go. I drink in every sensation: the warmth and pressure, the slight tickle of Ally's hair on my skin and the limp weight of his hand resting just under my ribs. I'm fighting the sleep I constantly crave. The minutes seem to be racing by, and it'll be time to get ready for work too soon. Ally stirs, shifts off my chest and limpets against my side. I touch his hair and kiss it because I can.

Just after five I hear the noise. Ally lives in a cul-de-sac, so the sound of a car is noticeable, especially to a bat-eared insomniac. I hear the car door shutting, close enough to assume it's outside Ally's house, and then the banging at the front door begins. Ally doesn't stir, he's sleeping deeply. I extricate my arm from under Ally's and slide out of bed. I leave him peaceful and safe under the quilt; I won't let anything happen to him.

The banging is persistent, getting louder. I pull Ally's sweater on and go downstairs.

Scott blanches and spits with anger when I answer the door. I open it just a few inches and block his access.

'Who the fuck are you? Did he pick you up somewhere on his way home from mine last night?'

Scott is that sickening kind of good-looking that even heavy drug use and sleep deprivation can't dent: James Dean jawline, big, dark eyes and architectural cheekbones.

I just stare. I won't move—I am not intimidated by him.

'Let me in. I need to speak to Ally.'

'No, you're not coming in.'

'Seriously, who do you think you are? Get out of the way!'

'No. I'm not scared of you. I know what you did to Ally, and unlike him, I'll press charges if you lay a finger on me, and then you'll really be fucked.'

Scott shifts his weight back on his heels but doesn't back off. 'You know fuck all. Whatever he's told you is probably bullshit. I need to see him.'

'You can't. Go home.' I start to close the door in his face.

'Chris?' I hear Ally's sleepy, confused voice from the top of the stairs. 'Chris, what's going on?'

I look over my shoulder to tell him to stay upstairs, and Scott grabs his chance, barging past me through the front door. I stagger but stay upright, grabbing the wall for support. Ally runs halfway down the stairs and stops, frozen with shock.

'Just tell him to go,' Scott orders.

Ally shakes his head. 'He's not going anywhere.'

'You said you'd call me. You said you'd call last night. You were ignoring me. If you'd just answered your phone, I wouldn't have had to come here. We can't just leave things like this. You owe me more than that.'

Ally shakes his head again, more firmly. 'I don't owe you anything.'

'You what? Are you joking? You don't owe me anything? This is what it's been about all along, isn't it?'

'About what?'

'About you using me to get what you want. As long as everything's coming your way then everyone else can just go fuck themselves. I want to be a teacher, Scott, so can you bankroll me through college? Can you pay my useless dad a good wage for a job he's too drunk to do and drop everything to come pick me up whenever I flake over some stupid shit? Oh yeah, and by the way, I'll just shag whoever I want while I'm at it. You think I'm an absolute fucking mug, don't you? You think I'll just put up with this? Just get your pal here to leave so we can sort this out.'

Ally stares at the carpet, and I can see he's clutching the bannister with white knuckles. 'You need to go,' he says, but I hear more fear than conviction.

Scott tuts and sneers. 'You're fucking pathetic, you know that? Look at you: you're absolutely shitting yourself now because you got caught! I knew you've been screwing around behind my back.'

I try to catch Ally's eye, to reassure him. 'Didn't you hear him?' I challenge Scott. 'He said you need to leave.'

'Shut the fuck up, no one asked you!' Scott spins around, snarling at me. 'I'll sort you out in a minute.'

'No,' Ally says. 'He hasn't done anything, but he knows... I told him what happened. I didn't go to the police, but the hospital took samples and stuff, so there's evidence. I can still—'

Scott laughs, a disgusted bark. 'Oh my God, you're such a fucking idiot, Ally! Evidence that you like getting fucked up the arse by every man and his dog isn't going to interest anyone, except maybe your pal here, but I'm sure he's found that out first-hand since you're so obliging. You know what, my darling? I've got some evidence too. Did you tell him about your birthday last year when we got high down in London and I paid that boy to come up to the hotel room for a threesome? Got all that on camera if he wants evidence. He fucking loved it, by the way!' Scott turns and squares up to me. 'Ally was getting fucked and sucking me off while I filmed it. Hard to tell which one is the professional from the video.'

I tip my head to one side, look him up and down. He doesn't know how to take my disdain. I can hear Ally's ragged breathing, but my own is deep and regular. I make a show of checking my watch. 'Are you done yet? Because it's getting cold with the front door open,' I tell Scott.

Ally flinches, expecting Scott to kick off. Instead he just stares at me, livid.

'You're a teacher too, aren't you?' Scott asks, inches from my face. 'I remember you—you were outside the school that time. Aren't you from Bridge of Layne too? I know your face.'

'I know yours too,' I say, matter-of-fact.

'Fucking smart-arse. Does your boss know you're into boys too?'

'Does yours?'

Scott lunges for me, makes a show of grabbing my arm and twisting it behind my back. I don't struggle; I don't want Ally to think Scott is hurting me.

'He's not—Leave him alone. He hasn't done anything.' Ally takes a few hesitant steps downstairs.

'It's okay.' I'm bleakly confident. 'He won't do anything to me, don't worry.'

Scott raises an eyebrow. 'Eh? I wouldn't be so sure, mate. You're as bad as him. You think I'm okay with you helping yourself to what's mine?'

'I don't see anything in here that belongs to you.' I can feel his fingernails piercing my skin, his grip is painful, but I won't struggle against it. I refuse.

Ally has come down the stairs now and is holding something out to Scott. 'This is yours.' He drops his phone into Scott's hand. 'You'd better take it back.'

Scott lets go of my arm and takes the phone between his thumb and forefinger as if it were filthy. Then he drops it on the hardwood floor and drives his heel into it violently, splintering the screen and case, before kicking it against the wall.

'You're going to be so sorry you fucked me over.'

Ally ducks, shrinking away from him.

'You're fucking pathetic! I can't believe I've put up with your shit this long. Ten fucking years, Ally! My folks know about you, so now I have nothing to lose. You can forget about getting a teaching job once I get this video edited and emailed around a few local worthies.'

'You wouldn't do that!' Ally's composure begins to dissolve. The minute contractions of his throat mean he's fighting his fear and losing catastrophically.

'No, he won't. He's all talk,' I tell him.

'What the fuck do you know?' Scott is scarlet and sweating. 'You're just a fucking teacher. You make thirty grand a year babysitting at some crappy high school and you're acting like you're so superior? I really don't like your tone, mate. You have no idea what's going on here, so just shut the fuck up and stay out of it.'

I smile because he's losing his shit because of me. 'Yes, I'm just a teacher, but I know you're bullshitting, and I know Ally doesn't want you here.'

Scott moves towards the bottom of the stairs, where Ally stands, dishevelled and vulnerable. I know Scott won't hurt me, but I won't give him any chance to hurt Ally.

'I will make sure that everybody who matters knows what you're really like, I swear I will. I should have worked out the kind of scrounging scum you are the first time I met your dad. No wonder you were always lying about your family. I'd be embarrassed too if I grew up in a shithole like that. I'd lie about my family too if my mum was a slut, and my dad was a drunk and my brother was retarded. No one else is going to employ your fucking useless alky father, and they'll probably take your brother into care when they see the state of that house and find your mum shacked up with her toy boy.'

I break in, but Scott shoves me sideways.

'You got above yourself, Ally, that's your problem. There wasn't a day went by I wasn't trying to look after you and help you, and all I expected was a bit of loyalty. You know, when I was watching you fuck that guy in the hotel room, I thought to myself, 'He doesn't care. As long as he's getting laid and someone's paying, he's happy as a fucking pig in shit.' I'll make sure everyone sees what you're really like: a greedy, twisted deviant who let me pay for cocaine and rent boys. Not a soul is going to want you near their kids after that, so you can forget your teaching bullshit once and for all.'

Ally sinks down on the step, protecting his face with his hands, his shoulders hunched against the tirade.

'Okay, you need to go now.' I step between him and Ally. 'He doesn't want you here. So fuck off.'

'Seriously, are you going to make me?' Scott squares himself up, the veins in his neck throbbing.

'No.' I shake my head, stepping back. 'But I'm not scared of you. You wouldn't dare touch me.' I smile just to infuriate Scott further.

'You're bang out of order, acting like you've got the moral high ground when you're the one that's got caught fucking my—' Scott stops.

Ally looks up from his hands. 'Your what exactly, Scott?' he says, with nascent challenge. 'Your what?'

'You know, Ally.' For the first time, there's something more painful than furious in Scott's tone.

'No, I don't,' he says wearily. 'I don't know.'

For a few moments no one speaks, and anxiety suddenly knots in my chest, because I don't understand what's passing between them. Scott is mouthing something to himself and shaking his head. *Ten years...ten fucking years.* He stops to pull a pack of cigarettes and a lighter from his pocket. Finally, he speaks through the corner of his mouth as he lights up.

'Fuck this shit. You know what, pal, you're welcome to him. He's nothing but a vicious wee slut. Not even twenty-four hours ago he had my cock down his throat, so I hope you enjoyed my sloppy seconds last night. In fact, I hope you used a rubber, because fuck knows where else he's been.'

A scarlet bead emerges from his right nostril, smearing its way to his top lip. It makes me laugh and Ally gasp.

'Need a tissue for that?' I ask, pressing him toward the door. 'I suppose you've got the cash for another nose job. Good luck with the rehab.'

Scott drags the side of his hand under his nose, which makes it bleed harder. 'Fuck you, mate. Hope the little faggot gives you AIDS.' Scott pinches his bloody nose before he slams the front door.

I lock the door behind him, then sit down on the stair with Ally.

'Fuck me. What a charmer.'

Ally is leaning heavily on the stair post. His skin is grey. I try to touch his face, but he shrinks away, flees back upstairs. I find him on the floor in a corner of his bedroom, hugging his knees and ripping at his nails with his teeth.

'He's right,' he says. 'I am a total slut. And I brought this on myself because I couldn't say no to him. All those things he said about me are true. It was all true. That stuff did happen when we were in London. I was drunk and high, and I did that, and he's got most of it on video. Oh my God, Chris, he even played it back to me.'

'It's history, isn't it?'

'You're so good, and I'm fucking disgusting. Scott just confirmed what you already know about me.'

'What do you mean?'

Ally grips his temples with his fingertips. 'You know, Chris. You know how much I used to fuck around behind your back. You caught me on my knees in a toilet. You know he's right.'

I edge closer, like you would to a wounded animal, and sit down beside him. 'You've listened to him too much; he's made you believe that he's right. He's not, though.'

'I really fucking hate myself,' he says, grinding his teeth. 'I know he'll do something with those videos.'

'He won't. Isn't he in them too? Why would he put them online or whatever if he's in them? I think he's all talk. Ally, don't let him mess with your head so much.'

He still won't let me hold his hand.

'You know, back then, when I was meant to be with you, Chris, I was doing stuff like... you don't know the half of it. When you were down in Glasgow, I was a total slut, and then I acted like your boyfriend over the holidays. I don't even know how many people I slept with. After I met Scott, I'd tell you I loved you over the phone then fuck him in the stationery cupboard after work.'

I feel drained of hurt now. I've let it bleed away. 'I don't need to know. It doesn't matter now. Like you said, everyone sleeps around at uni. If I wasn't such a loser I would have too.'

'No, you wouldn't have.' Ally leans on my shoulder, picking up my proffered hand. 'You're a case apart, Christopher James Elliot.'

'You mean I'm a freak?'

'You're perfect, honestly.'

I laugh and gently shove his shoulder. 'Yeah, I'm perfectly neurotic and uptight. Let's go back to bed. It's cold.'

'You were so calm. It was just the right way to be.'

'I teach Jordan Franks four times a week—Scott Binnie doesn't scare me.' I stand up and help him to his feet.

The sheets have cooled down again, and our cold hands and feet find one another under the quilt. I kiss him, and he grips me tight. He looks shattered.

'I told Louise about my love and sex theory, and she thinks it's hilarious just like you do. You know the one about chaste worship versus messy sex? It'll be in one of my old letters; sex is like *The Pearl*, and all that?'

'Oh yeah, I know it well.' Ally smiles against my skin.

'I think I'm ready to get messy now, though.'

'I'll mess you up alright,' he promises.

CHAPTER THIRTY-ONE

TUESDAY

Ally twitches as he sleeps next to me. It's enough to break through my own hard-won sleep. I lay a hand on Ally's hip to reassure him, but he jabs an elbow in my stomach, which knocks the breath out of me. Then he twists around and hooks one leg over mine, burying his face into the space between my chin and chest.

'Are you awake?' I whisper, kissing his hair.

He flinches and shifts away from me. 'No, Scott, I'm tired.'

Deflated, I stare into the darkness. Ally lashes out like this almost every night, flinching and frightened of his dreams, which are still haunted by Scott. We've spent the past fourteen nights together, democratically dividing them between my flat and Ally's house, and every night I kiss and soothe him to sleep before lying awake to fretfully watch him thrash out these translucent nightmares.

The nights are so long that even when I take the sleeping pills, there are several hours of frustration waiting for Ally to wake up in the morning. He's lying close, his skin touching mine, but I can't reach him. Finally, his blue-green eyes will open between long, sticky lashes, and, radiating relief at the sight of my face, he'll reach for me and we'll kiss and start chatting about anything other than what is really eating us both alive. Sometimes, I almost feel ready to ask about it, but then I catch Ally looking hollow and let it pass.

Yesterday I overheard Ally chatting to Louise at work over lunchtime, neither aware I was listening.

'Scott let me borrow his car last night, so I could nip home to see Jamie.' Louise paused, confused. 'You mean Chris?'

'Huh?'

"Chris leant you his car, yeah?'

'That's what I said, honey.' He carried on talking to her about Jamie none the wiser.

Tonight, a deep fear is gathering momentum. 'Ally, wake up!' I shake him until he sleepily responds.

'I'm tired, Scott, no!' He moans again.

'It's me, for fuck's sake! It's me!' I bring a tight-clenched fist down on the quilt.

'What?" Ally's eyes flicker open. 'What's wrong, baby? Can't you get to sleep?'

'No, I can't. Not when you're calling me Scott every fucking night in your sleep.'

Ally sits up, pushing his hair out of his eyes. 'Seriously? I am?'

'Yeah, you are. Every single night.'

'Are you sure?' Ally chews his lip.

'Yes, I'm fucking sure!' I'm shocked at the force of my anger. I pull back the duvet and go to the bathroom, slamming the door. I sit right in the middle of the floor, where I can't break anything, and grip my heaving chest.

'Chris!' Ally tries the door handle and finds himself locked out. 'Chris, I'm sorry. I really didn't know I was doing it.'

'I need a minute,' I choke out. 'Give me a minute.' I hear Ally pacing on the other side of the door.

'Chris... you don't really think I'm doing it to hurt you?'

'I don't know what I think. Go back to bed. Leave me alone,' I shout at him, and hear Ally retreat. My brain is a snake pit, shame and fear and jealousy all slithering over each other.

I'm jealous. I'll be like Scott, I'll take over where he left off, and we'll tear each other to bits. I don't even care that this will hurt and screw everything up, because I want it so much. Let him go, don't be so selfish. What are you doing?

Like a rubber band, a sickening snap releases the pressure of my dammed-up fury. 'I fucking hate him!'

My fist meets the wall with a sickening crack, but there's no sensation, just the sight of blood on my knuckles and the fist-shaped mess in the plasterboard. I'm pouring with sweat and dripping blood on the bathroom floor. I unlock the door to see that Ally's hovering on the threshold of the bedroom. He says nothing, just goes downstairs for something to stem the blood.

Wiping the last of the blood from my knuckles, he presses hard on the gauzy cotton wool. I bite my lip in pain and frustration.

'Ally, we need to talk about... you know, about how we haven't...'

Ally laughs. It's funny to him. He doesn't understand. 'I know,' he says. 'It's fine.'

"It's not fine, Ally, and it's not funny!' I snatch my hand away. 'It wasn't fine before, and it's not going to be fine this time.'

'Chris, stop it.'

'I can't. I'm going to fuck things up again because I don't know what to do about it.'

Ally cups one hand on the nape of my neck. 'Stop thinking about it. You're driving yourself up the wall.'

He kisses my mouth and persuades me to sit on the bed. 'You hate talking about sex, but I can talk about it for both of us. I want to have sex with you, I always have, but I can keep waiting, because I know we'll get there. We're not clueless kids now. I'm kind of scared myself, if I'm honest. It's become too big a deal, too much pressure. I think you need to stop thinking about it, because the only thing that's scary is what your brain is getting up to. I know this doesn't scare you.' He pauses and kisses me softly, squeezing my fingers in his. 'This doesn't either.' He pushes his tongue into my mouth, to which I respond tentatively. 'And this is usually okay for you.' He kisses as far as my belly button and stops. Then he slides his fingers under the elastic of my pants. 'This used to be okay?'

He holds my gaze, waiting. I tense, but say nothing, my heart thudding. Ally pushes his hand further and takes a firm grip of my cock.

'Sometimes this is okay.' He gives it a gentle squeeze and starts to let go. I strain towards Ally for another kiss. 'Is it?' Ally asks in surprise. 'Is this okay?'

I nod dumbly as Ally's hand begins to move. 'Is it okay if...' He tugs at the elastic and pulls them out of the way. I gasp and tighten my grip on his hand. Ally stops. I start my nervous apologising.

'I don't know... I'm no good at this, and I don't think I—'

'Shh,' Ally insists. 'There's nothing to be good at. I want to touch you, that's all.'

'It's fine.' My breath comes unsteadily.

Ally sets a gentle rhythm with his hand, working within the constraints of the cotton and Lycra. 'This shouldn't stress you out, Chris.'

I press in for the reassurance of Ally's mouth on mine, trying to relax. My hips want to move with Ally's hand. I look at him, wanting him so badly that I panic and stop him, gripping his wrist.

'You're having nightmares about him. About Scott. I'm guessing it's to do with what he did to you... what you told me about.'

Ally inhales sharply, his shoulders sinking. I want to protect him, not hurt him more.

'I think we shouldn't... I mean, it isn't right to just pretend it didn't happen, because it's still giving you nightmares. Maybe you're going to associate that with me, with sleeping with me, and I couldn't handle that.'

His eyes look shadowy and bruised. 'Don't make me think about it, Chris. I don't want to think about it. Not now. Not yet.' He slumps back against the pile of pillows behind him.

Bloodstains are peeking through the white gauze on his injured hand. I grip myself around the chest where the worst of the rage is burning.

'This is never going to work, is it? It's so fucking messed up.'

'Don't say that!' He grips me by both wrists, pushes me down and pins me on the bed. 'Honestly, do you really think that's all that matters to me? You know what? If we never get further than kisses and hand jobs, I couldn't care less. I just want to be with you.'

I'm struggling against him. Ally dips down and kisses me, pressing so hard that I struggle for breath.

'Stop fighting me.'

He invades my mouth with his tongue. I'm hard again, but so are my tense muscles.

With one hand pressing firmly on my collarbone to keep me still, Ally drops down between my legs to nuzzle and kiss my cock through my shorts. Then, with one quick motion, he pulls them out of the way and takes it in his mouth. I moan at the wet, hot sensation as Ally works expertly with his tongue and lips.

Ally shifts, takes me deeper, holding me fast. After weeks of frustration, my orgasm builds so quickly that I'm almost shut down by the force. I fight to keep my eyes open, so I can watch what Ally is doing and drink up every second. He swallows, then runs his tongue over the head of my cock, leaving it wet and clean before he slides back up the bed to lie beside me. His eyes are heavy with arousal. We kiss and kiss without saying a word. With only a slight flutter of anxiety, I reach for Ally and use my hand on him until he gasps and doubles up around me to his own messy climax.

'That just needed to be done. It was getting ridiculous.' Ally smiles sleepily, draping his arms around my shoulders. 'It wasn't so bad, was it?'

'Not bad at all. Thank you.'

'Oh God, like I did you a favour? You've no idea how long I've wanted to do that to you. I've gone through a lot of Kleenex thinking about your cock in my mouth.'

I laugh, relieved, and rest my chin on Ally's shoulder. His skin is clammy and salty. 'Yeah? I suppose I thought about it too.'

Ally kisses me with a wicked grin. 'Did you wank over me too? Really?' And when I blush and make a face, he shoves me playfully. 'You need to stop thinking about it so much.'

I adjust to being naked and coiled around Ally as we mouth and tongue and nuzzle at each other.

'When you sleep with girls do you stress like that?' Ally asks.

'No. Not at all,'

'Just me then. Great. I never asked you before. Do you fancy other guys? How does your brain work?'

'Not very well.' I yawn. 'I've thought about it a lot. Maybe I do, but I don't let myself go there. I think if Paul had walked in on me in bed with Carolynn, he'd probably have taken me out for a beer to celebrate, but he didn't. It was you and me he saw. He still hardly speaks to me, and I know he told my mum about us. You know I lived with Carolynn for four years, don't you?'

Ally's stunned shake of the head answers my question.

'My flat... well, I still rent it from her parents. She wanted to go travelling before we got married, but I couldn't go because I'd got the job at Aberlayne. She went with two friends instead, and then she met this guy in New Zealand. Now she's married to him and they have a baby. Even when I was with her, and we booked the hotel and stuff for the wedding reception, Paul must have been in my mum's ear about it, I know he was. She kept saying, Chris, is this really what you want? You're still young and Carolynn is your first real girlfriend, there's no rush.'

Ally looks crushed. 'Why don't I know any of this?'

'You weren't around when I was with Carolynn. We'd lost touch.'

'You were really going to get married?'

'Uh-huh.'

'Jesus.'

'Carolynn did Engineering at uni, so she got a really good job when she graduated, and we... well, she could afford to buy a flat, and our parents went halves on the deposit. When we broke up she signed the flat over to her folks and bought me out. I still rent it from them. It's handy for work.'

'So, you still live in the flat you bought with her? And you'd booked the wedding and everything? Jesus, Chris, this is a headfuck.'

'I don't call you Carolynn in my sleep every night.'

'Maybe if you ever actually slept you would.' Ally deflects my barbed comment. 'What time is it, anyway?'

I check my phone. 'Just after half three. Do you want some tea? I don't think I'll get back to sleep now.'

'I don't understand how you function. You're not even getting three hours most nights.'

'I just need to get used to sharing a bed. It'll get better.'

I seem to be accumulating more things at Ally's than Ally is at my place. There's more room, and Ally encouraged me to bring my guitar. I only play it when he nags me to. It sits in the corner of Ally's living room.

My sketch pad and pencils are littering Ally's kitchen table. The light is good there during the day. I spent last Saturday afternoon sitting there drawing while Ally took my car to get a new exhaust fitted. As I wait for the kettle to boil, I smudge a few lines with a damp finger and shade a tiny section that's irritating me. The last two weekends have been a revelation. I don't dread the days off, I don't cling to the structure of a workday. Being at Ally's house is like being on holiday. It feels okay to bend routines, be a little lazy, spend or waste time together.

I carry the two mugs of tea back upstairs. Ally's dozing with the light on. The cut on the side of his head is almost healed, but it still looks ragged now that the bruising has faded. It's scarring badly, the skin stretched and warped around the dark cut. I put his mug down as quietly as I can, but the movement makes his eyes flicker open again.

'Thank you,' he yawns.

'Sorry, I didn't mean to wake you.' I ease back into bed beside him. He's radiating heat.

'I wasn't really sleeping.' He sits up and wraps his fingers around his mug.

'I think I can fix your bathroom wall,' I say. 'I'm sorry, I've never done anything like that before.'

Ally squeezes my hand under the quilt. 'Don't worry about it.'

'What'll you do if they give you Fraserburgh or somewhere like that for your probation year? Would you move away?' I ask.

Ally shakes his head. 'No, if it's not commuting distance from here I'll have to go on the supply list and do it that way instead.'

'Good... I don't want you to move away.'

'I'm not planning to. Don't worry.' Ally drains his mug of sugary tea, freeing both his hands up to roam over my skin.

'Can you stay at mine tomorrow night?' I ask him. 'I've got another doctor's appointment after work.'

'Em, yeah. I said I'd go out with Louise tomorrow night, but I'll come round after that if you like?'

I nudge closer and lay an arm around Ally's waist. 'Come and stay. What are you and Lou up to tomorrow?'

'She wants to see this Spanish horror film, and no one else will go with her.'

'You're more sociable than me. I'd rather stay in and feel sorry for myself.'

'Anyone is more sociable than you, Chris. You even do your Tesco shopping online, so you don't have to speak to the checkout people. When you're feeling a bit better we'll do stuff together at the weekends.'

'Like what?' I ask. 'Actually go to Tesco?'

'Maybe even that,' Ally says, rolling his eyes. 'Scott and I could never do anything together, but he went nuts if I went out with friends. And there were so many conditions, like 'You need to text every twenty minutes,' 'You need to call me when you get home,' 'You can't drink,' or 'You have to be home by a certain time,' that I just gave up. Then I just got a bit obsessed with couples. When I was watching couples on TV or in the street or whatever, I'd get fixated on the stuff they do. Like that thing where you walk along, and his hand is in her pocket and her hand is in his? Or when you see a couple kiss each other goodbye in public? I was always looking at people holding hands. It's like, the most banal thing, but I've never done that, ever. I got off once fantasising about walking round home base with my hand in his pocket, my head on his shoulder, holding his hand. It's pathetic.'

'His hand?' The ambiguous third person reignites my jealousy. He doesn't hear me, so it simmers as Ally talks.

'You remember how I'm phobic of dentists?' Ally continues. 'I fucking hate dentists, but I had this horrendous toothache and I had to go. I was begging Scott to come with me. I was so scared, and nothing was helping the pain anymore. He said, 'Just take a Valium and you'll be fine.' He gave me a few, but he wouldn't even drop me off outside the place. I was so scared I couldn't breathe; I couldn't even talk. It was a massive abscess, and they had to sedate me to get the tooth out, but I didn't tell them I'd already had a couple of Valium. When they finished, I couldn't even tell them where I lived. They called my dad, but he didn't answer, and neither did my mum, because she was at work. So they were just going to get my address off my record and put me back in a taxi to get home and sleep it off. The dental nurse was really sweet, and she sat with me for ages. I asked her to call Scott, get him to pick me up, and I gave her my phone. She called him, and I heard her start to explain, but he hung up on her. '

'Well, yeah, he let you down. What did you expect?'

'Carolynn would just have gone to the dentist with you. Fuck me—I'm sure even Eilidh would have gone to the dentist with you. '

'Ally, any decent person would have done that. None of this is to do with the fact that you're gay, or that Scott didn't want to be your boyfriend. It's because he's a total prick. I know what you're saying, but you were never going to get that from him.'

Ally's lips are tight. 'You think I'm an idiot, eh?'

'Ally, I *know* you're an idiot.'

'Thanks.'

'You're welcome.'

I thumb Ally's face gently, attempt to smile. 'Are we actually doing this? Is this it?' I ask him.

'Eh? What do you mean?' Ally draws back.

'Are we... What is this?'

'You really need to ask that?'

'It's just... Eilidh said that I don't read things right.'

'You can read me, Chris. You always could read me. I can't believe you're really asking me what this is.'

Ally's right eye, the one with green flecks through the blue, tends to wander to one side when he's tired. He settles back onto the pillows and rubs it with the knuckle of his index finger.

'Maybe I just need to hear it from you. I always get it wrong.'

'It's love. I love you. There's nothing to get wrong, Chris.'

I flood with relief. 'I love you too, so we—'

'So we're okay then. You're on solid ground. Stop thinking.' Ally's fingers twine sleepily in my hair.

CHAPTER THIRTY-TWO

When Ally reached for his phone to switch the alarm off, his fingers found the mug of hot coffee Chris had set there for him. Sipping it triggered his nicotine craving. He pulled on a T-shirt and pyjama bottoms to go downstairs and smoke outside the back door, protecting Chris from his second-hand smoke. Chris was working at the kitchen table, having washed and shaved and dressed hours ago.

'It's freezing out there,' he said as Ally shuffled past him to pick up his fag packet from the window sill.

Ally let himself out the back door while bundling a coat on and lit up with Scott's silver lighter. The sky was dark with flurrying rain.

The door opened a fraction behind him and Chris passed his coffee mug out. 'You don't have to stand out there. It's your house!'

He shut the door again against the cold, leaving Ally alone with his coffee and cigarette. When he finished and peered through the small pane of glass in the door, he saw the blurred outline of Chris sitting over his laptop at the kitchen table. He closed it when Ally came back inside and stood up as if he had been about to do something else. Ally pressed himself against Chris's side, resting his chin on his shoulder.

'How's your hand?' he asked, examining it. The bandage was damp and stained.

'Hurts.' Chris leaned in to kiss him, then screwed up his face.

'What? I haven't cleaned my teeth yet!' Ally blew into the palm of his hand.

'You taste of fag ash. It's rank. I wish you didn't smoke.'

'I know. I need to stop.' He dropped his cigarettes on the kitchen table and put his arms around Chris's waist.

'I'm going to make toast, are you hungry?' Chris asked him, but Ally was distracted, pulling Chris's shirt free from the waistband of his trousers so he could run his hands up his back.

'If I cleaned my teeth right now, would you come back to bed with me?'

'No, go and get ready for work. You'll make us late.'

'We don't even need to go upstairs then.'

Chris removed Ally's hands from under his clothes and stepped back.

'Just not right now.' He smiled, one side of his mouth turning down in baffled amusement. 'Go and have a cold shower.'

'I can't believe next week will be your last week,' Louise said to Ally. She and Chris were perched on student desks in Chris's classroom while Ally cleared up after his class. 'He could come back, couldn't he, Chris?' she asked.

'No, he can fuck off,' Chris deadpanned. 'He's shit, and he gets on everyone's nerves, plus the kids all hate him.'

'That is Chris Elliot complimenting you, Ally,' Louise said. 'That's as good as it ever gets.'

'I hear Ally's buying you dinner, Lou, so make sure you take him somewhere really expensive,' Chris said.

'I think we'll just go for a pizza or something. The film starts quite early. Luca's gutted he can't come.'

Chris caught Ally's eye briefly.

'That's a shame,' Ally said.

'Okay, well enjoy yourselves. I need to leave sharp tonight.'

Chris left without saying bye, and Louise gave Ally a puzzled frown.

Louise drove a sporty little Fiat with red leather seats and Ally knew better than to ask if he could smoke in it.

'Thanks for driving. It's shit not having a car anymore.'

'Yeah, you're lucky Chris picks you up every morning now, especially since you live in the opposite direction. Hope you're giving him petrol money?'

'He won't take any, but I took his car into Kwik Fit and got that knackered exhaust fixed for him, and two new tyres put on as well. He's useless with cars.'

'That was good of you. He seems a bit better, the last few days. Maybe that's the antidepressants starting to work?'

'Maybe.'

'I can't believe Eilidh just cut him dead like that. What a bitch. You'd think she'd at least have the balls to tell him herself, not get Elaine to do it for her.'

'Yeah, she's a bitch. Chris deserves better.'

'Is your ex still being a total psycho?' she asked as she circled for a parking space.

'I haven't heard from him at all. I got my P45 from Binnie Group, but I expected that.'

'Good thing you aced your Crit lesson then. Sales and marketing sounded boring anyway. Teaching's bloody knackering, but it's never boring.'

She twisted around and reversed into a space in the multi-storey car park, and he noticed she'd smudged her eyeliner at the corners. 'Stay still,' he said after she pulled on the handbrake. He rubbed the smudges away with his thumb and kissed her cheek. 'There, you're beautiful.'

'Thank you, honey.'

As they walked through the car park to the lift, he held her hand and gave her a cuddle. In the mirrored interior of the lift they looked like a couple. A good-looking couple. He tried not to think about holding Chris's hand.

'I thought you were going to ask Chris if he wanted to come?' she asked. 'That was a bit awkward in his room. I thought you'd invited him.'

'He probably wouldn't have come anyway. He's always got an excuse not to go out. And I... well, I just wanted to talk to you.'

'Why? What's going on?'

She dropped his hand just before they walked into the restaurant. As they sat down he checked his phone briefly. Wondering how Chris had got on at the doctor's, he sent a quick text.

Let me know how it goes. See you tonight, gorgeous xxx

Louise raised an eyebrow as she watched him. He apologised but left the phone beside his plate. 'So, you haven't heard from Scott at all?' She eyed his phone suspiciously.

'No, not at all.'

'And?'

'And what?'

The waitress came, and Louise ordered a Diet Coke, tutting when Ally ordered a large glass of wine. 'On a school night?'

'Might make this film more bearable. Do you even know any Spanish?'

'*Si, me llamo* Louise, *donde están los servicios, por favor.*'

'Yeah, whatever. You're just showing off. I got an A in French, you know.'

'I bet you did!'

His phone lit up and he glanced over to see it was a message from Chris.

Went okay, thanks. I got more sleeping pills, but if they don't work I get referred on. Say hi to Lou. Don't be too late. I love you xx

Smiling to himself, he started to reply.

I love you too

Before he had time to finish, Louise snatched the phone from him. 'You're sitting there texting Scott, aren't you? Seriously, Ally, are you fucking retarded?'

'Louise, give me my phone back and stop making a scene. I'm not texting Scott! It's from Chris.'

'No, it is not. Since when did Chris sign off with...' She read the message as she spoke, then, frowning, handed him back his phone. 'Oh. What's going on then?'

'Well, you're snatching my phone and reading my messages as if that's totally cool, and it's not.'

'No, I'm not sorry. I was genuinely worried you were doing something stupid.'

The waitress brought the drinks and took their order, giving Louise time to calm down.

'So, are you two...?'

'Are we what, Louise?'

'Are you an item now?'

'Kind of.'

'Might have known it wouldn't be a simple yes or no. Since when?'

'Two weeks or so.'

'After you went AWOL?'

'Yeah, after that.'

Her eyes were wider than usual. 'Wow.' She sipped her drink, silent for a moment. 'So, you two have been seeing each other for two weeks, and its love. Wow. Are you having actual sex with him?'

'No. Just kissing, cuddling, hand jobs... kind of like teenagers at a Scripture Union camp.' Ally sighed.

'Oh dear. Chris told me about all that the night you disappeared.'

'All about what?'

'His Steinbeck theory about sex. He adores you and worships you and thinks the sun shines out of your arse, but if he gives in to his base desire to screw you, then you'll become a worthless and corrupt object, which he'll continue to desire and possess until it destroys you both. Did I get that right? It's difficult to keep up with Chris's fevered brain sometimes.'

'Oh God, yeah. He mentioned he'd told you that. Apparently, it doesn't apply to girls. He can screw them without theorising about it.' He drained his wine glass, tapping the table in agitation. The waitress noticed the empty glass and quickly replaced it with a full one.

'The theory doesn't apply to anyone but you, you idiot! You are the sole object of his worship and adoration, and I'm pretty sure you always have been. He loves you, and he knows that when two boys love each other very much they can have special cuddles with the lights off, but he's scared of that for the reasons mentioned above.'

'Did he say that to you?'

'What?'

"That he loves me?'

'No, he said he *loved* you, past tense, then you broke his actual wee heart, but he did say, 'If I start talking about Ally, I won't be able to stop, and then I have to admit to myself there's still something there.'. I think he's scared bloody shitless that you'll flake on him again, so this is a major fucking deal for him, Ally.'

The waitress brought their food, but Ally couldn't eat. Louise tucked into her seafood pasta, tasting a tiny sip of Ally's white wine with it.

'Do you think I'm flaky? Honestly?' he asked.

'Alasdair, my darling, I say you have flaky tendencies and a touch of the drama queen, which is charming and hilarious in a friend, but assuredly much harder work in a boyfriend.'

'I'm flaky and hard work? Thanks.'

'Seriously, if you flake on our Chris, I will hurt you. Hurry up and eat something.'

He picked at his Caesar salad to appease her. 'I stay at his one night, then he sleeps over at mine the next. Anyway... the sex thing is frustrating, but I can handle it. I know what he's okay with and I just let him call the shots.'

Louise listened intently as she finished her pasta.

'But last night he woke me about three in the morning really pissed off because he says I'm calling him Scott all the time in my sleep.' He didn't mention his nightmares.

'Ouch. Yeah, I had noticed that at work. You never, ever mentioned his name until recently, and just the last few weeks you've called Chris 'Scott' twice and not realised what you were saying. That's why I jumped to the wrong conclusion tonight, thinking you were back in touch.'

The waitress offered Ally another glass of wine. 'I swear I haven't seen him or heard from him. If I'm totally honest, I do still think about him. We were seeing each other for years, and I was pretty hung up on him. I think Chris feels—'

'Threatened? Jealous? Insecure? Yeah, probably.' Louise skewered a piece of chicken from his salad and ate it. 'Your ex is gorgeous and rich and you're still banging on about him all the time. Why wouldn't he be? Plus, from the outside looking in, it's like you cynically lined up Chris so you had somewhere soft to land, so to speak, when you were ready to dump Scott.'

'Why are you being such a bitch?' Ally laid his fork down unhappily.

'Why are you drinking like a fish and not eating anything? Is it your guilty conscience?'

Narrowing his eyes at her, he picked up his wine glass. 'You're right. God, I hate that you're right, you smug wee cow. I feel like shit for doing that to him. And now... well, yeah, I do feel like I've kind of exploited him, but I was desperate, and I do love him, so maybe the end justifies the means, you know?'

'Maybe,' she agreed without conviction. 'So, how did you leave things last night? You said he woke you up pissed off with you. Did you sort it out?'

'Yeah. I tried to tell him I had no idea I was doing it. I'm asleep, it's not deliberate. But then we did, well, we made a bit of progress anyway, but I'm not that chuffed with how I went about it. It wasn't how I wanted it to be.'

Louise stole another sip of his wine. 'Hmm, loving the euphemisms there. What kind of progress exactly?'

'Louise!'

'You don't have to become a prude just because he is. So why wasn't how you wanted it to be?'

'I don't know. I got a bit bossy, which I'm not proud of. I know he's not deliberately teasing me, but I've fancied him for half my life and we're no further on. I want him so much, and he... well, I know he wants me too. It's all there, but he fucking overthinks everything. It's so shit that Chris feels he's somehow in Scott's shadow, because it's completely the opposite way around, and it always was.'

'Tell him that!' Louise shook her head in disbelief. 'How is it possible that you two can't communicate? You are both ridiculously clever and articulate—just tell him everything you've just told me!'

Ally shrugged and stared into his empty glass. 'I think sometimes we overdo it with the communication.'

Louise fed him a bit more chicken and salad from his plate.

'Can we ditch the film and order another bottle?' Ally asked.

'No, we cannot. I've booked the tickets, and you've got 3L1 period four tomorrow, and believe me, there is only one thing worse than teaching Jordan Franks, and that is teaching Jordan Franks when you're hungover.'

'Yeah, I keep checking to see if I've missed something with him. I mean, he must have some kind of syndrome? Surely he has ADD or Tourette's or both, but no, he hasn't even got a Pupil Profile. He's just a good, old-fashioned, irritating wee shite.'

Sitting in the dark of the cinema holding Louise's hand, Ally worked and reworked the words in his head. After the film, he went to the toilet, shut himself in a cubicle and sent them to Chris.

In the mirror, he looked flushed and sweaty. Scraping his damp fingers through his hair, he resolved not to check his phone again. He tried to compose himself before meeting Louise in the foyer, but the fear had him running back into the cubicle and doubling over with the dry heaves.

He sidestepped Louise's questions on the way home, palming his nervous sweat onto her car seats.

'So where am I dropping you off then?' she checked as they hit the dual carriageway.

'At Chris's, please.'

'Do I have to pretend I don't know about this?'

'It's okay; he'll know I've spoken to you.'

'Thanks for tonight. Your choice next time.'

He kissed her goodnight before getting out of her car outside Chris's building. He didn't want Chris to taste his smoke, but the craving made him jittery. He lit up and paced by the door a few minutes before crunching extra strong mints. Chris buzzed him in and he climbed to the first floor, sick with nerves.

CHAPTER THIRTY-THREE

I read the message repeatedly, my mouth going dry. If they're leaving Aberdeen now, I've got about forty minutes. I pour a drink and knock it back. It dulls the burn of fear, so I refill and repeat, then use the time to shower, shave and clean my teeth. Then another quick drink. I'm reading the message again when the buzzer goes, making me jump. Ally's cheekbones are flushed from the cold, and he smells of fresh smoke and mints.

We stand awkwardly just inside the door. He looks as scared as I feel as I unwind the scarf from around his neck. Stepping nearer to reach the hook behind our heads, I press against Ally's shoulder. Ally catches my hand and presses it against his mouth. The skin on his face is cold, but his breath is hot. I unbutton his duffel coat and help him take it off, shuffling closer. My skin feels fiery. I just pulled a pair of jeans on after the shower, and his fingers are raking my arms and my chest.

Ally takes the first steps, leading me to the bedroom door, where he kisses me. It's a tentative kiss, and we're short of breath, our hands clammily grasping. It's almost impossible not to say anything and break the tension.

I push my bedroom door open and switch on the small bedside lamp. Ally turns me around by the waist and catches my wrists, easing me backwards against the bedroom wall. He rakes his fingers through my hair as he bites and kisses my earlobe, then down along my jawline to my mouth. We spend long minutes in deep, desperate kisses. My hand combs down Ally's back, clawing into a shoulder blade, then a hip bone, then the vulnerable hollow between ribs and waist.

Ally cups and strokes my face as he kisses me, fingertips on damp eyelashes and freshly shaved skin. My hand slips under his waistband, and he responds with a nudge of his hips. His hands drop to my collarbone, kissing my neck. I push him back, making space so I can undo the buttons of his shirt and slide it off. He feels damp and pliable, and I lay the flat of my hand against his abdomen to feel it rise and fall as we kiss again. Ally exhales raggedly, and I almost speak, but stop myself in time.

Ally guides me backwards, one hand on my shoulder, until we both tip onto the bed, Ally straddling me, his hands working on my fly. He returns to my mouth for more, one hand feeling for my cock as we kiss.

The vulnerability of being undressed, the fear of inadequacy... all my doubts are losing the battle for my attention as Ally lavishes his on me, first on my mouth, and then on my cock until I silently beg him to stop. I push him back, pressing urgently into Ally's thighs as I spoon against him. I lean into his wordless commands, his sighs and smiles and nudges.

This is what happens next. This is what is going to happen. I read Ally's message with its stark instructions, but now, as it's happening, it feels like a ritual, an observance. Ally coaches me gently with his own fingers first, lying on his back, holding me tight, and then he guides me. I think I am ready, I don't want to stop.

I let it happen, the way he asked me in the message he sent me. The sensation is unreal. I'm so overwhelmed that my eyes sting with tears as his start to glaze, and then we both relax. I know exactly why he wanted this, and why it is what we need.

I don't know if I can keep to the script, or lack of one. Ally reaches up, splays one hand on my chest and moans. He's sweating, radiating heat as I cling to him and we move. I'm losing control. I don't know if I'm saying words or just making noises, and then I stop caring, because Ally pushes back against me, his eyes losing focus, his mouth dropping open, and his chest flushing a deep, dark red. Ally's hand grips his own hard cock, and as he comes, the resulting spasm tips me over too. With violent shudders, I double over onto Ally's slick, sticky chest and rest there, breathless.

Ally drags me to him, lacing his arms around my neck. Between kisses he smiles—an intoxicated, blissful smile— and his eyes are wide and glistening. I trace the tiny cleft in Ally's chin, smooth over his lips and gently pull my fingertips through his hair, making him gasp. I settle at his side, our legs still tangled together.

We can't stop kissing, building to little peaks and letting the tension drop away again. I nuzzle into the space between Ally's shoulder and his chin and lie still. Ally's fingers keep massaging what he can reach of my back and neck, and he buries more kisses in my hair. Something barely perceptible makes him stop; he feels a shift, a release from me, into his arms.

CHAPTER THIRTY-FOUR

My darling Chris, this is what will happen tonight, and it's going to be beautiful.

No talking, no thinking out loud, not a word. We'll go to your bedroom and we'll undress each other, and we'll kiss like only we kiss.

This is what will happen. On the bed, let me get you ready. Let me take my time. Not a word. Do not speak, try not to think.

When it gets too much, push me away, but don't speak. What happens next is you get me ready, and then you make love to me. I will help you, my darling.

DO NOT SAY A WORD; DO NOT ASK ME IF IT'S OKAY. IT WILL BE OKAY.

Let it happen, because it needs to happen, because I love you.

Don't talk. Don't think. Tomorrow you can write it down for me like you used to.

Ally drew back on the pillow so that he could see Chris's face.

He was sleeping.

CHAPTER THIRTY-FIVE

THURSDAY

'I want to quit smoking,' Ally told Louise as he returned, windswept, from his lunchtime fag break.

'Good for you.' She looked up from her lunch. 'Have you tried to quit before?'

'No, but I've been trying to cut down and I feel like shit, so I probably need to get nicotine patches or something.' He shook off his wet coat and hung it on the back of the door.

'You could ask the school nurse; she'd probably get you them for free. I'll talk to her for you. Stick the kettle on.'

He put it on to boil, leaning against the filing cabinet as he waited. 'Where's Chris?' he asked.

'In a meeting. Something about Katia Kamisky,' she said. 'Callum's got football training. It's just you and me, pal.'

After making her tea and his coffee, Ally sat down beside her to eat his lunch.

'Any progress to report?' she asked as she pulled the cellophane off her salad.

He looked at her with a conspiratorial wink.

She clapped her hands, laughing. 'Really?!'

'Like you wouldn't believe, Lou. I'm exhausted. We've literally done nothing but make progress since Tuesday night.'

'Holy shit! Well done!' She high-fived him. 'Good for you, my darling. Are you happy?'

'Yeah,'

'You're going to cry, look at you!'

'Yeah, I'm really happy. You've no idea, I...'

'Here, have a tissue.'

'I love him so much, Lou.'

Louise dabbed his face. 'You're bloody lucky. Don't you dare flake on him now.'

'No. Never.'

'When are you going Facebook official?' Louise teased. 'How is he feeling about being your other half?'

'Give him time. You know how uptight he is. Please don't say anything yet.'

'I won't, because I surely do.' Louise ruffled Ally's hair and picked up the mugs to wash them.

'Is that your phone ringing?' Ally asked.

'No, it's yours. Mine is charging in my room.'

'Shit, I've got a missed call from Jamie.' He pressed redial.

'Alasdair, where are you?' Jamie was crying.

'I'm at work, wee man. What's wrong? Why aren't you at school?'

'I've been vomiting all morning—my head and my tummy hurt. There's no one here and I'm feeling so anxious. Can you call Mum please? Can you ask her to come here? Because I need her right now.'

'Jamie, Mum will be at work too. Where's Dad? Did you tell him you were ill? Why did he leave you alone?'

'I've been sick on the floor,' Jamie said. 'Between... the door of my room and the bathroom. I can't... walk past it. It's so messy and dirty and I don't know what to do. I need Mum.'

His sentences were peppered with pauses, indicating repetitions of his jaw-sawing tic.

'Jamie, I can get there, but you need to calm down, wee man. It doesn't matter about the floor. I'll clean it all up. I need to see if I can get away from work first, so just sit tight.'

'Alasdair, I wish Mum would just come home. I wish she would come back and be here with me all the time. I miss Mum so much; things just get worse and worse. Dad hasn't been home at all. Do you know where he is?'

'I'm on my way. Just stay by the phone, wee man.'

Louise got up and took Ally by the arm. 'Listen,' she said, 'take my car. You just have my Second Years this afternoon, don't you? I'll take them, it's fine. I'll tell Chris you had to go, and let's face it he's not going to throw the book at you, is he? I'll get you my keys. I'm sure Chris will give me a lift home.'

Ally nodded and dragged the palms of his hands across his knees. Louise passed him the car keys and he looked up to thank her.

'Just go,' she said, kissing his cheek.

'Tell him I'll just call him later. I—'

'It's okay. Just go. I'll tell him,' she said.

The house was shrouded in darkness, the garden scrabbling to get in at the dirty windows. Ally parked Louise's smart little Fiat and let himself in the front door. Inside stank of damp and bins. He called for Jamie, and his small voice replied from the top of the stairs. At the top of the stairs he almost stepped in the puddle of vomit. Jamie was huddled on his bed in smelly, stained pyjamas that were too small for him.

'Alasdair, did you see the mess?'

He laid his hand on Jamie's forehead. 'Are you still feeling sick, Jamie?'

'I don't feel sick anymore.' His nervous tic broke his train of thought. 'I just want Mum,' he started to sob and gripped at Ally's wrist. 'When will she come?'

'You're going to stay with me tonight, but she says she'll come and get you in the morning. She has to work late, and it takes two hours for her to drive here, remember?'

'I don't understand why she lives there. It's too far away. Why would she choose to live far away? I would like her to be close, so I could see her every day.'

'Well, you could still go and live with her and Mark. Remember we talked about that? They have a really nice house with a room for you.'

'It wouldn't be possible for me to go to my own school. I would have to change schools. Mark has a large dog and I am very afraid of dogs. It's not convenient,' he explained miserably.

'Did Dad say when he would be back, Jamie? Is he working the late shift? Did you try and call him?'

'Dad doesn't go to work anymore. Not since Monday. And he says he has lost his mobile phone, so I can't call him. Perhaps he has decided to move away like Mum? I'm thirteen and I don't think I can live on my own, Alasdair. I don't think it's allowed. What will happen?' His eyes were enormous with fear.

Ally was sick with anger. 'Jamie, no one's going to leave you on your own. I can look after you; Mum can look after you. Dad shouldn't have left you alone, but he'll come back.'

'We're going to run you a bath, change your sheets and get you clean pyjamas, okay? I'll clean up the mess, so you don't have to look at it. Do you think you could drink some water now?'

After a quick run to the nearest shop to get what he needed, Ally cleaned up around Jamie as best he could. The hall carpet was wrecked, but he tipped bicarbonate of soda over the vomit, then scrubbed the bath until he could bear to help Jamie into it. The kitchen smelled terrible and there was nothing edible in the fridge. He found sheets in the airing cupboard that seemed clean and made up Jamie's bed for him.

'Do you feel like eating anything yet?' he asked him. 'I got some stuff at the shop; maybe some toast to start with?'

'Is there toast?' Jamie asked. 'Really? There hasn't been toast for ages. I'd really like some toast. I'd like toast with lots of butter please. I don't suppose there is lemonade too?'

'I got Fanta for you. Don't you like Fanta anymore?' Ally forced a smile.

'Oh yes,' he said, beaming, 'I do, very much. Thank you. I feel so much better. Where will you sleep tonight, Alasdair?'

'I thought... well, I thought you could have a sleepover at my house actually. That'd be cool, eh?' he tried weakly.

'Oh.' Jamie looked down at his hands. 'The thing is... I need to be here for when Dad gets back, and for school tomorrow. All my things are here. It's better if I stay here. It's not very convenient to go to another house really.'

'I know, Jamie, but it's just for one night, and I can take you to school in the morning. We don't know when Dad will get back, so I need you to come home with me just this once. Please?'

Jamie paused intently, listening for something. 'There's a car coming. Maybe it's Dad now. I'll go to see.' Jamie got out of bed and crossed his bedroom to look out the window.

Ally followed him, and his heart sank when he recognised the car pulling up behind Louise's Fiat. He watched Chris get out, looking smart in his work clothes, navy wool coat and scarf. He locked the car and narrowly avoided stepping in dog shit on the pavement.

Ally pacified Jamie and went to the door, opening it a fraction.

'Why are you here?'

'Is Jamie okay?' Chris asked, hovering on the doorstep. 'Louise said you got a call from him. Is everything okay?'

Ally stepped outside and shut the door behind him. He was desperate for a cigarette and made Chris wait while he lit up. 'You should just go home. Jamie's not great with strangers,' he said, shuffling impatiently.

'What can I do to help?'

'Nothing.' He inhaled sharply, looking away.

Chris glanced around, and Ally saw him take in the overgrown garden full of rubbish bags. Ally stood awkwardly between him and the front door.

'Is your dad in there?' Chris asked.

He shook his head, enclosed in himself.

'At work?'

Ally shook his head again. 'Scott's had him sacked. I knew he would. Jamie's sick, and Dad's just fucked off on a bender, feeling sorry for himself.'

'Why don't you take Jamie back to yours?'

Ally snapped. 'For fuck's sake, Chris. Just go away! I'm trying to get Jamie to come home with me, and if he sees you he definitely won't.'

Chris took a step back, hands in his pockets. 'I'll try and find your dad. Jamie must be worried about him.'

Irritated, Ally flicked his ash just clear of Chris's shoes. 'Why do you have to get involved? Just go.'

'You said you needed me to help you, and I'm here. I'm trying to help.'

'I didn't mean help with...' Ally stopped himself.

Chris backed away. 'If I find him I'll call you, okay?'

Ally watched as Chris unlocked his car and drove away without looking back. When he went back inside, he was startled by Jamie, who was waiting silently on the other side of the door.

'I understand about homosexuality,' he began, matter-of-fact. 'It means you are physically attracted to someone of the same sex. It isn't anything to feel uncomfortable about, but some people have strong beliefs that it is morally wrong. These are beliefs; therefore, they are not based on fact. Dad says he isn't angry that you are homosexual, but he did say it made him sad that you never told him that you were, and that he found out because a lady at his work told him that you were having sex with her brother. That made him very unhappy, Alasdair. It would have been better just to tell him. Was that man at the door your boyfriend or just a platonic friend?'

Speechless, Ally shook his head. He sat down on the bottom stair and wrapped his arms around his knees. 'Shit, Jamie. I'm sorry. That was... that was Chris, and yeah, I suppose he is my boyfriend.'

'Okay,' said Jamie. 'Can I have some toast now?'

CHAPTER THIRTY-SIX

Bridge of Layne has a limited range of licensed premises, none of which I've ventured into since my late teens. There's one decent old-fashioned pub in what was the old village centre. The other two were tacked on in the early eighties when Binnie Homes tripled the size of the place with their monotonous new builds. Both are looking dated and neglected, and I imagine they are only busy when they show football, or when a local man dies, and the funeral goers have a respectful pint after the ham sandwiches.

Dave McClay is well known in all three, but I start at his local, the Bridge Arms. I don't spot anyone familiar. After a quick check of the gents, I ask the bored-looking woman behind the bar.

'I think he's barred? Hang on, I'll check. John... Johnny!' she yells through to the public bar. 'Is Davie McClay still barred?'

'We can't afford to bar Davie; he's too good a customer. We just threaten him with it every so often. Who's asking?'

'Try the Orchard. He sometimes drinks there too,' the woman says.

I don't find him in the Orchard or the Market Arms, and I call Ally just after seven o'clock and apologise for my failure.

'I know,' Ally says, sounding distant. 'He's here.'

'Is Jamie alright? What happened?'

'I can't talk just now.'

'Well, are you... will I see you later?'

'I don't know.'

'Give me a call when you get home?'

'I'll try.'

An agonising silence divides us until I can't bear it any longer. 'I just wanted to help.' My voice is strange and strangled.

'I need to go.' Ally hangs up on me.

Some instinctual haemorrhage of feeling takes over, scouring and numbing the places that hurt the most. By the time I've driven home, my body feels leaden and chilled. I mechanically remove my coat and scarf, hang them up, and go to the kitchen to get a drink. On the kitchen table is my monumental to-do list, comically annotated by Ally, who doodled all over it as he drank his coffee this morning. I trace my fingers over his writing a few times before sitting down at the kitchen table with a glass of red.

It takes me a long time, and most of the bottle, to start writing anything. I tear a piece of lined A4 out of the block and fold it. There are envelopes in my work bag, but no stamps. I address the envelope anyway, checking Ally's address and postcode against the details on the university report I'm completing for him.

A. S. McClay
17 Muir Road
Bridgend
Bridge of Layne

After pouring the remainder of the bottle into my glass I sit on the sofa, put on the TV for company, and flick through my phone to distract myself. I read the message

Ally sent me from the cinema on Tuesday night and analyse it compulsively. My thoughts are a warped and ravaged mess. I know the night spent without him will be interminable.

A lucid moment takes me back to the kitchen, where I remember one last emergency sleeping pill squirrelled away, and I wash it down with the last of my wine. Pulling the tatty throw over me, I hug a cushion to my stomach as I wait for it to work. When it doesn't work quickly enough, I hunt in the bedroom for *The Testament of Gideon Mack*. It's fallen between the bed and the wall. If I persevere, reading the first few pages slowly and letting each word disperse like a drop of cool water on my fevered mind, I can hear Ally's voice reading it to me.

I must have been sleeping heavily, because it takes a while for the buzzing noise to permeate my dreams. It really is the buzzer sounding. I heave myself off the sofa and to the door, where I flick the intercom switch.

'It's me, Chris. Can I come in?'

I press the switch that unlocks the front door, rub my eyes fiercely and open the door of the flat to let him in. The musty smell of the house Ally grew up in still clings to him—that of smoke and sweat and unwashed clothes. His work clothes are splashed and stained from cleaning up. He's white-faced and red-eyed.

'I'm sorry it's so late. I woke you, didn't I?' He leans against the wall, doesn't remove his coat. I'm scared he'll turn and walk away.

'I couldn't call you—my phone ran out of battery. Do you want me to leave?' Ally asks.

Bewildered, I wander back to the sofa, willing him to follow. Relief warms me from the inside when he does.

'After she gave him his P45, Serena told Dad about me and Scott. He was crying, Chris. He was crying because I didn't tell him, because he found out from her. I've never seen him cry before. He had me and Jamie together in the same room, and he was telling us how proud he is of us, and I'm so fucking... ashamed of him. I'm so embarrassed you came anywhere near my dad, that shitty house, poor wee Jamie. I know that's shallow and disloyal, but maybe I'm like that. Maybe I am those things, and it's a good thing if you see what I'm really like.'

I raise a hand to stop him. 'In your head, all you hear is him,' I say. 'It doesn't matter what anyone tells you, because all you hear is Scott Binnie. I can't get through to you.'

Ally slumps on the sofa beside me. 'That's not fair, Chris. You're making it about you when it's not. My dad would still be working for Binnie if it weren't for me, and he wouldn't have had to find out about me that way.'

'Maybe, but on the other hand he'd still have a drink problem and you'd still be lying to him. I get it, Ally. I know you. I heard what Scott has to say about you and your family. You take his word as gospel—that you're shallow, or slutty, or that your dad is a lost cause. I'm not buying it, though, because I actually know who you are.'

Ally swears under his breath, scuffing the heel of his hand along the cracked leather of the sofa arm. 'You can't blame Scott when it's me who's been lying to my folks for years and pretending they don't exist when it suits me.'

'What do you want me to do? Talk to you the way he did?'

Tears start to gather in the corners of his eyes, and normally this would infuriate me. 'I don't know. I'm sorry.

Tonight's been really fucking harrowing. I'm tired and I feel like shit, and I'm just taking out on you because I can.'

I sigh. 'I'm tired too.'

After a brooding pause, Ally leans over and picks up the paperback of *Gideon Mack* from the coffee table. I look at him sideways.

Ally says, 'I think I understand why you don't think Gideon was mad. Really, your argument is the same as mine. It's not about sanity. It's still about love. You think he just doesn't conform, he doesn't believe what he should believe, and I agree. He's so fucked up because of his childhood that he doesn't believe in love, and so he can't believe in anything. He has no solid ground, so he falls into the Black Jaws to where the Devil is. Then he believes in the Devil because the Devil is him. The Devil is his own pain and loneliness. Since he can really feel that, he can believe in it.'

'Love doesn't save people, unless you're reading a trashy novel,' I say.

'But I don't mean that. I mean, if you didn't feel it from your family or believe it was something that existed, that you could really feel, then there's nowhere to go, is there? Nowhere safe or solid. You can't thrive, because there's no making sense of life. You can't believe in anything.'

My arms are tight around my middle as I listen. 'I was wrong,' I whisper.

'Eh?'

'Nothing.' I scuff my feet on the tatty carpet.

'Can I stay over?' Ally asks, still thumbing the pages of the novel.

'Yeah, of course. Just don't fucking talk anymore, okay?' I throw a cushion at him with a twisted smile.

Ally lies down with his head on my lap, and every muscle in his face and neck softens when my fingernails rake through his dishevelled hair.

'You can stay over,' I continue, 'but go and have a shower before you come to bed, because you stink. Oh, and when you're finished feeling sorry for yourself, you can make me a cup of tea.'

'Yeah, okay, fair enough. I deserve that.' I can tell Ally enjoys the sensation of my nails on his scalp by the way he closes his eyes and exhales.

'I need to finish your PGDE report by Monday. Which box do I tick? Satisfactory? Very good? Excellent?'

'I think I have been an excellent student and I have lots of potential, Mr. Elliot,' he says facetiously.

'I think you have to.' I pick up his hand and kiss the back of it. 'You're a great teacher. Now go and make me a cup of tea or I'll fail you.'

Reluctantly, Ally moves from my lap and goes to the kitchen. I hear him switch the kettle on and tear open a fresh packet of custard creams. The crunching stops, and I smile because I know what he's found lying on the kitchen table.

'Can I open this?' he shouts.

'Open what?' I feign ignorance.

'This.' He comes to the kitchen door holding it, so I can see what he's talking about.

'Yeah, go on. If you want to.' I pretend to be busy on my laptop.

I hear him tear the envelope and pull out the folded paper. I know that we share a nostalgic anticipation for tearing open each other's letters.

Do you remember Mrs. Stewart reading us Sunset Song?

Home isn't the place, it's the person, and their feeling. Safe and solid ground.
You said I was your safe place.
You are where I live now. I don't want to leave.
Always was, always will be, yours, Chris.

CHAPTER THIRTY-SEVEN

LAST DAY OF PLACEMENT

I print a copy of the report for Ally's file and find a new A4 envelope to put it in. When I go to the printer in the English base to pick it up, Callum is sitting on his own, having his lunch and reading the paper.

'Where are Ally and Louise?' I ask him.

'Away uptown on some secret mission. Those two are all over each other,' he grunts.

'Yeah?' I make an effort to sound surprised.

"I can't believe you haven't noticed. They go about holding hands and everything. Your head is right up your arse, Chris. I thought you'd have been in about Louise by now, but I think you're way too slow off the mark there.'

I shrug and slip the printout into the envelope while looking for a pen to write Ally's name across the front.

'I'll miss the wee fucker. He's a good lad, eh?' Callum says.

'Yeah, he's not the worst, I suppose,' I say. 'Are you coming to his house tonight?'

'Yeah, he says Anna can come too, which is decent of him. We're getting a lift with Lou.'

Anna is Callum's acerbic PE-teacher wife, who drifts into the English base periodically to steal biscuits and ridicule her husband for our amusement.

'I bet he and Lou get off with each other tonight. I'll put money on it. She's been sniffing after Ally since day one, the wee slapper.' Callum snorts with laughter.

'Yeah, maybe.' I sit down and start unwrapping my sandwich.

'You need to get back on the horse yourself, Chris,' Callum says. 'We'll get a night out organised. Christmas parties soon, prime time to get you hooked up.'

'Nah, it's alright. You're a shit wingman.' This is true, but nights out with Callum are great for the drunken banter.

Louise's giggles echo down the corridor, and Callum looks at me knowingly. Ally comes in first and hangs a carrier bag behind his coat, helping Louise off with hers before hanging it up for her.

'We got cakes for everyone.' He rips open the baker's paper bag and spreads it out on the coffee table. 'Help yourselves.'

'Nice one, thanks. Hands off the jammy donut, Elliot!' Callum swipes it before anyone else has a chance.

'I wish we could keep you,' Louise says, resting her head on Ally's shoulder. They're totally inseparable at work.

'Fucking get a room, you two!' says Callum.

I put the kettle on, check if the milk is still okay.

Callum begins messily devouring his donut. 'Who's all going tonight then, Ally?'

'Just us guys, Anna, Luca and eh... I don't know, but my new boyfriend might appear. He's not sure yet.'

I turn away, blushing, and pretend to be busy making the tea.

Callum's jaw drops, revealing a half-chewed jammy mess of donut. 'What? You're winding us up? Since when did you bat for the other team, Ally?'

'Since I first laid eyes on you, Callum. I was devastated when I found out you were spoken for.' Ally blows Callum a kiss across the coffee table.

'Did you two know about this?' Callum says.

I turn around as Louise whoops with laughter.

'Nobody tells me anything,' Callum grumbles. 'Bunch of tossers. Aw, well, that's good, Ally. Fair play to you. 'Mon the gays, I say. Frees up more fanny for the rest of us.'

'That's your bet off then, Callum,' I say.

'What bet?' Ally asks.

'He said he'd put money on you getting off with Louise tonight.'

'I might jump ship for her.' Ally smiles, putting his arm around her.

Louise laughs and shoves him away. 'In your dreams, old man.'

As Louise reaches for a blueberry muffin from the array of cakes on the coffee table, I hand out mugs of tea, swiping a chocolate brownie for myself. I sit down between Callum and Ally, stealthily inhaling him as he reaches forward for his mug of coffee, a tiny fix of promised intimacy. I can't wait to be alone with him. I can't even think about it here.

'Your report.' I pass the brown envelope to Ally.

'Thanks,' he smiles. 'Thank you so much.'

Ally can't speak on the drive home, and I know how upset he is that his placement is over. He's laden with cards from the pupils and staff, and the brown envelope with his final report is resting on top of the pile. We're halfway to his house in Bridgend before his fingers settle on top of mine on the gearstick.

I glance at him, already imagining the moment when the front door closes behind us. His expression is set, distant, the way Ally looks when he's sleeping. It's the best time to study the bones under his skin, the shadows under his eyes and the exact spacing of the tiny gaps between his front teeth.

'Okay?' I ask him, squeezing his fingers.

Ally nods dreamily.

I concentrate on reverse parking in the driveway of Ally's house. I'm impatient now that the front door is in sight. Ally catches my gaze and I catch his smile. There are bags in the boot to unload for the party later tonight, so I grab a few while Ally unlocks the front door.

'Have you read your report yet?' I ask him, dropping the bags in the hallway. Ally locks the inside bolt and wraps his arms around my waist. It's a relief to touch him again.

'Just give it to me orally. You're getting good at that; a solid pass, I'd say.'

I make a face at him. 'You have sex on the brain, Ally.'

'Says you! I'm just not buying your prim and proper bullshit anymore. You may be an insomniac, but that doesn't mean I can function on three hours of sleep to meet your incessant demands, my darling.'

'You seem to be functioning pretty well.' I kiss his mouth and start undoing his tie, so I can kiss his neck and throat. I tied the knot for him this morning.

'Chris.' Ally stops me. 'You rent your flat, yeah?'

'Uh-huh.' I'm not really listening as I undress him, so Ally presses his fingers fiercely into my scalp until I look up into his wide eyes. 'What is it?' I ask.

'Would you move in with me? There's more room here, and I'm not renting, so it makes sense. I mean... not right away, but would you think about it?'

'Yes,' I say. I've made myself breathless. 'I will think about it when I'm not so horny.'

In truth, I know there is nothing I want more.

CHAPTER THIRTY-EIGHT

Louise arrived just after seven with Luca, Callum and Anna crammed in her Fiat. Callum shouldered in a case of beers as Luca carried Louise's clinking bags into the house for her.

Once everyone had a drink in their hand, the girls wanted a tour of the house, so Ally took them upstairs to see the three small bedrooms and bathroom, wondering if they'd notice Chris's glasses beside the bed, or his work clothes on the back of the chair. Ally was coming back downstairs with Louise and Anna when he saw Luca make a beeline for Chris's guitar, which was on its stand in the corner of the living room.

'I didn't know you played,' Luca said to Chris.

'I don't...much. I mean, not recently.' Chris was still shy, transitioning out of work mode. Ally watched him blush and mutter and spoke up for him.

'Chris does play. He's shit hot. Grade eight, aren't you?'

'Holy crap, I'll not bother asking for a shot then,' Luca said.

'No, help yourself. I haven't played for ages,' Chris said.

'Where's your lad then, Ally?' Callum asked. 'Are we getting to meet him?'

'Shut up, Callum!' Anna shot him a well-honed death stare.

A few hours later, Anna and Louise had settled into a tipsy conspiratorial conversation on the stairs, Luca was playing Kings of Leon songs on Chris's guitar and Callum was shouting random requests at him. Chris was sitting

on the sofa, hugging his knees and trying to sober up. Ally
began to hand out book- shaped presents wrapped in brown
paper, a card taped to each one.

Louise opened *Little Birds* by Anaïs Nin, Anna the
latest Ian Rankin, Callum an Irvine Welsh, Luca a book
of Lou Reed's photos, and Chris *The Private Memoirs and
Confessions of a Justified Sinner* by James Hogg. Louise
hugged Ally tearfully, and they whispered in the corner for
a few minutes before Ally settled on the sofa next to Chris,
who was thumbing through his book.

'I'm pretty sure it was an inspiration for *Gideon Mack*.'

'Thank you.' Chris smiled at him, shiny-eyed. 'You can
read it to me once I've finished reading you *At the Loch of
the Green Corrie*.'

Ally wondered if they glowed with feelings, if it was
obvious to everyone that he was stupefied with loving and
being loved. 'I've got another present for you in the kitchen.
Come through with me,' he whispered, brushing the back
of Chris's hand.

A flicker of anxiety crossed Chris's face.

'It's okay, come on.' Ally got up and disappeared into the
kitchen. When Chris followed him a few moments later,
he wore an apprehensive smile. 'Seriously, Ally?'

'Come over here a minute. Stop stressing.'

Chris crossed the kitchen and, checking behind him,
held both of Ally's hands to give him a brief kiss.

'Here.' Ally took Chris's fingers and ran them down his
arm, so he could feel the slight synthetic wrinkle under his
thin sweater.

'Is that where you went with Louise at lunchtime then?'
Chris asked.

'I need to quit because you hate it,' Ally said, squeezing Chris's fingers and leaning across to catch his mouth in a kiss that was insistent and involved. He pressed against Chris, arms draped around his neck.

'Ally, are there any more beers in the—holy shit! Fuck's sake. Sorry! Sorry!'

Callum spun on his heel and backed rapidly out of the kitchen.

Ally and Chris froze, still gripping each other. They listened intently to the conversation unfolding through the doorway in the living room.

'Jesus, Callum, what the fuck have you done now?' Anna yelled at him.

'You alright, Callum?' Luca asked. 'You look like you saw a ghost, pal!'

'Ally and Chris are in there and they're—oh my God. I can't unsee that! I mean... giveus a fucking warning, boys, seriously!'

Then they heard Louise laugh at him. 'Did you get an eyeful, Callum?' she asked.

'An eyeful of what?' Anna asked her.

Chris stroked his fingers once more across the alien texture of the nicotine patch on Ally's arm. Then he laced their fingers together and gripped Ally's hand tight as they left the kitchen and re-joined the others.

THE END